The Boy with a Bird in His Chest

a novel

EMME LUND

ATRIA BOOKS

NEW YORK   LONDON   TORONTO   SYDNEY   NEW DELHI

An Imprint of Simon & Schuster, Inc.
1230 Avenue of the Americas
New York, NY 10020

First Atria Books hardcover edition February 2022

ATRIA B O O K S and colophon are trademarks of Simon & Schuster, Inc.

For information about special discounts for bulk purchases, please contact Simon & Schuster Special Sales at 1-866-506-1949 or business@simonandschuster.com.

The Simon & Schuster Speakers Bureau can bring authors to your live event. For more information or to book an event, contact the Simon & Schuster Speakers Bureau at 1-866-248-3049 or visit our website at www.simonspeakers.com.

Interior design by Kyoko Watanabe

Manufactured in the United States of America

1 3 5 7 9 10 8 6 4 2

Library of Congress Cataloging-in-Publication Data

Names: Lund, Emme, 1985- author.
Title: The boy with a bird in his chest : a novel / Emme Lund.
Description: First Atria Books hardcover edition. | New York : Atria Boks, 2022.
Identifiers: LCCN 2021034476 (print) | LCCN 2021034477 (ebook) |
ISBN 9781982171933 (hardcover) | ISBN 9781982171957 (ebook)
Subjects: LCGFT: Bildungsromans.
Classification: LCC PS3612.U535 B69 2022 (print) | LCC PS3612.U535 (ebook) |
DDC 813/.6—dc23
LC record available at https://lccn.loc.gov/2021034476
LC ebook record available at https://lccn.loc.gov/2021034477

ISBN 978-1-9821-7193-3
ISBN 978-1-9821-7195-7 (ebook)

For Stelleaux,
who taught me how to love the bird in my chest

The Boy with a
Bird in His Chest

0.5

A java sparrow lives inside of Owen's chest. His heart is pushed down so that it sits above his belly and his left lung is shoved against his sternum. Between the two organs his skin is pulled back, and inside the hole is a bird named Gail. She has been there since he was born. She'll die when he dies. Three ribs stick out from his skin, swim in the open air, and then sink back beneath the skin on his left side. The bones are a dull gray, and the space where the skin meets bone feels natural, like the webbing between fingers or toes.

Owen has one week left to live. He is going to California, where he will walk off the side of the Golden Gate Bridge. He is seventeen, and many will assume he is being dramatic, but he's simply being a realist. He has felt a strong pull to deep water ever since his birth, and he is simply giving in. He knows his story ends in the water. His body will remain in the bay, resting among the mermaids.

Under the Sea.

The bus groans and pulls over at the top of the Rob Hill, the base of the Coyote. There is no sidewalk here, only gravel and the sienna dust that covers everything in Montana. He kicks dirt and gravel onto the grass of someone's yard and sets his bag on the ground. A left rib creaks from an injury that never quite healed right. His knuckles are swollen and bruised, and he fingers the cuts. Gail runs her beak along his spine. The wind blows a warm breeze, and Owen turns to face the town. He stands with his back to the west, makes sure no one is looking, and lifts up his tank top. There it is, the space with no skin, just ribs and the small bird who lives inside his chest. Most of her feathers are a light gray. She wears white feathers below her eyes like a mask and deep black feathers on the top of her head like a bad toupee.

He and Gail look out over the valley one last time. The Rockies sweep across the landscape, and it seems as though the town is molded into the side of the Coyote, couched in its soft hills. A mild gray film covers the valley like smoke, and Owen is not sure if it's always been that gray or if his colorblindness is getting worse.

Morning, Montana, has always been that gray.

He pulls his shirt back down and picks up his bag and crosses the street. Beyond the street is a small ditch overgrown with grass, and past that is I-90, his ticket west. The long grass brushes against his elbows, and Gail squawks beneath his T-shirt.

"Are you going to do the classic right thumb out, walking backwards, or the walk forward, but turn every time you hear a car? I think eye contact is key here. You want the driver to see you." Gail's words tickle the tops of his ribs.

Owen slides down the small bank. "Walking backwards will take us twice as long," he says, dripping the words down his throat to her. "I think it's better to just face forward and hold my thumb out. Hope someone picks us up." Rocks slide down the other side of the ditch, and his boots dig into the dust. He stands at the side of the railing. It is only briefly, but for a moment Owen considers those he is leaving behind: his mother, Tennessee, the boy.

"Owen, you don't have to go," Gail says. She's reminded him a thousand times he doesn't have to go if he doesn't want to.

"I do." He climbs over the steel rail and onto the side of the two-lane highway.

"Just be careful. Trust that gut of yours."

Gail is thinking about serial killers again. Cars race by. None of them are even close to slowing down. "You're my gut," he says, and he sticks his left thumb out and walks towards exit 82, out west.

Book One

Childhood

(How to Make It to the End of the Day)

1

There is a tradition in Morning, Montana, that goes back so far no one can pinpoint the first time it was ever observed. The McCullough Bridge sits at the town's lowest point, 2,500 feet above sea level. The mountains on the west side of the bridge collect and preserve snow and ice over the winter months. When it snows it is like a door is open from another dimension and peace and quiet are allowed into the mountains. Then there are days of sun. The ice and snow start to melt. At night, the temperature drops and everything freezes again. The cycle continues, so on and so forth, until there is a slick and crunchy layer of ice that seems like it will never melt.

The mountains give in to being covered in ice and snow, summer forever just past the horizon. This moment, when the mountains finally give in to being covered in ice, is when the rain starts to fall. Then it is like another dimension is torn open, a world filled with water. Buckets and buckets of rain dump onto the mountains and onto Morning. The snow melts. The melted snow joins the rain, and together they barrel down the hill, a force known as Beaver Creek.

Every year, without fail, Beaver Creek floods the McCullough Bridge, and every year, the town gathers days before to watch. The creek climbs the concrete pillars of the bridge, carrying branches, soil, and rocks. Folks take off work. Schools are closed for days at a time. News crews stand next to the water at all hours, day and night. Lawn chairs scatter the roadway leading up to the bridge, and the chairs are striped and woven with cheap plastic of nearly every color. Red, white, and blue for the patriotic. Teal, orange, and white for the adventurous. Mrs. Jones weaves between the families with her thermos full of hot cider, filling each cup and adding small nips of whiskey into the mug of anyone of age. They all wait.

Anyone who sees the bridge flood at the exact moment when the water spills up and onto the road has good luck for the year.

Owen was born on March 3, 1997, four weeks late and on the first day of the absolute worst flood of '97.

2

The baby wailed and wailed on Janice's shoulder in the back of her station wagon. Rain thundered the tin roof of the car. Her neck was craned, her eyes on the bridge. The water spilled onto the road and with it, sticks, mud, and pine needles. It crept along the road, coming for family dens and church basements. Owen howled at the sight of the water, wailed at the feeling of fresh air in his lungs.

Someone yelled at somebody else to get Janice to the hospital, to get her and her newborn baby there as soon as possible. People clapped. Janice could only smile, because Owen had been born right at the magic moment when the water spilled onto the road, and she felt the lucky flood flowing inside her son. She knew he was special.

The boy born during the flood.

• • •

The bird did not show up in his chest for five days. In that time, Owen was diagnosed (incorrectly) with an extreme heart murmur and was given anywhere between one week and eighty-five years to live. The hospital room was a rotating door of doctors and nurses and social workers and grief counselors. Janice called the barrage of specialists trying to remove her son the *Army of Acronyms*. The Army of Acronyms was strong at the hospital, third in the world to police stations and city hall. Janice sat in bed with her boy on her shoulder and answered their questions and let them administer their tests. But each was a soldier moving closer and closer to taking her boy away from her. So, on the second night, she got out of bed, dug her car keys out of the bottom of the hospital-issued plastic bag that contained her personal items (leaving behind her wet jeans and parka), and she left the hospital, vowing never to let another doctor near her child.

She prepared to grieve.

She thought, at worst, Owen could die at home as comfortable as possible. She turned the living room into a living memorial, placed peonies at the foot of his bassinet, cleaned his toys and arranged them near the television as an altar, and she smoked cigarettes like each one was a prayer that she whispered to the wind and blew out the dining room window. But each morning he woke up next to her. She got up, reheated a casserole left for her by a coworker, and put the coffeepot on. With each day that he survived, it seemed his luck increased. She investigated her son, his little toes like pebbles, microscopic toenails, and skin somehow paler than her own, so pale and new it was pink. On the third day, she woke up and found something seriously wrong with her boy.

A large hole in his chest. Three of his tiny, baby-sized ribs were exposed, and inside the rib cage, next to his heart and lungs was a baby bird.

He was the luckiest boy in the whole world.

3

Owen continued to survive and grow and so did the bird in his chest. Each day, bird and boy getting bigger, both getting chattier, developing a rapport.

When Owen was three years old, he already knew two things:

The first thing was that he was not, under any circumstances, allowed to talk about or show anyone the bird in his chest. His mother told him so one night while Owen was tucked small in the folds of the couch, the bird named Gail tucked tight asleep in his chest. His mother's elbows were on her knees, leaning forward, her face lit by the one lamp in the corner.

"No one can know." She tapped her chest with two fingers.

"No one?"

"No one, never." She leaned in closer to Owen, set a hand on his knee. "No one," she said. "They'll take you away from me, away from everyone, and they may take her away from you." She tapped her chest with two fingers one more time.

The second thing Owen knew was that his lungs didn't always work right. Sometimes, he and his mom would be at her friend Elayne's house. He'd be playing in her living room, running in circles while Gail told him jokes in his chest, whispered the punch lines up his throat so only he could hear them, and before he knew it, he'd be in a fit, wheezing and coughing. His lungs clamped shut.

Some nights he woke up in the bathroom, the yellow light harsh against the cream tub. He could barely open his eyes. The bathtub faucet was a thunderous creek, and the applause of water running against the bathtub echoed off the bathroom's tiled walls. The water was so hot it burned to the touch. Even with the bathwater near boiling and his lungs clamped shut, Owen felt a pull to the water, like all would be better if he could climb in and let it hold him.

His mother sat behind him, rubbing his back. She shushed him. "It's okay, just breathe in the steam. Breathe it deep into your lungs."

Steam rolled across his face and his face grew hot. He opened his eyes wide and let the bright room crawl into his brain. He tried to breathe in all the steam that rolled off the hot water. His lungs wouldn't listen. He breathed in short, quick breaths.

His mother wore a nightgown printed with small lilacs from the frill collar down to the hems. She stared blankly at the wall, rubbing his back and turning the water hotter and hotter. His skin reddened.

Gail ran her wing down his spine, careful to leave his lungs alone. "Shhh," she whispered. "Shhhh."

They sat in the bathroom until the water ran cold.

Then they would move into his bedroom and his mom would prop him up in bed to massage VapoRub on his chest. She crawled into his tiny bed built for a child and sat up next to him. Her left leg hung off the side of the mattress. She stared at the wall. His breaths grew deeper. His ears were cold, still wet from the steam.

Like the sunrise, everything slowly settled until it was day again and he could almost breathe like normal, and still his mom would sit next to him. She'd take the day off work and they'd sit in bed together, watching the wall and listening to Owen's breath.

4

When both her parents died within two days of each other, Janice determined that the world was absolutely, under no circumstances safe for her son. Her brother, Bob, and his daughter, Tennessee, who was a whole one year and nine months older than Owen, came out to grieve. Owen's mom and Bob got drunk as skunks in the living room, singing and dancing and bawling their eyes out. Owen and his cousin sat in the corner, not saying a word to each other.

Two days after the funeral, Owen's mother took him out for a last hurrah, a day to experience everything he'd miss after he was locked away. Her face was still blistered red from three days of crying. They sat in a booth at the diner where she worked, sharing a plate of steak and eggs. Once, between bites of steak, she leaned in and whispered to Owen. "Any of these people could be in the Army of Acronyms." She pointed her fork at a man walking briskly to his car with a briefcase. "People like him. You got to be careful." They both tapped their chests with their two fingers.

After lunch, the afternoon sun still high in the sky, they left the car parked in the diner's lot and went across the street to the Thelma to watch *The Little Mermaid*, his mother's favorite movie which was being reshown twelve years after its release.

The inside of the theater was dark and cold. Owen stuffed Rolos and popcorn into his mouth and felt a stomachache coming on but ate more anyways.

The lights went way, way down and the movie started.

The Little Mermaid showed Owen what was possible beneath the ocean. Fish that talked to birds. Birds who talked to humans. Humans with half a fish hanging out their tail end. He saw himself on the screen and he was giant, the size of four humans put together. He felt the warmth of the ocean, how it cradled everything. He wanted nothing more than to disappear under the sea. He passed the feeling of being seen down to Gail and she danced in his chest, flapped her wings for a moment. His mother gripped his hand when Ariel agreed to give up her voice, and Owen wondered if she felt seen, too.

After the movie they drove the winding road up the Coyote. The night sky was black above them, and the headlights of the station wagon cut like two knives onto the road. His mother turned the radio on and sang along with the Rolling Stones. She pulled off the road and there was nothing but trees, the moon, and the town's lights far beneath them. "Something for Gail," she said.

She gripped his shoulders and walked him into the forest. It was so dark he had to put his hands out in front of him to keep from walking into a tree. They stopped in front of a monstrous pine whose branches swept out low to the ground. His mom hefted him up into the air and onto a branch. "We're going to climb this tree," she said. "It's special." She climbed beneath him and hoisted him up, branch by branch, until they were nearly fifteen feet off the ground. She sat him down on a limb. It was knobby and cut into his thighs. They couldn't see much from where they sat. The trees were close to one another. He knew the town was out there somewhere, that beyond the trees was the diner they'd just left, that even their house still sat there without them.

His mom reached over and unbuttoned his jacket slowly. The wind rushed in and stung his belly. Once his jacket was unbuttoned, she pulled up his shirt. "We're only doing this because no one is around. Never do this on your own." She lifted his shirt up to his chin. It bunched up around his armpits. The air burned it was so cold.

Gail got a good look at the forest. "Holy cow," she said, "it feels good to be in the woods." She chirped and whistled and sent out a loud *POE-TWEE-TOE-TWEET*. Owen's arms felt longer, his head lighter, and an easiness spread across his shoulders and out his finger-tips. Gail flitted from side to side in his chest, prancing between his ribs and his lungs. She poked her beak between his ribs so when he looked down all he saw was the tip of her nose. She felt at home in the tree, where a bird should be. She let out another song.

His mother sat next to him, grinning from ear to ear. "She really is something," she said. She leaned down until she was face-to-face with Gail. "I love you, Gail, and I'm glad you're here."

5

After Owen's last hurrah, it was total lockdown. His mother strengthened the security of the house, including a clasp lock with a chain at just the right height for Owen to lock and unlock each day when she came home.

Something about both her parents being dead made his mom superstitious of ghosts. (The only form in which her own mother could return.) She painted the front porch and the small two steps leading to the backyard a deep blue, confusing ghosts into thinking they lived on a houseboat. (Apparently, ghosts were terrified of water.) She filled a glass with tap water and set it on top of the refrigerator to trap evil spirits. Over the front door she hung bulbs of fennel, a horseshoe, several mirrors, and a broom. She stopped short of hanging a crucifix. "That crosses a line," she said. She set an acorn on every windowsill in the house. And one sunny Monday afternoon, she found an old thick tree limb that had fallen in the woods at the base of their hill. She dug a hole in the ground in the front yard and planted the bare limb so that it looked like a short tree in January when the leaves had fallen. She pulled the paper bag full of empty glass bottles out from under the sink and brought it with her into the yard. She placed the bottles over the bare branches. The sunlight bounced and cascaded off the blue and green glass and the bottle tree filtered the light like leaves.

After the house was locked down and secured, Owen's mother sat next to the dining room window in her rocking chair. Owen sat at the table. The television flickered in the corner of his eyes. His mother lit a cigarette and blew the smoke out of the corner of her mouth and out the window. Owen's hand was under his shirt, Gail nibbling his finger.

His mother told him about the Army of Acronyms, how they were part of a system that removes children from parents. "Doctors are a strong arm of the Army of Acronyms," she said. "You must never see a doctor under any circumstances."

He nodded.

"And cops, too. Cops are worse than doctors."

He pulled his hand out from under his shirt and sat on his fingers until they fell asleep.

"You don't have to worry though. We'll keep you safe in this house. You're safe here."

Gail ran her wing down his spine. His mom stared off in the distance like she saw something on the horizon. She stretched her right arm long in an attempt to keep her cigarette next to the window while she reached for more wine on the table. Her body was contorted, pulled in two different directions. She poured the rest of the wine into her glass and finished her cigarette.

"Rules," his mother said, "No one, never." They both tapped their chests with two fingers. "Never open the door for anyone. The world is lousy with the Army of Acronyms, and they are looking for you. They will kidnap you the second they have the chance, so don't open the door for nothing."

Owen nodded a sheepish yes.

"You gotta trust that bird of yours. She's smart. Animals know things we don't. The bird's in charge." She leaned over and patted Owen's knee. "No baths or showers, bub. You'll get water on your organs and you'll never be able to get it all out. Mold and rot will find your insides."

This was the most difficult rule for Owen to accept. He got not going outside and talking to strangers and listening to Gail, but the urge to sink into water grew each day. He was the boy born during the flood. It was in his bones, but he didn't want his insides to rot, either.

His mother continued, "You can have a little coffee, but it has to be watered down."

She stood up and slapped the table, satisfied with the rules she'd laid out. She drank more wine and went into the living room, where she swayed to the radio and turned it up loud. She motioned for him to come join her, and so he stood up with his shoulders slumped. Slowly, he twirled and fell into the rhythm of the Talking Heads, and soon they were both spinning themselves silly. Gail spun in his chest, a dizzy bird.

6

I t was ten long years that Owen stayed locked in the house, never feeling concrete under his shoes, never seeing the sky above him. He woke up each morning and his mother was already off to work at the diner. A half-drunk cup of coffee left on the floor by the couch was the only evidence she'd been home at all. Every single day for those ten years, he felt a strong urge to open the door and walk outside, but he remembered what waited for him: doctors, police officers, scientists, and social workers, all itching to rip Gail from his chest and keep him from his mother. Just thinking about it worked him up so much, he had to take a puff on his inhaler.

His school was television. The British narrators of the nature documentaries taught him about instincts, the things Gail was interested in, even though she claimed they were wrong half the time. "That's not why we fly in flocks," she scoffed. Owen's favorite was the specials on ocean animals. He loved the way the screen filled with aqua blue, how sea otters and penguins and whales danced underwater. Even when he saw specials on killer whales or sharks, he thought the ocean seemed like a safer world, and he remembered *The Little Mermaid*. One afternoon he learned about circus "freaks" (one-armed men; a woman with webbed toes, *half duck*—squeeze the boy with a bird in his chest right in there). Another afternoon he learned about the Tuskegee Experiment, and he knew his mother was right about the Army of Acronyms.

The closed captions taught Owen how to read, and soap operas were the best for his reading lessons. Dr. Paul Jones taught him that a double *S* can make the *shh* sound (think: *passion*). Jenny and Sarah Brentworth (twins) taught him about *UR* and *ER* (*murder*). He loved the way the letter *L* rolled off Donovan's tongue and out his mouth in so many different ways (*love, world, betrayal,* and *lioness*).

After the soaps, Owen and Gail practiced the migratory patterns of other birds together in the living room. The front door was southern Mexico, and the back door was Winnipeg. His mother's bedroom transformed into British Columbia, his bedroom Havana.

Gail instructed him as he walked the paths from one end to the other. "It takes a long time," she said. "Walk it slowly." They set up glasses of water, short mugs of coffee, and bits of banana along the way. "Lots of stops for food and drink and sleep," Gail said. He took a nap somewhere in Nevada (just south of the couch).

• • •

Owen and Gail taught his mother the bird migratory pattern game on her day off. She followed him along the route with a fan, insisting that it was the only way to really capture the feeling of wind under his wings. "Can you feel it?" she asked, and then, "Yes, Owen! You're soaring," and it really did feel like he was flying.

Later at night they walked the house and shut off every light until the house was pitch-black, save for the bit of orange glow cast from the streetlight through the kitchen window. His mother placed her hands on his shoulders and walked him into the living room. "The secret to seeing in the dark," she said, "is closing your eyes and imagining your legs as roots digging deep, deep down into the ground. You have to feel the earth beneath you." He closed his eyes. Gail closed her eyes in his chest. He imagined his feet bursting through the wood floors and then the house's foundation and eventually the soil, where they spread and dug into the ground. "Now," his mother continued, "you are going to count to thirty and I am going to hide. Your eyes will adjust to the darkness, and when you're finished counting, it will seem bright as day."

He counted to thirty, eyes sealed shut, so much darkness it hurt.

When he opened his eyes, everything was clear, the couch and behind it, the dining room table, his mother's rocking chair next to the window, and no mother, gone like a ghost. He went from room to room until eventually he found her under her bed.

Next, she showed him how to hide. "The secret to disappearing is becoming invisible." She counted to thirty loudly in the living room, and he slipped as quietly as possible into a kitchen cabinet, the one to the left of the sink that held only a baking sheet. He held his breath and tried to imagine he was completely gone, disappeared. Even Gail played along, becoming a rock in his chest. His mom opened the cabinet and got on her knees. She leaned in, inches from his face, trying to make out the shapes in front of her. Owen thought for a moment that he had, in fact, become invisible. He couldn't hold his breath any longer and he found it funny, his mom so close without seeing him, so he laughed, spitting on her face by accident. She laughed, the three of them on the kitchen floor, melting into a puddle of laughter on the linoleum.

7

At the end of those ten years, two days before his fourteenth birthday, the urge to be outside was a burning in Owen's chest that had grown to a forest fire, his whole insides ablaze with the desire. Gail said nothing, and the inferno grew, the flames licking his throat while they watched an informercial. He sat on the floor only two feet from the television, like a knife that could slice a shoe in half was the most interesting thing in the world. Eventually, without saying a word, he stood up and went to the back door. He didn't see any kidnappers crouched behind bushes. No cops waiting for him. No doctors in lab coats. Only blue skies and dew dotting the sliding glass door. He worried the Army of Acronyms could be hiding around the corner, but he couldn't stand the stale air of the house for one more second.

The metal rails were sticky from years of nonuse, so he had to push hard to get the glass door open enough to stand in the doorway. The relief was like pouring cold water on flames. The days had been sunny, and the world was alive but still cold. Birds chirped.

"Take off your shirt," Gail said. "Let me feel it too."

He pulled his T-shirt over his head, and she bounced up and down on his heart. The air nipped at his bare rib cage, and he shivered.

The blue paint on the back steps was chipped and faded. Owen saw it like a ghost would, as a wide, uncrossable ocean, and so he stayed inside.

A bird flew up and out of the neighbor's tree. It flew over the roof of the house and then back into the yard. It perched on the electric wire. Owen was cold, and he tugged on the door to close it, ready to go back inside. The door stuck on its rails and he had to push it back open to get enough momentum to hop the sticky part. The bird flew down into the yard until it was nearly in front of him. He thought it an auspicious sign, that he really should go back inside and not stay a second longer in the big, wide world. He pulled harder, but he couldn't get the door to budge. He was still wrestling with it when the bird flew up and over his head and into the house.

"No, no, no, no, no, no, no, no, no, no, no, no, no, no, no, no, no, no, no, no." He followed the bird inside. "No, no, no, no, no, no, no, no. Oh, shit. Goddammit. No, no, no, no, no."

The bird fluttered near the ceiling and then to the television, where it landed on top of the set. It was small, but larger than Gail, maybe five inches long. Its belly was a soft white with dark brown feathers worn long down its wings. Owen stepped slowly towards the bird. He thought maybe he could get close enough to catch it, to hold it in his hands and take it back outside. But when he got near it, it took off again and flew right at him. He ducked, and the bird ran into the window and fell to the floor. It pulled itself up and careened into the glass again.

"Close the blinds," Gail yelled. "This bird's an idiot." Owen pulled the blinds closed. The bird flew over his head and to the kitchen, where it flitted from window to window. He ran around the house closing each of the blinds, save for the pair that covered the back door that was still wide open. The bird hovered in the kitchen, wings beating. He worried it would stay there forever. Maybe his mom would come home and it would still be there, uncatchable. They'd have to walk around it, avoid it in the hallway. They'd live under the loose bird regime for years.

"Chill out." Gail poked her beak out between his ribs. "It's just scared."

He walked towards the bird slowly, his hands swept wide at each side. It flew towards him. He froze, ducked. It landed on the kitchen counter.

"Get it towards the back door," Gail yelled. He walked around the bird, keeping his back to it. Once he was on the other side of the crea-ture, he extended his hand and herded the bird towards the back door. It let him get within a couple feet before it flew up from the counter and over his head and out the back door. He ran to the door. The bird flew high up into the sky, a celebration. Owen pulled his T-shirt back over his skinny body and followed the bird, stepping onto the back step without even realizing it.

His awareness lagged behind his body, so it was a full beat before he realized he stood outside for the first time in a decade, exposed.

The breeze blew against his long hair and it startled him. He'd for-gotten how long his hair had grown, tickling the tops of his shoulders now. He forgot how far the world stretched, past the neighbors, out towards the mountains, and once the world got past the mountains, it just kept going. He'd forgotten how tall the trees were and how it smelled differently outside.

The desert sands brushed against his lungs, the fresh air so startling. He peeked around the side of the house but still didn't see anyone waiting to steal him away, only packed mud and patches of dandelions.

He stepped onto the back lawn.

He had the impulse to spin, and so he did. The grass was long but heavy with frost, and it lay flat on the ground. It crunched beneath his feet. He stretched his arms out long and looked up to the sky and the sun whirled around in a blur, he spun so fast. When he slowed down he wobbled a bit, and Gail bumped into his spine and then ran into his ribs. He plopped down on the ground, drunk on dizziness and surprised by how sharp the earth was.

He petted the grass. Beads of dew wetted his fingertips.

He stood up to walk to the corner of the yard. A dog barked. Gail welled up inside him, happiness brimming out of the hole in his chest. "Oh, this guy thinks he owns the place, huh?" she yelled. She chirped loudly, *POE-TWEE-toe-TWEET-TWEET-tweet*. His nostrils pulled in the scent of pine. The earth still wobbled. Air swirled around him, full of microscopic bugs and atoms and emotions. He sneezed.

He closed his eyes and passed Gail the feeling of a planet swirling beneath him, of his feet firmly in the soil and the air biting at his bare elbows. He thought of the Army of Acronyms and how bare he was outside, but then he imagined growing roots and standing tall like the trees around him. *Open your eyes and it will seem bright as day.* He imagined not being afraid of the Army of Acronyms. He imagined Gail living open and free, and him living open and free in turn.

The cold air sank past his skin and settled in his meat. He rubbed his neck.

"Let's get you inside," Gail said. "Your mom's coming home soon."

At the door, he turned and looked out across his yard one more time before sliding the glass door closed behind him.

He and Gail collapsed on the couch. The television now played an informercial for a ladder that fit under a sofa. He couldn't believe it. All those years and nobody was waiting to kidnap him, only fresh air and a world alive with sound and scent and color.

The illusions of his mother's rules were shattered.

He felt the bird all over the room. The house was different, contaminated, and he thought his mother would know as soon as she came home. She didn't notice, though. She came in swirling on beer like she always did. She kissed Owen on the forehead and ruffled his hair. She put on another pot of coffee.

Later that night, Owen and his mother walked the house together. They made sure all the doors were locked tight. His mom wiggled the handles to test their stay-putted-ness. They ensured the stove was off, fridge door was shut, and lights were turned off. Owen shut the window in the dining room. His mother sang out good night to him and went into her bedroom to collapse on her bed. He hung her coat, placed her purse on the table, and straightened her shoes near the front door. He felt like a ghost, haunting her by picking up after her.

8

O wen decided to ask his mother to start going outside officially, eventually working up to school and regular teenage boy things. He knew only what he'd seen on the reruns of family sitcoms: *The Fresh Prince of Bel-Air* and *Full House*. He wanted the drama: the two dates in one night, the bully who learns his lesson, and the opportunity to be caught cheating on a test, all to be wrapped up in under thirty minutes.

Two days later, and it was his fourteenth birthday. He sat at the table in the kitchen, his mother scrubbing the dishes from all the meals she had cooked throughout the day: oatmeal from the bottom of the pot, bits of bread crusts from plates, lasagna from forks. The question was lodged like a tennis ball in his throat. Gail sat cross-legged in his chest, tracing a wing on the top of his heart. Owen gulped, swallowed hard past the lump, and then forced it out.

"I've been cooped up too long and I think I'm old enough to go out in the world," he said. "I'll keep the bird on tight lockdown. We can start with leaving me in the car. I can't get into trouble in the car." He tapped his chest with two fingers and said, "No one, never." He sat back in the chair, satisfied with his pitch.

His mother stared at him, blinking once, twice. The faucet ran water over a spatula encrusted with lasagna. He wished he'd swallowed the lump, let it sit in all his stomach acid until it was nothing at all. His mom cleared her throat, turned the sink off, and wiped her hands on the dish towel that hung on the oven door. She walked towards him, ruffled his hair, and then picked up her keys and left through the front door without saying a word.

He stood up from the table, picked up his piece of pie, and walked into the bathroom to take a full, water-to-the-brim bath. He turned the faucet on hot. Once the water pounded the tub, Owen felt the urge to crawl in grow exponentially. He wanted to know what it was like to be completely submerged in water, to feel its warmth, and to know what it was like to have every bit of his skin feel the water's embrace. The urge to be in water had been with Owen since his birth, but he had no clue how or why it started. The desire to crawl into the water was a lot like Gail in that way.

He slipped out of his jeans and T-shirt and stood in his underwear. His shorts hung loosely off his rear end. His skin was pale, and he felt like a monster, a skeleton barely inhabited.

The water running in the tub was a roar like the creek in the winter, and steam crawled out of the bath and into the room. He leaned over the sink and bent down until he was real close to the mirror, right at the hole in his chest, where there was no skin, just bones and bird. Gail looked back at him. She winked. Her eyes were bright, full of excitement. The black mess of feathers on top of her head like a cheap bicycle helmet. His meat moved beneath her feet, lungs grew and shrunk, heart pumped, stomach folded. The steam rolled across the mirror and soon he couldn't see Gail, and it was like she was covered in smoke. The tub was more than halfway full, so he turned the water off. The silence following the cascade of sound stung his ears, but then it settled into his bones.

He considered his mother's warnings one last time. She believed rot would find his organs, green and black flecks of mold speckled on his heart and lungs, but she had been wrong about what waited for him outside. There had been no Army of Acronyms or doctors or social workers waiting to kidnap him, so he figured she was probably wrong about baths, too. He thought about all the baths everyone in the world must have taken with no problem at all. Kings and queens and poor folks and artists and science-fiction writers and waitresses. Why did they get to take baths while he couldn't? There it was again, the deep pull he felt when he was next to water, the desire to climb in, *the boy born during the flood*. One foot and then the other, and he sank down into the hot water.

The water was warm on his skin, and he closed his eyes and tried to feel where his body ended and the water began. Gail asked him to go under, so he plunged deep. Everything grew louder and quieter simultaneously. Gail tapped on his spine and the knocking sounded like thunder underwater. She was out of breath. He came up and pitched himself forward. Water sloshed out of the hole in his chest and ran over his ribs like the creek over logs.

A child of the flood, water was his equalizer. He was home.

He brought his birthday pie into the bath; bits of chocolate pudding and whipped cream clung to his chin. Piecrust littered the bathwater.

"How many flies does it take to screw in a lightbulb?" Gail shook out her feathers and kicked the water off her toes.

"How many?" Owen asked.

"Two, but no one knows how they got in there."

Owen laughed, snorting at the image of two flies having sex in a lightbulb.

His mother entered the house and closed the door quietly behind her. He heard her set down her keys. He was quiet in the tub, just the occasional drip from the faucet, while his mom roamed from room to room until she found him in the bathroom. He braced himself for her anger at him in the tub, ruining his insides and making a mess of the pie in the water.

His mother came in, still in her coat with a bottle of red wine, a mason jar, and a slice of cream pie. She set everything on the floor next to the tub and then plopped down next to him on the ground, her back against the wall. She stared forward, poured a glass of wine, and took a bite of pie. She cleared her throat. Took another bite of pie.

Owen couldn't take it anymore. "Mom," he said. "Helllllllooooo. Are you going to say something?"

She set down her plate and took a long gulp of wine. "Don't you ever wonder where she came from?" She leaned forward and turned around and peered at Gail. "Like, where'd you come from, Bird?"

Gail shuffled in his chest. "I woke up here. Always have been here."

"Exactly," his mom said. "That's how I remember it, too. It was just one morning, things were regular—well, almost regular. The Army of Acronyms said you were going to die, but you were regular, like no talking bird in your chest, just a boy with a heart condition. And then, one day, poof, there's a hole in your chest and a baby bird inside—just like that." She snapped her fingers.

"Just like that," Owen said. He pushed himself up, and the tub squeaked under his naked body. He knocked a piece of piecrust away so he could lean back.

"I tried to do research when Gail first showed up, but I was terrified of someone finding out you were here, a boy with a bird in his chest, in *Montana*. I was too scared to check out a book from the library or even pay cash for one in a store. You should have seen how they were at the hospital." She took a long drink of wine and then refilled her glass. "Just doctor after doctor and social worker after counselor, and they each told me you were dying. That has never left me. So I researched alone on the floor of the library and read what little I could find."

"What'd you find? How'd she get here?"

Gail leaned forward, her wings folded over her crossed legs.

"Who knows? Everything I read called it a phenomenon, unexplained. The only thing I can think of is this one time before you were born: your dad and I got drunk as skunks one night and drove way up the Coyote, where we used to climb trees together. And that's what we did that night, climb trees and drink gin, but at some point I felt light, like I could float off the branch and fly away—I swear it's true—I floated up and off the branch, but I didn't fly away, we were already so high off the ground, Owen, high in the tree. Instead—" She took another drink of wine. "Instead, I floated a few feet to where your dad was and I landed right on his lap, and I felt different for a moment." She paused and set her wine down. Her eyes were wide and cheeks flushed. "Owen," she said, "do you know how babies are made? Do you know what sex is?"

Owen's cheeks turned red, and he thought of flies in a lightbulb. "Yes." His knobby knees poked up out of the gray water. "I watched a PBS special."

His mom laughed. "A PBS special, okay. Well, your dad and I had sex in the tree that night, and I swear I just kept flying and I felt like I could fly for weeks afterwards."

Gail ran her wing down Owen's spine.

"I would have dreams where flocks of java sparrows were swirling around me. That's what Gail is, you know." His mom leaned forward and tapped a rib. "Like a java sparrow tornado. I used to worry that I put Gail there, that I ruined your life."

"Gail doesn't ruin my life."

"Sure, but she doesn't make things easy."

"What do the books say?"

"The books are bullshit." She scraped up the last bits of her pie. "Most of them say you developed a bird in your chest because your dad left shortly after I became pregnant with you, that you were cursed because I had you out of wedlock. The nice ones say you have a bird in your chest because you don't have a strong male figure, that you developed her to take on the role of father. It's all bullshit. They do say that there are other people born with animals inside them. They don't know how many, but they think others like you exist. They call them *Terrors*. That's how I know they're all wrong." She leaned far forward and scooted around, rotating to meet Owen's eyes. "No matter what, you are not a Terror. You are a delight, and so is Gail." She smiled, and her teeth were stained a dark red from the cheap wine.

"So you don't know how Gail got here?" He looked down at his chest, ran his finger along a rib that swam in open air.

"I do not, but this is what I do know. I know that you two are connected, that she makes you special, and that you are intertwined in a way that means you can't live without each other. The books say that you'll die when she dies, and vice versa; when you die, she dies. I know the way the doctors treated you. I know how rare it is, to get something like a bird in your chest, and I know what they will do when they find you. They will not let you go. It will be experiment after experiment until there is nothing left to test. No bird. No boy. The Army of Acronyms is relentless."

"Relentless."

"Which is why you can't go outside, even for a moment. What if a neighbor sees you? All it takes is for one person to find out and then it's all over. Gail is yours to protect, to keep safe. You die when she dies." His mom leaned hard against the wall and stuck her bottom lip out, blowing a stream of air to knock the hair out of her face.

"No one, never," Owen said.

"No one, never," his mom said, and she tapped her chest with two fingers. She stood up and leaned over the tub, scooping out bits of piecrust from the water. "My little Pisces fish." She ruffled his hair. "Born during the flood." She gathered her wine and the empty plates and left him in the bathroom. "Hope you don't rot your insides," she called, closing the door behind her.

9

Owen started off slow. He thought a lot about what his mother had said about the string of doctors and nurses and social workers and counselors and how they had been relentless, but his desire to be outside and to roam the big, wide world was stronger and bigger inside him, so every day he opened the door a little wider, and before too long, he was outside again.

He pushed the invisible boundaries he allowed himself to travel. Soon it was the front yard. And then, when he went unnoticed in the yard, it was the street. And eventually, by summer, it was the small woods at the bottom of the hill, where the street ended and a path wove through the trees along the creek.

He stood at the mouth of the path every day for one whole week.

At the end of the week, the June sun turned the air dry and hot, so when Owen closed the front door to their home, the doorknob was hot to the touch. He turned left. He walked slowly down the street. Most of the blinds were shut in the neighbors' homes. The air smelled of pine and cedar.

He stood at the barrier between road and woods. The small path at the bottom of the hill was dark and cold with shade, but the wind was calm. Mist rolled off the creek. He listened to the small crawl of the water and could barely hear cars on either side of the woods. The sun buzzed and birds chirped wildly in the trees, and Gail flitted back and forth in his chest. "Holy moly, this is something, isn't it?" she whispered.

He took a deep breath and stepped forward, moving from the hard asphalt to the soft dirt path. From this moment, the world expanded greatly for Owen.

He walked along the small path until he heard voices echoing through the trees, and so he stopped and placed his hands on a large oak. The trunk was smooth, save for a few rough patches of knotted bark. He thought of all the worry his mother carried inside her, of her warnings about what other people would do to him if they found out his secret. His two fingers tapped his chest and his heart quickened. Anyone could grab him out here. He wanted to run home, to flee.

"Climb this tree," Gail said. "We're always safe in trees."

He remembered his last hurrah and sitting in the tree with his mother. Then the memory was gone. It may have been a dream, not rooted in reality. He remembered the story his mother had told him months earlier about her and his disappeared father, um, *copulating* in a tree, drunk as skunks. From the bottom, he climbed slowly. Its branches twisted and turned around the other trees. Gail encouraged him to go higher still. About halfway up, a small set of pops erupted in the distance. The pops were far apart at first, and then quicker in succession, like popcorn popping in the microwave. Boys whooped and Owen climbed higher. He thought the higher he got, the safer he and Gail would be. Owen reached the top of the tree. He was so high, and the branches twisted in such a way that he couldn't make out the path or the creek below.

The view was far out across the small valley. To his left, beyond the trees, was a large field, and in front of him was historic downtown Morning. Just past the small park was the Wyden's Pharmacy building, and the Thelma neon sign ran along the theater's side and bookended the right side of downtown. The tall buildings lasted only a few blocks and then it was homes and churches until the mountains, which huddled around the valley. Forests peppered their sides, and Owen imagined each of the trees to be just like the oak that he sat in now. It seemed impossible that the world could be so big.

More pops in the distance. He turned to a clearing in the park to his left where the voices were coming from. There were two boys standing in the meadow holding a rifle. It was nothing like the compact handguns he'd seen on his soap operas. The gun was slender and long, and they took turns passing it back and forth, pumping and then firing at unseen targets. After each pop they would laugh, and one would knock the other on the back. Whoever wasn't shooting would take long drinks from a can. They swapped the gun and the can back and forth like this for a while, drinking and shooting in turn.

"Boys will be boys," Gail said.

The boys were older than Owen, their shoulders broader than his. Would he look like that in a few years? Their bodies were infused with confidence, their stance tall. Even from the tree he could see that they knew they belonged in that field, in the world. He couldn't fathom taking up space like that, not caring if you were noticed. The mountains turned orange in the waning sunlight, and a breeze blew cold over the tops of the trees. "Still not sure what it's like to be a boy and exist in the world," he said to Gail. The two boys in the clearing plopped down on the ground and set the rifle down, each laughing and opening up another can.

"Climbing a tree is a good start."

His foot fell asleep, so he pulled it out from under his leg and let the tingles dissipate down his calf. He pulled at the hem of his shirt and pulled the cotton T-shirt up to his neck, displaying the scene for Gail. It felt like he was showing the whole world what it was like to have a bird in his chest. He felt cradled and hidden in the tree's leaves, while also having the sensation that he was on top of the world.

Gail chirped a loud *POE-chirp-chirp-CHIRP-poe-poe-POE-TWEE-TOE-TWEET-tweet-tweet*. A declaration. He whistled a similar tune, and she thought it was one of the best jokes ever told. "Listen to you," she said. "That was funny."

When Owen climbed down the tree, the stars had barely started showing. The woods were dark in the twilight and the streetlamps had turned on by the time he reached the house. His bones were sore and his skin salty with sweat. He ran the bath cooler than usual, hoping to pull the sun's heat from his body so his mother wouldn't notice he'd left the house. His insides had remained the same, no mold, and so he'd discovered another way his mother was wrong. His hair still smelled of mountain air after he got out of the bath, but his mom didn't say anything when she got home. She rustled his wet hair and went into the kitchen to put on a pot of coffee and reheat food from the diner for Owen's dinner. He felt the air of the outside settling into his lungs, so he snuck away to his bedroom to puff on his inhaler.

10

Most days for the rest of the summer, Owen and Gail walked to the woods to climb the oak tree and watch the boys play target practice by shooting at beer cans after emptying them. The boys were loud, always hitting one another and screaming insults. Their idea of horsing around. Owen was uncomfortable by the sheer destruction of the boys, the mess they left behind, the space they took up. One afternoon when the sun was high in the sky and the heat almost too much to bear, the boys took off their shirts and sprawled out in the clearing. They sunbathed for a good part of the afternoon. Owen felt drawn to the boys, something in the danger of the gun leaning against the tree stump mixed with the vulnerability of them lounging in the field with their shirts off. Something made him want to get their attention.

"A BB gun like that can kill me, and you die when I die," Gail whispered up to him. "Anyways, you don't want their attention. Trust me. With boys like that, it'd be the wrong kind of attention."

"The wrong kind of attention," Owen repeated, dripping the words down to her.

Every night he ran a bath and took a spurt of his inhaler. He melted into the water: bones, skin, bird, boy, and bath all one, a soup of sorts, the boy born on the flood, his mother's Pisces fish.

All those baths meant that each day he got a good look at his naked form in the mirror. His body morphed and grew in ways that were strange to Owen, out of his control. He noticed that when he climbed down the tree each evening, a scent akin to the compost pile revealed itself in his armpits. Molehills popped out of nowhere along his forehead. His voice cracked.

Worst of all, though, was the way his penis behaved without his permission. He'd be in the oak tree watching the boys shoot their gun or his own scent would catch his nose, and suddenly his dick would be reporting for duty, standing at attention. It stood so straight and so hard that it seemed military metaphors were the only ones that would suffice, despite their cliché. Even Gail took to teasing him by announcing, *"BUMP-BADA-DUH! CHARGE!"* whenever he got an erection.

. . .

One afternoon on her day off, his mother walked the house, replacing each acorn on the windowsills. She dusted the bottle tree. She brought down the broom that hung above the front door and she swept every corner of the house. Owen helped her move furniture so she could sweep. Afterwards, she hung the broom back up in its place above the front door and went around with a burning bundle of sage. He asked his mother why the sudden attention to the house, and all she could say was, "Something's coming. I can feel it." She painted smoke in the corners and over Owen's body. She even had Gail poke her wings between Owen's ribs, so she could cleanse each wing, one at a time. The house smelled like fresh smoke, entirely different from the stale cigarette smoke that generally clung to the walls.

The house was quiet and clean. His lungs stung worse from the sage smoke, and so he puffed more on his inhaler, the third time that day.

. . .

It was a morning in August when he opened the front door and the air was gray and the light held a strange orange glow. His mother had just repainted the front porch, but the blue paint looked drab, not like the vibrant blue he knew it was. No breeze. The air felt stagnant like the world had fallen asleep.

"Shut the door," Gail said. "I don't like it. Something is wrong." She shared everything in the air with him, and he felt loneliness and a sense of death coming, and it scared him, but he thought it better to die in the oak tree than to live for a hundred years as a shut-in in that house. There was no going back to days of listlessly watching soaps and pretending to be a bird in the confines of a two-bedroom house. He laced up his sneakers and went outside.

The air was thick, and a dense layer of clouds covered the valley. He climbed the tree and his lungs clamped shut. From the top of the tree he could see the world was painted with a gray film, like a painter was trying to wash out the landscape they'd painted when they were a younger, more frivolous artist.

No boys in the field.

He could barely see the field from the tree. The air smelled like a campfire.

"We need to go," Gail said. "I don't like it out here."

He wanted to leave but didn't want it to seem like it was because of Gail. He was tired of her bossing him around. "Just a few more minutes." He inhaled the air deeply. It burned his lungs, and he wondered if it was poisonous gas.

"We have to go," Gail said, "like, yesterday." It felt like nothing moved, like the world was empty.

"In a minute," Owen said.

"I know you can feel what I feel. I know you can feel my panic." She started shaking in his chest. Her feathers vibrated.

"I have my own feelings. Not everything I feel is yours to have."

"Owen, we need to leave or I am going to throw a tantrum like you've never seen." She puffed out her chest and wings. His blood raced. Birds flew overhead.

"Oh, you only want to go home because that's what other birds are doing. You just want to be a bird in the sky." The air *was* poison, and it had seeped into his brain, made him say things he didn't mean.

"Of course I want to do what other birds do. Like it or not, I'm a bird." She rammed herself into his lungs and the air drained from his body. He tried to pull in more oxygen, but the air was too thick. He needed to go back home, and fast. He made his way down the tree. His eyelids burned. Gail knocked around in his chest from side to side.

She pushed her weight down on his spine and spread out her wings as far as she could. He thought she might burst. Her eyes rolled into the back of her head.

Gail rattled his ribs like the bars on a jail cell. "Let me outta here. I need to get away. We need to get away." He felt her breath shorten. The poisonous air had gotten to her, too. The desire to do anything drained from him, and he thought maybe it'd be okay if he just lay down on the dirt and waited for it all to end. He reached the base of the tree and forced himself to continue the rest of the way home. The asphalt was sticky, and the air was worse at the top of the hill. The sky was an orange glow and it all felt like a terrible dream, beautiful and deadly.

He walked in the front door and let his body go. He crawled to his room and puffed three times on his inhaler, his whole body sapped of everything: water, oxygen, energy.

Gail dissolved into a pile of bird. "We're gonna die. I die when you die, and vice versa, and we're as good as dead."

Owen went into the front room and lay facedown by the front door. He sank into the floor. He felt the whole planet beneath the floorboards rocking him. He closed his eyes and started counting to thirty, tried to imagine his limbs growing roots in the ground but got to fifteen and it was lights out.

11

Owen slipped in and out of consciousness in the car. Gail too. One would be awake, while the other passed out, and they traded off that way like they were keeping watch over Owen and his lungs.

The vinyl seat crinkled under his back. His only view was of the red fabric ceiling and the gray sky, split by the doorframe. The earth bumped and rolled and tossed him around, and it was a familiar sensation that he couldn't place.

Gail was silent, her lungs burning, too. His mom slammed her hands against the steering wheel and careened the wagon around corners. Soon the car stopped and his mother jumped out of the driver's seat. Owen propped himself up on an elbow in the backseat. It took nearly all his strength to do so. Gail was asleep. His mom was crying and she hugged her friend, Elayne. They stood in front of a large gray apartment complex. His mom backed away. Elayne pulled out a cell phone and called somebody. His mom was shaking. Snot ran from her nose to the back of her hand. Elayne hung up and hugged his mother one last time. Then she looked over at Owen and lifted her hand just an inch or two in a wave. Her eyes were damp with pity.

. . .

Time passed in more snippets.

. . .

They pulled up to a massive brick building, parking around back near a dumpster. His mom got out and leaned against the door, her back to Owen. She lit a cigarette.

A man in scrubs came out, ready with a syringe. The man's hands were thick, and a tingling spread through Owen's arm where he grabbed him through the car window. "It'll be quick," he said. He rolled up Owen's T-shirt sleeve, and before Owen could protest, the man drove the needle into his bicep. He plunged the syringe, removed it, and placed a bandage tenderly where the needle had been. He handed Owen a medical mask. "Wear this." The mask rubbed against Owen's nostrils, slightly too big.

His mom leaned against the car and finished her cigarette and talked to the man. They argued. His mom shouted, "No doctors, never," and Owen thought she might hit him, but she didn't. Instead she cried again, but not as hard as she had with Elayne. The man handed her a piece of paper and put a hand on her shoulder.

• • •

Later, his mom hovered over him in his only view out the window. She pumped gas. Dusk was settling, but the haze was so thick that time passed, the sun set, and nothing seemed to change. The earth stopped spinning.

• • •

Later still. There were no stars in the sky. The road bumped beneath the car's tires and Owen was floating. He'd grown used to the mask over his mouth, and his arm ached where he'd gotten the shot. He was carsick. They drove through the mountains, and Owen realized it was the furthest he and Gail had ever been from home. He thought of their house, how it was abandoned, how easily that one bird had flown into it, and he wondered how many more could fill the house. Gail was asleep. That damn bird.

Owen sat up. Outside the window a hillside was painted black from a fire. A few orange sparks still danced between trees. The highway was sectioned off with cones down to only one lane, and the line of cars stretched forever. Firemen in ash-covered yellow suits directed cars through the narrow lane. On the other side of the road, all the trees and brush were still green and brown, untouched by the fire. The black bones of a small house sat at the top of the hill. It was empty except for what looked like a couch that had partially been charred. He wondered where the people were.

12

He was still awake when they pulled into an empty parking lot early the next morning. His mother's eyes were wild from no sleep and cigarettes as her only sustenance. Her pupils darted to the building and then the steering wheel and then to the rearview mirror to check on her son. The earth was flat. It spanned in every direction with almost no hills and certainly no mountains. Owen felt closer to the sky, like the sky was close enough to crush them. He spotted only a couple of trees. Clumps of dried grass popped up along the side of the road, nearly no plants, just dry dirt, with the exception of the small manicured lawn on either side of a stout brick building.

"They don't open for another couple of hours, so we're just going to have to wait." His mom turned the car off and turned around to face him in the backseat.

"What are we waiting for?" His lungs were sore and his breaths were short, but it was better.

"A treatment to make sure this attack is beat. What the fuck were you thinking? I made it clear. This could have been it. I could have lost you, and then what?" She flung a few strands of hair out of her eyes. "Why don't you listen to me?"

His mother's tone shifted so suddenly, zero to sixty, a teakettle from tap water to boiling over. "I'm sorry."

"The whole town has to stay inside. You're lucky you're not dead."

Gail placed her beak between his ribs. "It's my fault, Janice. I let him go out in the first place."

"I don't care who told who what. You should have listened to me. I'm trying to keep you safe, goddammit." She turned back around and faced the empty building.

"I know." He pulled the mask off his mouth, swung his legs forward, and sat up. His mother popped the door open and climbed out. The door slammed shut, and she leaned against it, lighting a cigarette. The smoke swirled around and then disappeared. The wind did not carry it. It evaporated.

*   *   *

Three hours later he held his mom's hand and they walked into the brick building together. Owen had never been in a doctor's office before, only heard about the horror stories from his mother each night. Gail sank deep into his chest, made it so he could barely feel her. He'd never felt that before either, no stirring, no whispering words up his throat, only stillness, empty. So, so quiet inside.

The waiting room was harshly lit, like a supermarket. Rows of seats lined the wall and were arranged in the middle of the room. Different framed posters hung on the walls, encouraging healthy habits. *Try Something New Today* under a woman in leggings in a yoga pose. *Take a ME Moment* under the simple image of a cup of tea.

His mother instructed him to sit in one of the brown chairs against the wall. She walked up to a woman who sat behind a large desk. They spoke in hushed tones. She slipped the woman a piece of paper.

His mom walked over and sat next to him. "It'll be a minute." She placed a hand on his knee. The phone rang and someone in another room answered it. The clock ticked behind the desk. Nine-oh-five-A.M.

Soon they were called in. A nurse named Olivia carried a clipboard tight to her chest. His first instinct was to turn and run. *The Army of Acronyms is relentless.* His mother pushed hard against his back, moving him forward. She had to press so hard he nearly tumbled over. The nurse ushered them into a room off the main hallway.

The walls were mint green, and an exam table took up nearly all the space in the small room. A poster detailing tartar buildup in arteries hung near the door. Owen remembered a commercial for an antacid, firemen hosing down the inside of a heart on fire. He struggled to place himself here, in a doctor's exam room. None of it felt real, and he hoped he would open his eyes and wake up on the couch at home.

"Climb up here." Nurse Olivia patted the parchment paper on the table.

The paper rustled under Owen. He searched for Gail in the space above his heart, but she was still too small.

Nurse Olivia asked his mother a barrage of questions. His mom responded with short answers. Janice crossed and then uncrossed her legs, she fidgeted with a pen from her purse. "Really, he's usually pretty okay, and he's better now, but he needs this nebulator thing and then he'll be good as new."

"A nebulizer treatment is important for children with asthma, and he should be getting one every week. Who is his doctor in Morning?"

"He doesn't have one."

"He doesn't have one? When was his last checkup?"

"He's never needed one."

"What do you mean never? He has asthma."

"Not once. Never." His mom clicked her pen one last time and flung it into her purse. "Look, I was told you could give him the treatment and it would be no big deal. You can't make us see the doctor. I looked it up."

"With all due respect, ma'am, you brought him to us." She stood over the sink washing her hands. "And besides that, I think the most important thing is your son's health." She sat down and rolled her stool over to Owen, the wheels swooshing on the floor. "I'm going to listen to your breathing." She unwrapped the stethoscope from around her neck and reached for his shirt.

Owen jolted backwards on the table. "Wait," he said. "Don't." He thought he might have another asthma attack. Gail stirred in his chest. He whispered down to her, dripped the words down his throat, "Gail, what do I do? I don't know what to do, Gail," but Gail didn't move a muscle. Everything was bright and cold and the air smelled like popsicle sticks, and he knew they were here to take him away from his mother, and then they'd take Gail away from him. *Relentless.* The two adults stared at him. "I'm cold," he said to the nurse. "You can't touch me there. Don't." He scooted further back on the table.

"It's okay, Owen. I'm a nurse. Your mom's right here. I'm just going to listen to your breathing."

He turned to his mother, waiting for a sign for what to do next. She sat with her mouth agape, frozen. He considered running out of the room. He thought if he could muster the oxygen, he could scream at the top of his lungs for help, but he wasn't sure what he'd do when help arrived. It was all too real. Every scenario his mother had painted for him involved medical exam rooms just like the one he was in. This was the center of the Army of Acronyms. For the second time in as many days, he considered lying on the ground and going to sleep, giving up.

Nurse Olivia leaned back on her stool. "Owen, why don't you want me to listen to your breathing? Is there something wrong?" Her voice was softer now.

"Nothing's wrong. You just can't lift up my shirt." Gail shuffled uneasily in his chest.

Olivia turned towards his mother. "Is he always this skittish? Can you explain what I need him to do, that it'll be all right?"

He was sitting right there on the table and they were talking about him like he wasn't in the room. He wondered if he had suddenly vanished, a ghost.

"Just don't lift up his shirt. He's got a thing about taking his shirt off." His mother's voice cracked, and there was a quiet pleading.

"Okay." The wheels swooshed again on the linoleum floor.

His mother nodded an okay. He stretched his T-shirt out enough for Nurse Olivia to slide the metal ear of her stethoscope up to his chest. It was cold against his skin. She placed her right hand on his back over his shirt and used her left hand to maneuver the stethoscope over his lungs, his right side first. Her embrace was soft and deliberate. He breathed deeply when she asked him to and tried to breathe normally in between. When he breathed down deep it was the desert sands, a whole forest fire in his lungs.

She moved the stethoscope over his rib cage on the left side, and he held his breath, waiting for her to notice there was no skin there, just bones, but Olivia didn't say anything. "Breathe," she said.

Owen pulled in air and he felt the pressure leave his shoulders. He was going to get out of here without Gail being found out. The three of them would be leaving shortly.

Gail patted the top of his heart and brushed her head against his lung. "Good job," she whispered up to him. The words, as always, climbed up his throat slowly until they found his eardrums. "We're almost out of here." Owen felt relief in feeling Gail in his chest again. He sat up straight, smiled.

The problem was, Olivia had heard Gail's voice in the ear of her stethoscope. She popped up in her chair. "What?" She squinted her left eye and scanned the room.

Owen and his mother stared at each other and then looked back at the nurse.

"What?" his mother asked.

Olivia looked down at the stethoscope that stretched from her ears and still snaked under Owen's shirt like the instrument had betrayed her. "Never mind," she spoke the words slowly, pronouncing each syllable carefully.

Owen breathed again. Olivia tried to reposition the ear of the stethoscope to find his left lung, but she went too far left and the lip slipped into the space between his ribs. Her right hand was still on his back and she pressed more firmly. He held his breath again. She slid the instrument further to find his left lung, and in doing so, her finger slipped between his ribs and was, for a moment, inside his chest.

Gail responded the only way she knew how, and she bit the nurse's finger.

It wasn't hard, a nibble really, but Nurse Olivia shrieked and ripped her hand out from under Owen's shirt. "What the hell was that? What's going on in there?" She rolled her chair against the sink and stared flabbergasted at Owen's chest. She turned to his mother. "I heard a woman's voice, and then something pinched my finger. What's going on?" She stared down at her hands in disbelief. A small drop of blood formed on the tip of her ring finger.

His mother stared blankly at her. "What? I mean, what could you mean? I mean, really? What?" She placed a hand to her chest. "Lordy," she said. "I've never."

"What is wrong with your son? Lift up your shirt. Let me see." Nurse Olivia waved both of her hands upwards, trying to use telekinesis to get Owen's shirt off.

Olivia's freak-out ramped up Gail, who had a lot of pent-up flutters from remaining calm over the past twenty-four hours. Gail started shaking her feathers out at news that there might be something wrong with Owen. She chirped loudly. Olivia scanned the room for a bird that had somehow gotten inside. Janice did the same to seem inconspicuous.

Gail blasted a loud *POE-TWEE-TOE-TWEET-TWEET-TWEET* out of his chest, and it felt like a gust of wind escaping. She was so big then, a bird who couldn't be denied. Owen was unable to run out of the room and unable to stay and fight. No fight. No flight.

The doctor, a tall man with flat hair and wiry eyebrows, opened the door to find his nurse pinned against the sink in horror, a boy on the exam table trying to keep his upper body from twitching and convulsing in random directions, and a mother who scanned the room for a loose bird trapped inside. He ran over to Owen, his first instinct to take care of his patient. "Are you okay?" he asked, but before he could reach the boy, Owen's mother leapt up from her chair and blocked his path.

"You are not taking him away from me." She threw herself on top of her son.

Gail was completely unsure of what was going on, but she was certain that she and Owen were being taken away from Janice, and she welled up inside him and started pumping her wings like little fists.

The doctor took a step back. "What is going on here?" He turned to his nurse.

She pointed at Owen, who was still lying flat beneath his mother on the exam table. "He's got something wrong with his chest and won't show me. It bit me."

"His chest bit you?" The doctor raised a wiry eyebrow.

His mother's breath was warm against Owen's ear. "Never show them, never," she whispered, and then, "Gail, calm down." She slowly climbed off her son. She raised her hands high in the air, a surrender. Owen's eyes took a moment to readjust to the fluorescent lights. Gail settled down, quietly air-boxing.

He pulled the shirt down past his rump, stretched it as far as it would go. He sat up. "No one, never," and he tapped his chest with his two fingers. His mother could only shake her head.

The doctor took a step forward, his hands at his sides where everyone could see them. "No one's taking anyone away. Everything is okay." He put his right hand out front and petted the air slowly. It was a futile way to keep everyone calm since Gail couldn't see any of it, and really, she was the one controlling the energy in the room.

Possessed by curiosity, Olivia lunged forward and grabbed Owen's collar, trying to get a peek down his shirt. His mother jumped forward and tugged at Owen's arm, trying to pull him away and out the door. Owen stayed planted, doubling down on stretching his T-shirt over his stomach, keeping firm. The shirt was old, the hem was ratty, and so it ripped easily, tearing at the collar and down across his chest.

"Olivia," the doctor shouted. "What has gotten into you? My god." He stepped forward to intervene. Owen's mother let go of his arm.

Owen's first thought was that his mother didn't really have the money to buy him new clothes, so he blurted, "You're going to have to pay for that."

But no one said anything, only silence. The room was full with static. The air-conditioning unit clicked on. It was then that Owen realized his torn shirt hung wide on his left side, and these complete strangers, a doctor *and* a nurse, stared at his open chest where there was no skin, just bones, and the gabby bird who was not too happy.

"Now you've done it," Gail shouted. "Now you've really done it."

The doctor and Nurse Olivia looked at Owen in horror. There was nothing in their medical training that could have prepared them for the monster they were witnessing here in their very own clinic. Owen understood why people like him were known as Terrors. (*Their word, not ours.*)

The doctor leaned down so he was eye level with Gail. "My god, it's true. You do exist," and he reached out to try to touch Owen's rib cage.

Owen jumped back on the table. "You can't touch her."

"Yeah, don't come any closer," Gail said, like she had a gun and wasn't afraid to use it.

Nurse Olivia stared openmouthed, tongue hanging out. She sat frozen for what felt like a lifetime, and then her eyes rolled back in her head, the stool slid out from under her, and she passed out onto the floor.

The doctor grabbed Owen's wrist. "Stay right there," he hissed. He turned to check on his nurse, placing a finger to Olivia's neck for a pulse.

Gail shook in Owen's chest. "Janice," she yelled. "We need to get the fuck out of here." His mother sat in a stupor in the chair under the poster for tartar buildup. Owen wondered if she was thinking about how it'd be easier to lie down right there, to give up. "NOW," Gail yelled. A phone rang at the receptionist's desk and it woke his mother up, brought her into the present.

The doctor turned back to Owen. "Oh no you don't." He gripped Owen's wrist tighter and pulled him towards him on the ground. "We've been trying to find a Terror for decades. Research has been limited. No Terrors to be found. We thought you had all gone extinct, all dead. You cannot leave." His eyes were green, and they turned like gears. His lower lip quivered and Owen thought the doctor might cry, but the air was full of anger and he knew the doctor was quaking mad at how Owen *was*, mad at the bird in Owen's chest, mad that after eight years of med school and residency, he was stuck in this dump, but no longer, because here was his ticket out.

His mom shot over to the exam table. She wrapped her arm around Owen and placed her white Keds on the doctor's chest and kicked as hard as she could. The doctor fell back, surprised more than anything, but it was all they needed.

"Up, now," Gail yelled in his chest.

Owen was up and off the table in no time. They slammed the exam room door behind them. His mother pulled a chair from across the hall and placed it under the doorknob, just like on television.

"Go," she whispered to Owen, "go, go, go. Don't run, but move quickly."

He speed-walked and tried not to think about what would happen if they caught him: experiments and taking Gail away. The linoleum of the hallway became the carpet of the lobby. A back door in the hallway opened, and the doctor shouted after them.

"RUN," his mother yelled, and so they ran. Owen's shirt flew out at his sides like wings and he wished he could fly, but it was just pavement under his feet now, the sun flaring and stinging his eyeballs. No trees, no grass, nothing. His mom threw open her door and started the car. Owen was barely in the seat, door still open, when she put the car in reverse and tore out of the parking spot. The doctor pushed out of the lobby and ran towards them. He slammed his fists on the hood and his anger shook the whole car. He ran to Owen's side and grabbed for the door, tried to reach inside and pull Owen out.

"Mom," Owen yelled, "now."

His mom kicked the wagon into gear and took off towards the highway. The doctor lost hold of the door and it swung wildly. The doctor ran after them. He got to the road's end and screamed like an animal, slamming his fist against the yield sign. His mother slowed down enough for Owen to heave the door shut, and then she took off.

13

The flat ground slowly slipped up and up and soon they were climbing again, out of the deep, flat valley. Gail curled tight in Owen's chest, and when he searched for her to see how she was holding up, she retreated further. It felt like calling out into a canyon and hearing only the faint echo. His mother turned up the radio loud and clenched her jaw. Pearl Jam blasted over the car's speakers and the song came out gritty like playing through gravel, the speakers were so lousy.

Owen realized they were not heading home, the gap between the wagon and the comfort of their living room widening with each mile. He did not ask where they were going. His mom muttered, "Shit, shit, shit, shit," under her breath like she was keeping time. Her metered profanities turned to ramblings and she spoke to the road. "I can't do it anymore, nope, no way, no how. That man won't stop. Shit, shit, shit, shit." She shook her head back and forth. "He'll be better off with someone else. Almost anyone else." She turned and ruffled Owen's hair. "You'll be better off."

Somewhere near Yakima they pulled over at a Walmart. She left him in the car and was gone for nearly an hour. The sun was hot against the windshield and Owen cracked a window for air. He took a puff of his inhaler. His mom returned with shopping bags full of clothes, underwear, socks, pants, shirts, a coat. "Put a new shirt on." She handed him a sandwich wrapped in cellophane. He took off his torn shirt and slipped a new one on, a green T-shirt two sizes too big, stiff in the collar and sleeves to the elbows. "You'll grow into it," his mother said, and she pulled back onto the highway.

Soon the landscape turned into green forests and mountains, like home, but not. It was that way for hours, the ground slipping away from them and then back up again. No matter the miles between them, Owen felt the chase of the doctor behind them. Certainly the search had already begun. They'd gather statements from witnesses. They'd call in the hounds. No one would believe the doctor, and it would only make him more determined to track Owen down.

• • •

The sun was just beginning to disappear below the horizon and saltwater was in the air when they pulled off the road and onto a gravel driveway. Finally here, Owen asked where they were going.

"Your new home," his mom said. "This is your new home." Twice she said it, and the sting of *your* not *our* knocked him in the chest and he could not breathe.

Book Two

Teenaged

(How to Hide the Bird in Your Chest)

14

The house sat deep in the woods, the driveway long and flat, ending in a large circle. A truck sat parked near the driveway's edge; on the other side, a stack of wood. A small garage stood next to the truck. Inside the garage was a small hatchback car, packed in by boxes. The covered porch was cluttered with a couple chairs, stacks of firewood, and used mason jars and coffee mugs. White smoke puffed out of the small chimney and rose into the air in the early moonlight. The air smelled dirty and fishy.

"Seawater," Gail said.

The screen door creaked open and Owen's uncle, Bob, a tall man with a ponytail and beard tight to his chin, and his daughter, Tennessee, a girl an inch taller than Owen in a flannel shirt and two long braids, walked out of the house. They met in the middle of the driveway and took turns each exchanging hugs. When Owen hugged Tennessee, she smelled like soil and tomato plants in the summer. For the first time in two days, Owen felt his body settle a little. The sky was a dark aquamarine and creatures darted overhead. He ducked down when one flew a little close. "They're just bats," Tennessee told him. "They're out every night. Harmless." They walked towards the house together. Owen kept his eyes upwards, watching the bats fly into each other, dodging and ducking at the last moment. The trees were tighter in the Puget Sound, full of water and not afraid to huddle around one another. He had the feeling that no one could find him here, that this was a place where he could truly become disappeared.

Nearly the entire house could be seen from the front entryway. The walls were covered in a warm wood paneling. A fan whirred loudly in the window. On the left was the kitchen, where a boombox played public radio near the sink. Bob poured two cups of coffee, one for his sister and one for himself. He made tea for Owen and Tennessee. A small island separated the kitchen from the living room, and there was no television but a woodstove in the corner instead. Owen and his mother plopped down on the corduroy couch, Bob sat on the armchair in the corner, and Tennessee dragged in a barstool from the island.

The four of them (plus bird) sat in the living room and the adults caught up. Tennessee traced her tennis shoes with a blue marker. The fogginess of drifting in and out of sleep, of all the events of the past twenty-four hours, flooded Owen's mind (breathing in the poisonous air high in the tree, letting go, the car ride, the forest fire, and that morning in the doctor's office, *terror, terror—Terrors*). He slipped his shoes off and tucked his feet under his mother's legs like he used to. Gail fell asleep in his chest.

Hours later his mom nudged him awake and walked him into Tennessee's room where he'd sleep on the floor. A pile of clothes was clumped in the corner. It was obvious the clothes had been kicked out of the way to make room for his sleeping bag. There were two posters on the wall, one detailing how to differentiate between species of ferns and another charting the lifespan of Douglas-firs. He took two spurts on his inhaler and swallowed a pill with water.

His cousin turned on a small clock radio that sat next to her bed. "Hope you don't mind. It helps me sleep." The music was turned low, only loud enough to cover up the wind outside.

Owen said he didn't mind, and he rolled over. Soon Tennessee fell asleep and he was left alone. He wondered what the doctor was doing at that moment. Did he have a family? Had he shared the events of the day with his wife? She wouldn't believe him. He'd probably already contacted law enforcement, other scientists, DHS, CPS, MDs. The image of the doctor slamming his fist down on the hood of the car, of the absolute panic in his eyes, played over and over again for Owen.

Fuck that bird that flew inside and then left like it was nothing.

His heart beat so loudly it woke Gail. She sleepily ran her wing along his ribs. "It's okay. We're safe. We're cocooned in a sleeping bag. A bird in a boy in a bag in a house deep in the woods. We'll just lay low. Forever if need be. We will survive this."

His shoulders and sternum shook with the possibility of being found, of having Gail taken from him. The soft static of the radio covered the sound of his shaking. He was an earthquake in a sleeping bag. He rolled over onto his stomach to face the ground and felt the floor through the thin pillow. He pressed his nose into it.

He spread his arms wide and imagined roots growing from his fingertips and toes deep into the earth. They'd have to tear him out like an old stump if they were ever going to remove him. He thought of himself as an old-growth tree, living for hundreds of years on this bedroom floor with a bird who tickled his spine and a cousin who snored on the bed above him. He thought of decomposing and becoming bug food, and it soothed him.

15

The next morning Owen ate fresh raspberries from the garden on the couch, and Tennessee sat on the floor near the woodstove. His mom and uncle smoked on the back porch. They were so similar, when they talked, their mouths moved in the same way. His mother's crow's feet dipped down, but Bob's were deeper, ridges higher. They shared the vein that split across the forehead like an estuary. Owen thought he saw his mom cry, but it must have been smoke in her eyes, because she wiped her left eye and put out the cigarette. When she came back in, she seemed as peppy as ever.

Later they cleared out boxes in the garage, eventually unearthing a VW Rabbit. Bob pulled the hatchback into the driveway and Owen's mother parked the station wagon in the garage, hiding it away. She ran her hand along the rear window. "Goodbye," she whispered to the car, "you were a piece of shit, but you were my piece of shit." Then she wiped her hand on her jeans and they went into the house.

Once inside, his mom had him climb onto a kitchen stool. Tennessee grabbed a pair of old hair clippers from under the bathroom sink. The clippers buzzed loud in his mother's hand and vibrated along his skull. Clumps of hair floated down to the linoleum floor.

Gail whispered in his chest, "Bye-bye, hair."

Owen ran his hand along the short hair, all of it buzzed close to the scalp, a disguise.

That evening, they built a fire in the backyard. The sun poked its last rays before dipping into the Pacific, and swallows swirled around in the sky. Soon bats mixed in. Then the swallows were gone and there were only bats dodging each other and diving for bugs. Owen felt a sense of quiet in the woods next to the fire. Tennessee brought out the boom box and put on *Abbey Road*.

His mom held her beer high above her head. "To my son," her voice cut through the trees and Owen wondered how far it could travel, "who is more like his grandfather than he'll ever know."

Bob lifted his beer up high, too. "And quite a bit like his dad."

Owen's mom raised her left eyebrow. They clinked their bottles together, held eye contact, each tapped their beer against their knees and took a drink. Tennessee rolled her eyes.

The fire popped and cracked in the metal bowl in the middle, and the sky was saturated in starlight, more stars than darkness. Owen hadn't seen stars like that in a long time, maybe ever. His neck hurt from staring up at the night sky. Soon his mom and uncle were red in the face and shouting about their own parents, how gone they were.

His mom lit a cigarette and leaned forward, meeting Bob's eyes. "I always thought Dad would meet Owen after Mom was gone, like maybe he'd be free to be around us again. Kinda wished they'd at least gotten to meet him once, even if it meant Mom had been there."

Owen didn't know what to do, his mother talking about him like he wasn't right there, telling his uncle things she'd never said to him.

Bob set his beer on the ground. "Well, if it's any consolation, Mom and Dad met Tennessee, and all Mom did was criticize me and Marie. It was an awful trip that I regretted for a long time."

"I don't know. At least they met her. I thought I had time, but Dad only got two days without her. It doesn't seem fair."

Tennessee stood up, slinked next to the fire, and went inside. She returned a moment later with a beer. She took a long pull on it and then passed it to Owen. He checked in on his mom, but she was waving her cigarette around in the air like a sparkler on the Fourth of July and beer sloshed from her bottle. Bits of tears like dew dotted the corner of her eye. He took a drink and gulped the beer down his throat. He passed the beer back to his cousin.

His uncle Bob and his mother grew silent for a moment. A log popped in the fire. Owen ran his tennis shoe along the ground, drawing spirals in the dry dirt.

"It's fucked," Bob said, suddenly clear minded, "so fucked what I'm going to say. It's just—" His face was red with beer. "Dad's better off."

"Dead," Owen's mom said.

"Yeah, he's got to be happier in the ground."

Bug food, Owen thought.

Both Bob and his mom took long gulps on their beer, and the sound of the beer sloshing could be heard over the fire. Bob burped loudly. His beer bottle swung loosely between his middle and index fingers.

The carbonation from the beer bubbled up in Owen's stomach and lifted his head so it floated ever so slightly off his neck, like a balloon tied to a fence post.

It was nearly midnight when Bob went inside, where he clanged pots and pans and exploded across the kitchen, cooking and folding quesadillas for everyone. Tennessee got up to help him. "He'll set off the smoke alarm otherwise."

It was only Owen and Gail and his mother. "This is it?" Owen asked his mom. "You're leaving and now I live here in the woods in hiding?" He almost said the word *Terror*, but he stopped a millisecond before it leapt from his mouth, a sign of restraint.

His mother handed him his inhaler. "Take a puff, honey." She pitched herself forward, leaning on her knees. "I need to go back." She set her beer on the ground and moved to the chair next to his. "I need to go back to work. You need to be somewhere they can't find you."

"You really think they're looking for us?" The doctor's office felt like a lifetime ago. They were in a different world, an alternate dimension.

"Don't be naïve." She shook her head in disgust, picked her beer off the ground, and took a swig. "We might never be safe together again." She tapped her chest with her fingers.

"No one, never," Owen said, a reflex. "Can't we prove them wrong? We can lift my shirt up real quick and there'll be no Gail there, an optical illusion or something." He imagined a papier-mâché sculpture of a regular boy's chest covering the hole and bird above his heart, maybe a series of mirrors.

"They will always see the boy sitting in the doctor's office that first day. They will never un-see the bird in your chest. Once that secret is out, it's out." She looked over her shoulder at the kitchen. Bob and Tennessee were laughing, and Bob was trying to flip a quesadilla in the pan without a spatula, just a flick of the wrist. His mother looked back at the fire. "You'll be happy here. You'll have a fuller family."

"You're my family," he said.

She set her beer back down and stacked her hands on his knees. Owen watched the fire. His mom leaned down until her face took up the entirety of his view. "I'm sorry it's this way. So, so, so sorry." She sat up and watched the fire with him. "At least you're getting your wish. You get to start school next week." Bob and Tennessee were plating the quesadillas and getting ready to bring out the late-night course. "Just listen to Gail. You've got to blend in." She propped her left elbow on her right knee and let her wrist fall limp.

• • •

His mother left the next morning to no fanfare or to-do. She ruffled Owen's hair and tapped her chest with two fingers. The air was warm and muggy. Clouds hung like a gray film above the tree line. His mother went to the garage and climbed into the station wagon, grabbing two packs of cigarettes from the glove box and the pine tree air freshener that hung from the rearview mirror. She slid her body through the tight space between the boxes and the car. She got into the GMC pickup and pulled out of the driveway, waving once before turning onto the road.

He stood next to his cousin and uncle and stared at the space where she had been, where he had last seen her.

16

Owen missed things he never thought he'd miss when he moved to Bob and Tennessee's. His mother's footsteps. Owen woke up the first few nights wondering what strange man was walking down the hall. (*The doctor? The doctor? The doctor?*) He stayed motionless on the floor with the sleeping bag zipped all the way to his chin until he heard his uncle's cough. When he woke up, it was not to the morning news and his mom asleep on the couch, but instead to the sounds of Tennessee's clock radio or nothing at all, maybe chirping birds and squirrels running through the branches. He missed his neighbor's car pulling into the driveway every evening at 5:52.

There were some things that were almost like the old house, but slightly different, lost in translation. Small rocks and crystals lined the windowsills instead of acorns. A recycling container in the front held empty bottles instead of a bottle tree. (Although there was a glass wind chime off the back porch that caught the light like the bottle tree used to.) The French press sputtered when it was plunged, and it almost sounded like the last sputterings of the old coffee maker.

The first few nights in the new home, Owen walked around and shut the house down like his mom used to make him do. He locked all the doors, fastened dead bolts, checked the range, shut all the windows, and turned off each lamp. The house was completely shut down and dark, save for a sliver of moonlight that came in through the window. He was safe; no doctor could reach him. He stood in the living room and relished in the safety, but when he climbed into his sleeping bag, he worried he'd missed something, a window unclasped, the woodstove open. On the third night, he woke up to his uncle pounding on the bedroom window, locked out of his own house. After that, Owen let someone else shut down the house each night, and often he woke up to unlocked doors and lights left on for no one. And so soon Owen also missed the feeling of safety, that moment when the house was shut down and dark, the outside world disappeared, and with it, the Army of Acronyms.

He missed how his mother swirled in the living room on wine. He missed her contorted body while she ranted about how dangerous the world was, the drags of a cigarette her only punctuation. He missed playing hide-and-seek and feeling like he'd actually become invisible, the way the game made his mom laugh every time. He missed living with someone who knew about Gail.

Owen found some comfort in the ritual of Bob and Tennessee's house.

He and Gail spent the week before school started hiking through the woods with Tennessee. Their boots clomped through forest. Tennessee bent down and pet the leaves of certain plants, naming the ones she knew. "Pacific bleeding hearts. English ivy. Red alders." She reached out and placed a firm palm on the tree's gray bark. She bent down and touched the leaves of a plant growing at the base of the tree. "This is a sword fern, also known as a pala pala plant."

He bent down next to her, curling his ankles over his feet. He ran his fingers along the fern's rough leaves and passed the sensation to Gail, so she could know what it felt like to touch the leaf of a sword fern when the sun cracked and split through the leaves. For a moment he thought of returning home and telling his mother about what Tennessee had taught him, and then reality clicked back into its slot.

17

Owen found that the best way to remain incognito was to pretend there was no bird in his chest. He imagined he was like every other boy, nothing but a beating heart in his chest and skin that covered all the right parts, and definitely no talking bird.

He locked himself in the bathroom and practiced hiding Gail while the bathtub filled up. He walked circles, stopped to look at himself in the mirror, drank water, did anything he might do at school surrounded by humans. He farted. He burped. He scratched under his armpits. He bent his knees and hunched over the sink like he was stationed at a desk.

Gail watched for any indication that he was carrying a bird in his chest. She'd tap his spine at the first sign that he was giving her away. "Stand up straight," she said. "Only someone ashamed of a secret holds their shoulders that way." When he got really good, Gail stopped hiding herself. She went wild, knocking around his insides, trying to turn him inside out. He reminded himself that there was no bird flapping her wings in his chest, nothing to see here.

Soon his denial of Gail was somewhat of a comfort to him, a shawl he could wear out in the world. He grew easier while eating dinner with a plate on his lap next to the fire pit, easier on his hikes with Tennessee. The hardest part was first thing in the morning when he was truly relaxed, the moment just after waking up when he felt regular, normal, no pretending. It felt like everyone knew he had a bird in his chest and no one cared. A twitch from Tennessee while she slept or the screen door slamming behind Bob on his way out, and the feeling was gone.

• • •

It turned out that school was, of all the places in the world, one of the easiest to disappear in. The hallways were overstuffed with teenagers, each squeezing past one another in a hurry to get to a classroom. All the bodies pressed up against each other made Owen bristle. A knobby shoulder cut into his chest. Most of the kids had their head down, a cell phone in front of their face, somewhere else. Classmates stepped on his toes. Gail pushed up against his chest and spread her wings across his rib cage, worried he was being trampled. He ignored her and made his way to room 106. When Owen got to class, there were more students than expected, so they spent the first hour locating enough desks. By the time everyone had a place to sit, it was on to the next class. Owen stood up with the others and moved quietly among the throng of students.

He was relieved when he found Tennessee at lunch. She patted the beige linoleum tile next to her on the ground. Owen sat down, his boney rump not much of a cushion. He met his cousin's two friends: Dean, a boy with dark hair to his ears, a light-brown complexion, a safety pin in his left earlobe, and a wide smile; and Ava, a girl with white, white, white skin, and despite the warm day, a long, black cape. Owen was the youngest, a freshman, while Tennessee and her friends were all juniors, but no one seemed to care. They sat under the trophy case displaying black-and-white photos of the 1954 basketball team and two full-color photos of choirs from 2010 and 2011.

Tennessee leaned over and pointed out people to avoid. "That's July. Prick," she said about a boy with short hair, dark brown eyes, and a chain hanging from his left ear. "Clyde. Evangelical blowhard. Lives next door. Different kind of prick." Clyde's skinny arms poked out of an extra-large T-shirt with an image of a jar of pickles that read RELISH SWEET JESUS. Clyde lifted his index finger in a wave in their direction. Tennessee ignored him. Cheerleaders and football stars. "Pricks,"

Tennessee said. AP history kids, "Bigger pricks. Not our people," Tennessee whispered. Owen wondered how many of these "pricks" were related to the Army of Acronyms. *Not our people.* He wondered if there was anywhere he was truly safe.

Near the end of the day Owen's head buzzed with more social interaction than he'd encountered in his entire life. How could he be around so many people and still feel so lonely? *Maybe the world is too big*, he thought. And of course, there was still his last class of the day, certainly the worst: gym. He had been instructed to dress down, even on the first day. "It's easy," his uncle had said. "All the other kids will be in their underwear, too. It'll be over before you know it."

He and Gail devised a plan to change in the bathroom stall to ensure she wouldn't be seen. It would be over in a few minutes: slip into the stall, change the clothes, flush the toilet (to avoid suspicion), and voilà, ready for class, his classmates none the wiser.

The problem wasn't Owen, but Gail. She couldn't see any of the boys in towels or whitey-tighties, but their mere presence was enough to ruffle her feathers. By the time Owen reached the stall, she was bouncing up and down inside his chest, knocking her head against his clavicle, slamming her feet against his stomach.

"Quiet, girl." He swallowed the words down to her. He shut the stall door and put his index finger under his shirt to let her nibble. She almost bit it off with excitement.

The stall was skinny and long. He nearly fell into the toilet pulling his pants off. His ass slammed into the stall door when he pulled up his gym shorts. The door shook on its hinges. When he pulled his shirt off, Gail peeked through the gaps in the stall and saw a boy's bare shoulders (a garden of freckles) and she went bonkers. She'd spent her whole life locked up in his chest, never really seeing something like a dozen naked boys in one room, only their skin and hair, muscles. She flapped and squawked and the wind from her feathers blew against his heart, and before he could pull the T-shirt over his head, she slammed against his lungs so fiercely that she knocked the wind right out of him.

He squatted down on the toilet in his gym shorts and put his arms over his head, trying to get his breath back. He didn't have his inhaler.

He focused on his breathing. Sweat poured from his forehead. His heart pounded and knees ached. It felt like he'd run a marathon. His body buzzed with pain and static. His brain pounded against the inside of his skull and he thought he might vomit. He wished for vomit. He flushed the toilet and went to class.

The next day, Owen averted his eyes, stared at the stall wall, away from the door. It meant more of a cramped space. He hit his head against the wall, knocked his knee against the toilet paper dispenser, but it kept Gail quiet and he didn't have to worry about seeing those freckles.

18

The first weekend after Owen started school, the rain began. The gray clouds were taken over by a sky that was black and purple and rich with water. It came down like Owen had never seen before, not even when the creek would flood. It was like something in the sky had been ripped open. The downpour was in his bones, and blood ran through his veins like flooded streets. It felt like it was raining for Owen. For those moments, it felt like the world was righting itself and telling the truth.

It felt like home.

The boy born during the flood.

A pan was placed in the living room to catch water that dropped from a small leak in the roof. Bob sat next to the woodstove for two days, feeding wood into the fire and blowing cigarette smoke up the chimney. Owen and Tennessee sat at the island and did homework. They listened to the radio turned low with the window open. They took the bag with all the collected chicken bones from their dinners over the summer and emptied it into the slow cooker on the counter. Tennessee filled the water to the top of the pot. They placed carrots, onions, garlic, celery, elderberry, dried mushrooms, and lots of salt in the broth. It simmered on the counter for two days. The house smelled like fresh rain and soup.

On Sunday Owen and Tennessee hiked through the woods. Water poured down every leaf and branch. His new parka sent the rain running along his hood and down the side of his jacket like Beaver Creek in the winter.

Usually when they went on their hikes, they walked past the garden and down into the woods. They'd turn right at the small creek and head towards the water, balancing on the small creek's stones and wobbling down to the Sound, where the water was a slow spill for miles. This time, they stepped over the creek and kept walking straight, deeper into the woods. Clyde, the boy Tennessee referred to as an *evangelical blowhard*, lived on the adjoining property, and soon they reached the fence that ran between his property and their own. There were two thin electric wires that surrounded the property on all four sides. The electric fence weaved into chicken wire at places and strung between rotten wood slats at others.

"We stay off their property," Tennessee warned, nodding to the other side of the fence.

"Trouble," Gail whispered up to him.

"Not our people," Tennessee said.

Owen added Clyde to the list of people who were not *his people*. On the list were the other boys at school who called out after him and others in the hallway, yelling *bitch* with a hard *B* and *fag*. (He had not stayed *entirely* disappeared.)

A border collie came careening down the hill, barking and yapping to high heaven. Owen jumped back, startled. He was always on edge outside the house.

"Jeez Louise," Tennessee said. "She's a loud dog, but really, she's fine."

The dog's teeth were bared. Her gums were black with spots of pink.

"She just wants you to throw a stick for her." The dog ran back and forth along the electric fence, getting as close to it as she could without actually touching it.

Tennessee picked up a stick and flung it over the fence. The ends spun around each other and it crashed somewhere in the distance. "Go get it, Jeez Louise. Leave us alone." Jeez Louise turned and ran off to retrieve the stick.

• • •

Despite the return of the water and the hominess of living near the Sound, Owen couldn't find comfort like he'd known at the old house. Thoughts flashed like oil in a pan and he would see the Army of Acronyms kidnapping his mother and interrogating her about his whereabouts. If he closed his eyes for too long, his mind shimmered with the image of the doctor sitting in a car on the other side of the driveway, waiting for the right moment to nab Owen and begin his experiments. Owen had to puff on his inhaler several times over the weekend. He hoped his mother would call. He thought if he could hear her voice and know she was okay, it would ease his thoughts. He thought she'd call soon, but the phone didn't ring.

Life ticked on.

Each morning he had oatmeal with his uncle and cousin. He took his time getting ready while Tennessee knelt in front of the small altar she'd built with sticks and rocks and a Prince postcard kept on top of a short table next to her dresser. Owen watched the rain drip down the window while his cousin drew a card from her tarot deck.

On days when the rain was at its worst, Bob would drive Owen and Tennessee to school. The drive was short. They pulled out of the driveway and down the hill like a roller coaster. At the bottom of the hill was an open field. Nearly every morning, rain or shine, Clyde sat on his horse in the field. He was such a skinny white farm boy, his elbows pink, always in a T-shirt, even in the downpour. Clyde watched nothing in the distance, a rifle slung across the back of the horse's saddle. The rifle looked like the same one Owen saw all summer in the field in Montana. *The wrong kind of attention.*

19

One night in mid-November, they put shovels, flashlights, and a tin pail into the trunk of the Rabbit, and everyone climbed in.

Tennessee pushed the front seat back and sat down. "You're in for a real treat." Her neck craned backwards to meet Owen's eyes.

It was nearly eight at night when they reached the highway. The moon was crescent and shone above of the sparse clouds, creating a silver ridge that sliced through the black sky. Bob turned on his brights, and the light woke up the forest. Tree trunks shone gray and brown in the Rabbit's headlights. The highway curved and snaked for nearly an hour. Tennessee turned the radio up and the three of them sang along with Paul McCartney and Led Zeppelin. They belted out loud with Hall and Oates. Owen remembered those times his mother came home and had just the right amount of wine so that she was loose but not weepy, when she would twirl in the living room in her underwear and T-shirt. Gail twirled in his chest now.

Bob pulled the Rabbit onto the side of the road. The trees had grown much sparser, now a mix of pines and birches. Long, thin grass swept along the side of the highway. A stone wall lined the road, and the air was nearly pitch-black on the other side of the wall.

They climbed out of the car. A static roar rose up from beyond a hill and Owen was astonished by how loud it was, so loud Tennessee's voice came out muffled. She yelled at him to put on his parka and grab a shovel. Bob switched on flashlights and passed one to each of them.

The light beams cut through the darkness, bobbed up and down with each of their steps, and crisscrossed over one another. The air was water. Owen walked with the shovel on his shoulder, exactly like his uncle and cousin. He waited for the roar to stop or soften, but it only grew louder.

They climbed to the top of the small hill. Owen couldn't hear anything over the static roar now, not even Gail, even though he knew she bounced around, a cacophony of freaking out in his chest.

The roar reached its apex when they crowned the hill and nothing stood between them and the monstrous ocean. The ocean crashed. The water glistened white in the moonlight. Truly the edge of the world, nothing out there but crabs and whales and singing mermaids.

Tennessee and Bob threw their shovels and flashlights down in the sand, arched their backs and let out a vicious howl that stung the air. They laughed, and Tennessee elbowed Owen. *Come on*, she mouthed, and the three of them howled at the crescent moon. "Louder," Tennessee said, and so he really pushed his voice his hardest and belted out a loud, sustained howl. *AaaaAAAAaaarrrroooOOOOOOooooooOOOO ooooOOOOoo-ooooooo.* Gail did the same in his chest. It was a funny thing, a bird howling at the moon.

Bob bent down and lit the small propane lantern, and they walked the rest of the way down to the beach. Small pools of water dug their way out of the sand. There were a few other groups of people with lanterns, flashlights, and shovels.

Tennessee stood on the shore and she spread her arms wide. "North America's cunt," she yelled.

The three of them laughed, but Bob shushed her between laughs. "Not everyone loves that word like you do."

Owen leaned over so that his mouth was right next to Tennessee's ear. "The end of the world," he said.

Tennessee turned and faced him. The wind knocked a few loose strands of hair into her face. "Or the beginning."

The waves crawled up the sand. Owen always felt the pull to the deep water tugging at him and calling his name in the background of his life, but he had never felt the desire so strong as it was here, next to the roaring ocean, and he had the urge to wade into the deep water, to keep going until he was completely submerged and he could live there forever. *Under the sea.* It seemed to Owen that he belonged to the water, or that he *was* the water. It felt like something he was born with, something inherited. He shoved the desire to wade into the sea deep down and walked next to Tennessee and Bob. They stopped at one of the small pools.

"This is perfect." Bob set the lantern on the ground and pointed his flashlight at the sand. "We want to dig where these small holes are, Owen. See it there?" He pointed at a tiny hole the size of a pencil's head. "We're going to have a bucket full of clams by the end of the night."

They took turns digging the first hole, each one taking a small scoop of sand with the shovel and letting the sand fall from the scoop, making sure there were no clams. "Be gentle. We want the clams in one piece," Tennessee instructed. Soon they found a small clam, maybe an inch across.

"Perfect," Bob said, and the clam's shell tinned against the galvanized metal pail. They each split up and took to digging holes separately.

The ocean's waves were a constant stream of water, each one tumbling over the other, like the sea only knew one action: spitting waves at the shore. Gail yelled up to him through his throat. "This is a moment. Remember it," she said.

"A moment for what?" Owen asked, throwing the words down his throat back to her.

"Just a moment. You should store it for later."

He shoveled and shoveled the sand, hoping he could find a clam to contribute to the bucket, really just ignoring Gail.

"This is magic," Gail continued. "This is how magic is made. Keep this moment with you, carry it in your brain. If you get to be out in the world, experiencing things, you have to remember the experiences."

He stopped shoveling and leaned on the handle. Gail got ideas like these stuck in her craw and there was no avoiding it, like *go outside and climb a tree*, and then later, *TAKE ME HOME NOW*, and always, *what is it like to fly.* He'd learned to lean into it, so he scanned the scene, downloaded the moment for later. The wind was something fierce now and it mixed with the waves, and together they created a wall of sound. The hood of his parka whipped into his face. Bob and Tennessee stood just a few feet away, but he nearly didn't recognize them. The lantern on the ground cast a strange glow when it stirred with the moonlight. "Pick up a small stone," Gail said. "Take it home with you. It'll help with the magic."

He picked up a tiny pebble and placed it in the pocket of his jeans. His voice was strained from yelling down the back of his throat to Gail, so he turned his attention back to the clamming. He leaned far, far forward and scanned the ground with his flashlight, looking for another small hole. When he found one, he dug and dug. He was worried they would go back to the house and he would have found no clam at all, contributing nothing. He was surprised when he unearthed a clam at the bottom of the hole. He brought it over to the bucket and dropped it in with the others, happy he'd found at least one.

Tennessee clapped her hand against his back. "Hey, most folks don't find one on their first dig."

He beamed as wide as the flashlight.

On the way back, Tennessee let him sit up front. She fell asleep in the backseat with her forehead against the window. Bob turned the radio down so it was a quiet whisper. "Did you have fun?" he asked Owen.

"Yeah. I've never seen the ocean before."

Bob stared at him for a moment, taking his eyes off the road. "No shit. I'm surprised your mother never took you." Owen tried to imagine his mother on the beach, the wind whipping her hair while she hunched over the sand, searching for clams, but he couldn't picture it. Bob turned the wiper blades down and placed both hands on the wheel.

"Did you and my mom ever go to the beach together?" Owen said the words quietly, cautious to invoke his mother. He thought talking about her would make him cry.

"Yeah, when we were kids. Our dad used to take us clamming, too, and your mom loved the beach so much that when it was time to leave, she kicked and screamed and threw such a tantrum, our dad had to carry her back to the car."

Owen laughed at the notion of his mom kicking and screaming when it was time to go, but he couldn't imagine her as a child, so when he pictured her it was as she was now, a full-grown adult throwing a tantrum because she didn't want to leave the beach. "I like the ocean, too," he said.

"It's a magical place," Bob said, and then, "You're a good kid."

Owen traced lines in the condensation on the window, warmed by the idea that he was like his mother.

The clouds huddled around one another in the sky and grew closer together until they were one large cloud. Bob pulled the car into the driveway well past midnight, and the rain had started up again. They unloaded the trunk. Tennessee went right to bed. Bob built a small fire and started his ritual of rolling cigarettes and then smoking them in quick succession. Owen wasn't tired and a chill sat in his bones, so he turned the bathwater on to take a bath, a substitution for walking into the ocean.

He stripped down and looked at his naked body in the mirror. His clothes, crumpled on the floor in the corner of the bathroom, looked like the remains of someone who'd spontaneously combusted.

Gail laughed, the black feathers mounded like a bad dye job on top of her head bouncing up and down. He closed his eyes and felt the cold linoleum beneath the pads of his feet. He pushed his weight down into the floor and felt rooted, tied to the ground. He felt the space he occupied, and for a moment, he felt at home in his body. Without any warning, he stood at full attention.

BUMP-BADA-DUH! CHARGE!

Normally he would ignore it and eventually his dick would grow soft. Instead, he looked straight down at his hard dick pointing at itself in the mirror. He reached down and touched it. He placed his hand firmly around it. He remembered what the air felt like flowing freely through his lungs when he'd howled at the moon. He climbed onto the counter, his back to the mirror and his legs swinging freely.

His heels kicked the cabinet. The mirror and the counter were cold on his skin but he ignored it, then embraced it. His mind wandered. He thought of gardens of freckles and bare shoulders. He thought of no one in particular. He thought about a weight on top of him. He thought of swinging breasts, of kisses along his neck, of the vinyl backseat of a car, of bodies fuller than his. A stillness entered him. His mind went to the woods, branches as hands reached out and ran fingers along his shoulders. Roots tickled his calves. He was at the beach and algae slipped in and out of his toes. The ocean was inside him and he matched its rhythm, in and out with each wave, back and forth. The sound of the tub running matched the ocean roar in his ears. The whole world rocked inside him. He was warmth. He was shaking when he opened his eyes. The air swooshed inside him. Everything felt easier than it'd ever felt before. He came.

It was the first time since arriving at the house on the Puget Sound that Owen was able to let go of the fear of the doctor. For a moment he didn't feel the deep longing for his mother. It was only himself and the kernel of desire that had been lodged behind his thighs. He basked in the roar of the tub, the stillness of the room. He pinched the tip of his dick and moved the come around for a second before cleaning it up. Parts of his spirit had been blasted around the room. He collected a few of the pieces. Before he flushed the mess down the toilet, he thought about the rock from the beach, a small piece of magic, and now parts of himself scattered across the room, another small piece of magic, like giving himself away, a sacrifice.

"Can I see the rock?" Gail asked. He ran his hands under the faucet, toweled off, picked up his jeans off the floor, and dug the stone out of the pocket. It was smaller than his pinky nail, a copper brown with flecks of black. He handed it to Gail. She held it between her two wings, right in front of her face. Then she placed it in the tip of her beak and tossed her head back, swallowing it whole.

"Not even going to let me say goodbye, huh?" He shook his head and stepped into the hot bath. He closed his eyes and imagined he was in the ocean, living under the sea.

20

A month later Owen got the call from his mother he'd been wait-ing for. He was napping on the couch when the phone rang, shaking him awake. No one ever called the landline, save for telemar-keters or occasionally Ava to tell Tennessee to hike to the water to meet her. His mother's voice was calculating and quiet, and her breath passed through her lips fast.

"Owen?"

"Mom?"

"Yes. But we can't talk long. I'm calling from a pay phone, last one in town. It won't be long before they follow me here and tap it. I'm watching the doctor's movements on the internet. Owen, he's asking a lot of questions. He's still looking for you."

Her voice was soft in his ears, and it sounded higher than usual, like a poor impersonation of his mother, the way that no one's voice sounds quite right over the phone. Gail sat cross-legged in his chest, leaning hard against his spine at the place right below his throat.

"Can't talk long. Just wanted to say that we don't live at the house anymore. I'm living somewhere else. We can't go back. It's not safe. You're safe there, though. Are you being safe?"

"I'm safe," he said. The fog of his nap was lifting, and he came to understand he was talking to his mother for the first time in four months. What did she mean the doctor was still looking for him? "Mom, are you okay?"

"Me? I'm fine, never been better. I mean, I've been better, but you get the idea. Don't worry about me." A large truck or a gust of wind passed on the other side and static bloomed in Owen's ear and then wilted. "There's no time to talk about me," she said. "I only called to tell you the old house is done. It's still there, just I'm not there anymore. I'll keep renting it to throw them off the scent. I live somewhere else. You live somewhere else. I need to go."

"Okay." He tried to clear his still cloudy mind, but he couldn't. "I miss you."

"I love you." She hung up, and a loud *click* popped in his eardrum. He set the receiver down.

A part of him assumed when his mother called, she would realize that she needed to be with him and would move here, or maybe she would pick him up and take him back to Morning, where he would be more appreciative of his time in the house, no more long days staying disappeared. He thought of the doctor's eyes, the way he'd held Owen's wrist. A panic spread like static electricity across his chest and around his back, as wide as his shoulders.

"Sit down on the couch," Gail instructed. "Both feet on the floor, hands on your thighs." Owen sat down and focused on the couch's corduroy fabric running stripes down his back. Gail ran her wing along his spine. "Pretend like you're playing hide-and-seek and it's your turn to seek."

Owen closed his eyes tight, so much darkness it hurt. He imagined his feet digging roots through the floor and past the floor and into the earth. His feet dug deeper and deeper into the earth's crust. He counted to thirty. When he opened his eyes, the room was filled with white light. His eyelids fluttered. His fuzzy vision and the rain outside meshed until there was no world beyond the rain or even the back door. It was just him and the living room, a small fire popping in the corner. He went into the bedroom to puff on his inhaler.

The panic quieted to the low rumble that was its constant. Owen had nightmares, well not nightmares, per se, since he wasn't asleep. They weren't daydreams, either, since daydreams implied happiness. From time to time Owen's mind wandered. He imagined what it would be like to be taken away by the Army of Acronyms. He imagined the doctor and nurse had finally tracked him down and were ripping him away from his life in Washington. In his nightmares, Tennessee was always confused, and rightfully so. She baffled at Owen as he was dragged backwards down the beach, his heels digging two parallel lines in the sand. She would run up to him and scream at the Army of Acronyms, ask why they were doing this to him. She'd beg the police to let him go, adamantly protesting that he'd done nothing wrong. Sometimes, he imagined his cousin didn't chase after him at all but instead watched him with a perplexed look on her face as he was dragged away, and then she always placed her right hand to her forehead to shield her eyes from the sun: the last image before the day-mare was finished. Owen always felt sadness here, not at his imagining being taken away, but because this was how his cousin learned about Gail. He didn't want her to find out about Gail this way, kicking and screaming, the cousin who simply vanished one day on the beach or was stolen from the bedroom late one night. Wake up in the morning and TA-DA, cousin gone.

Gail took the phone call seriously and she made herself so small that it felt like there was nothing but a rock in his chest. He reached down towards her, dripped words down his throat, but there was no response. He couldn't draw her out with jokes. He ran his finger along his rib and couldn't get her to nibble. She began what she called *Gail's vow of silence for an undetermined amount of time*. It seemed everyone disappeared: Gail, his mother, and maybe someday he'd disappear, too.

For the first time in his life, he was alone.

21

After Owen's mother called, panic and loneliness swirled a hurricane in his chest. When he found quiet moments alone to masturbate, it was like he was in the eye of the storm, and everything grew quiet. He knew there was more wind and rain and destruction on the other side, but the moment of peace was enough. He spent the winter break masturbating in as many new locations as he could muster. The backseat of the station wagon. Once behind a large Douglas-fir, feeling the bark under his fingertips. He came on the forest floor and left it there for the rain to wash away. His favorite place to masturbate was on the bathroom counter, right before he climbed into the bathtub. The tub ran loud, and he thought of other, faceless bodies on top of him, of standing dripping wet in a rainstorm, and of the boys in the field with their rifle. He climbed into the tub afterwards and was held by the warm water, and he felt so clean, so empty.

No matter where he masturbated, afterwards Owen always knew that bits of himself were broken and then left around the place he'd done it, and if every time he came, he left bits of himself places, then he also always felt a little bit of the place inside himself. Like the stone from the beach Gail had swallowed, but it was something microscopic, pieces of the forest or the backseat of the station wagon, like the more places he did it, the more he melded with everywhere around him.

22

The day before winter break ended, Owen, Bob, and Tennessee went into Olympia. *Futzing around town*, they called it.

The city was crowded with the Army of Acronyms, and Owen thought he saw the doctor three different times during their futz, but when he got closer, he realized he was mistaken. It turned out the doctor looked like a lot of other middle-aged white men. He saw several cops and even a herd of nurses in scrubs. Every man carrying a briefcase sent his heart racing. Gail still observed *Gail's vow of silence for an undetermined amount of time*, so he was grateful he'd brought his inhaler. Without Gail's presence, it was the only thing that could ease the desert sands of panic in his lungs.

He tried his first cappuccino, and it tasted like caramel and dirt and toasted almonds and cherry pits. The coffee shop was covered in warm wood and the bar vibrated against his palm every time the steam wand bubbled in the milk.

Outside, the sky was open and blue, and he wanted so badly to share it with Gail, but she wouldn't have it.

They ate free bread from the bakery.

They ended at the record store. In front of the store was a tree with a dozen different tennis shoes, all run-down and dirty, tied to its branches. The shoes hung like smelly old fruit. "Art," Bob scoffed. He pushed open the door and a bell hanging from the jamb rang. He pulled both of them aside and smiled widely. "Never gave you your

Christmas presents." He opened up his wallet and handed each of them a fifty-dollar bill. Owen's mother always had to work the lunch shift on Christmas, and so for most of his life the holiday passed by like any other day, the only difference being the soap operas ran reruns through New Year's. He had been surprised when Bob had come home with a tree no taller than three feet, and the idea of celebration grew on Owen, even when the tree sat undecorated for its first week in the home.

Owen held the money for a moment. "I can't," he said. "It's too much."

"Don't be ridiculous." Bob's eyes were deep hazel, and he placed a delicate hand on Owen's shoulder.

Tennessee gripped Owen's hand loosely and dragged him around the record shop, shoving CDs into his arms. He didn't recognize a single album she handed him, and this made her smile every time.

Radiohead. Sleater-Kinney. Car Seat Headrest. Bikini Kill. Dirty Projectors. The Smiths. The Stooges. Fleetwood Mac. Beat Happening. Prince. Queen. Sufjan Stevens. And motherfucking Björk. Bob gave them more money, to make sure they didn't have to put anything back. Owen thought he felt Gail twitch with excitement, but he wasn't sure.

Later, Owen sat on the floor with his head against the bed, Tennessee sat cross-legged in front of him. A new CD player sat where the clock radio used to. Only the string of Christmas lights and the lamp were turned on. Tennessee had draped a lavender scarf over the lamp's shade. She sat on the floor, shuffling her tarot deck before drawing a card and placing it on the floor in front of her. She did this two more times, and after each card, she sighed heavily.

Owen didn't ask what that was about. He was too lost in all the new sounds. He kept thinking about how much his mom would have loved all this music, and part of him wanted to call her, to break their pact, doctor be damned, so he could play the Dirty Projectors over the phone, but he didn't have a number to call if he'd wanted to. He imagined his mother swirling in her underwear in their old living room, the way Gail had swirled in his chest. He let the music into his skull, felt it sink under his skin and wiggle his muscles. The guitars and drums and pianos and voices hummed along the walls and the whole house felt different. The music cracked Owen open, and now he thought it was such a shame that he couldn't share it with Gail. He knew she must be experiencing it, too, but she was so shut up in his chest, he couldn't say for sure. He wondered if Tennessee experienced the cracking. What did it mean to listen to something that could crack open your chest, if there wasn't something inside of you that could mirror that cracking, like who was it for, then?

He stood up and slipped his boots on.

Tennessee rolled over. "Where are you going?"

"Outside."

The forest floor crunched under his boots. The day had opened him up so wide that he couldn't stand it anymore. "Gail," he whispered down his throat, "this sucks."

She took her vow of silence so seriously that she didn't respond, and so he kept walking. It was dark in the woods, so he stood next to one of the trees, the one he'd masturbated next to maybe, and closed his eyes, counting to thirty. *Bright as day.* He kept walking, and when he reached the small creek, he turned towards the Sound. He placed his hand under his shirt and felt his heartbeat and traced the edges of his ribs with his fingertip.

The water was gray and dark. The clouds parted for a moment and the moon lit up the sand. Owen climbed up onto the fallen tree and hunched over. He bent his knees and tiptoed until he was near the water. The tree was sturdy beneath him. He straightened his legs and put his hands to his hips. When he closed his eyes, the cold cut his earlobes into icicles. He let his knuckles grow numb. He shivered. Even on a freezing day in December, he had the desire to keep walking until he walked off the log and into the water. It was even harder to ignore with Gail so quiet, the urge like a calling of his name or a tugging on his waist. He resisted. He sent everything down to Gail until he didn't have to even think about it. Everything he felt, she felt as well. Then he spoke: "I get it. I get it. I mean I really do. But it sucks, and I don't know what to do about it. You are a part of me. You ARE me. I can't ignore you, but I need to stay disappeared. I can do it. I can live like this some of the time. I can live like this at the house and even in the bath and definitely at school or the grocery store and sometimes at a coffee shop, but I cannot live this way all the time." A large wave broke right beneath his feet on both sides of the log. "So, what do you say? How do we fix this? You gotta give me something that reminds me you're there, that I am not all alone. Because really, I don't give a shit about feeling safe if it's just me and no one else, no bird, just a boy."

The air smelled like seaweed, and he pulled it into his nostrils and down to Gail. And she sent back nothing. His shoulders fell down from his ears and he relaxed. He thought again of walking off the log and into the water.

Gail let out the faintest of chirps.

It was quiet at first. He couldn't hear it over the wind or the waves. It was nearly nothing, but then she chirped louder, and it was *tweet-chirp-chirp-tweet-tweet-tweet-chirp-chirp-tweet*. It messed with his brain to hear such a soft birdsong when it was so dark out. The tweets and the chirps swirled around each other and he saw the sound like ribbons, one orange and one purple. They danced in circles out onto the water: two strands of rope that loosened and spread and flew apart until somewhere out there, they split up completely and then they were gone, and he remembered he had a bird in his chest. No matter what, she'd always be there.

From then on, he walked to the water every other day, alone, so that Gail could chirp softly. Nothing felt better than the moment after, when it was quiet and there was no one but him and the bird.

23

Owen turned his attention away from the bird in his chest and this sent it to his fingertips and toes, to the top of his head.

Owen grew like a beanstalk.

His new perspective sent cramps to his calves and thighs. His newly found height meant he noticed things he'd never seen before. There was a small row of rocks that sat on the hood above the stove. Citrine, rose quartz, an agate, a geode, and some obsidian all lined up in a straight row. The part in Tennessee's hair curved slightly to the left in the back. There was a basketball wedged between the eaves of the house and the aluminum roof of the back porch. His new height also meant he could see above the bathroom stalls in the locker room.

One afternoon, Owen changed before gym class. He did his best to keep his eyes away from the crack in the stall door and the top of the stall walls. He didn't want to repeat the first incident, bird going nutso and knocking into his rib cage, so he studied the plain white tile floor. His head knocked against the stall and his ass against the door. The door rattled on its hinges. Bare feet slapped on the wet tile floor outside the stall. His jeans got caught on the heel of his foot and he pitched forward to meet the toilet bowl, stopping himself short with a hand on the wall. He paused for a moment. His breath was deep and full.

Someone shuffled in the stall next to him. Nothing special here. Boys shuffled into the stalls while he changed nearly every day, but this was different, there were no low grunts or sniffles to cover up their discomfort. It was someone like Owen, someone making the distinct shuffling sounds of getting undressed and then dressing again in new clothes. They were nearly silent, hoping to go unnoticed.

Owen knew it must be another Terror. He felt it in his bones.

Owen had to know who this boy was, maybe his only chance at meeting another Terror. He forgot where he was. He poked his head up and tried to peek down into the stall next to him, but all he saw was a mess of brown hair. He got down on his knees. The tile was hard against his kneecaps and cold against his palms. The floor smelled like a chlorinated pool. From here, he saw nothing but two dirty socks, each a light gray with three yellow stripes running at the ankle, no other clues, no shoes, no pants.

Gail tapped Owen's shoulder blade and he turned around, saw the bathroom stall from the floor, the toilet only inches from his face, and he scrambled to get up, suddenly aware of where he was and what he must look like. He slipped on his shorts and laced up his tennis shoes. By the time he was dressed and out of the stall, the boy in the stall next to him had already left and gone to class. When Owen got to the gym, everyone ran laps around the basketball court and their tennis shoes squeaked on the gym floor. Owen tried but he couldn't spot a single pair of yellow-striped socks.

· · ·

The idea of other Terrors had always been abstract for Owen, long distant. His mom had talked about books she'd read, but he'd never *known* another Terror, and he thought for sure he'd never meet another Terror, and even if he did, how would he know it? But once he thought that maybe he went to school with someone who had an animal wrapped up inside, he started to suspect everyone was carrying some animal deep in their bodies. The thought snuck into his brain, and like a woodpecker, it pounded on his skull, keeping rhythm and time. To an outsider, Owen looked like he was somewhere else, but in reality, he was relishing the idea that there could be someone who was different in the way he was different. He stared at classmates and teachers and wondered what creatures they carried in their bodies. He stared so hard he tripped over backpacks. Once, he walked into the janitor's closet instead of homeroom.

Everything stacked up and piled on to make Owen anything but disappeared: his new height, his lack of attention to his surroundings, the way he stared at his classmates, imagining the animals they could be carrying. And since Gail was still practicing *Gail's vow of silence for an undetermined amount of time*, Owen had no one to correct him, no one to tell him to stand up straight, keep his eyes to himself.

It was how he found himself after school one afternoon, closing his locker to three boys staring at him, standing far too close for comfort. He scanned the hallway in each direction, but it was empty. Even the janitor who at this time of day usually walked the hallways with his push broom had vanished. It was only Owen and three boys. In front was Jon (the one most frequently calling him *fag* and *queer* and *nerd* and *geek* and *asshat*). The two boys who flanked Jon on either side were Troy (short hair and a long, long rattail braided down his back) and July (a chain hung from his left earlobe).

Lately these three boys had been flinging more insults in Owen's direction, but they were always spitting insults at anyone who crossed their path, a shotgun spray of hurting as many of their peers as possible. The insults weren't inventive. *Asshole. Dildo. Homo. Fucker. Little fucker. Gay-wad.* Quantity over quality.

Owen leaned back against his locker and it clicked shut. He told himself he was just like them, no bird in his chest, and if he were just like them, then they wouldn't hurt him. Owen wanted to lie down on the linoleum floor and give up. It was that same feeling he'd felt during the asthma attack and again in the doctor's office. He kept his hand on the locker, a way to tether himself to the ground. The locker door was cold against his fingers and elbow.

Jon took a deep breath and brushed the hair out of his eyes "What's your deal?"

"What's my deal?" Owen thought hard on how to answer such a question. He wasn't sure he had a deal, other than the bird in his chest, and no way was he sharing that.

"Yeah, asshole. What's your deal?" Jon tilted his head a little to the left like he was reading Owen like a book and was ready to turn to the next page. His breath smelled like parmesan cheese.

"I'm not sure what you mean," Owen said.

Troy chimed in from the back. "He means you're a weirdo and no one likes weirdos. No one likes you."

Didn't people like Owen? He whispered to his right shoulder. "People like me." It didn't come out all that convincing.

Jon turned to his co-conspirators. "Hear that? People like him." He turned back to Owen. "You gonna cry about it?"

By now, Owen *was* holding back tears. He tasted their saltiness in the back of his throat. "No," he said, his voice cracking like it was tripping up stairs.

"Nah, no one likes you. Stop. Staring."

Owen nodded slowly, like his head was on a rocking chair.

Jon held out two fingers, nearly poking Owen's eyes. He pointed down to the ground. "Eyes. Down."

Owen looked down, studied the three sets of shoes, a pair of hiking boots, black Vans, and a white pair of Nikes. The shoes pivoted a full 180 on the green linoleum floor and left him standing there, looking at the ground.

Safe, he puffed on his inhaler in the empty hallway. Owen had always assumed it was only adults who could be in the Army of Acronyms. He'd been cautious around other students since they certainly had parents in the Army of Acronyms, but he never thought he had to really worry about someone his age.

He wasn't sure why the boys had singled him out. He didn't think they knew about Gail. It felt more like a general hatred, not the pointed disgust he'd seen on the doctor's face. Could they really tell he was all that different without even knowing him? Was it that obvious? From then on, it was head down, barrel through to class.

• • •

Owen asked Bob to get another key to the house, so he could lock the doors nightly again without locking his uncle outside. He buried the key in a planter on the back porch, deep in the soil, so only Bob and

Tennessee would know how to find it. He imagined the key sprouting a small bush that would bear dead bolt locks as fruits. He reinstated his nightly ritual of shutting down the house, clasping windows, triple-checking the stove, locking every door. Every day added new dangers. The Army of Acronyms, the doctor, and now, three boys.

24

A week later Tennessee and Owen sat next to the woodstove. It was a Saturday, so he'd let his panic from the week settle, convincing himself he could feel a little at ease in the house next to his cousin. He stared at her and wondered what kind of animal she would keep in her body if she were a Terror. He imagined a salamander in her thigh. She looked up from her textbook. "What are you staring at?"

Oh no, Owen thought, *not her too.*

"Sorry. I'm somewhere else," he said.

"Where?"

He shrugged. He ran his hand along the rug and felt its buzz on his palms.

"I get stared at all day. Maybe I can have a break when I'm in my own home."

He nodded. "Why do people stare?" He meant the question in general, because he felt their eyes, too, but he could guess why they stared at him, the unnamable thing that obviously separated Owen from everyone else, the thing that drew the three boys to him, *something different. The wrong kind of attention.*

But Tennessee thought he wanted specifics. "Because I'm queer." She turned back to her math homework.

There was a sharpness to her admission. The way she said it was not like an insult, but like the word was a crystal she carried in her pocket. He wondered how she could admit something like being *queer* and mean it like an asset, despite the boys who threw the word around like it was the worst thing someone could be. He reached out and placed a hand on her textbook. "I don't mean to stare, and if I do, it's not because of that."

"I know," Tennessee said. She ran her pencil's eraser along each of her eyebrows, and the fire purred and cracked in the woodstove.

25

Owen wanted Gail back. Missing his mother and the talking bird in his chest was too much to bear for him, and the moments when she chirped over the water were not enough. He tried all sorts of things to wake her up, to shake her out of her shell. Anything to end *Gail's vow of silence for an undetermined amount of time*. He stared at her in the bathroom mirror, cooed at her in his chest. She just turned around and faced his back, not even giving him a chance. One afternoon he walked into the woods towards Clyde's property. He stood at the part of the fence that was all chicken wire woven with the electric wire. He hovered his hand above it. He placed his pointer finger on the electric fence, and a jolt of electricity ran up his arm and spread across his chest. Owen thought the electricity would wake Gail up, bring her back from the dead, like the electric paddles on TV. She stayed curled up tight in his chest.

A man on a horse crested the top of the hill, Clyde's dad. The horse blew angry out its nose. Clyde's dad wore his hat low, low on his eyebrows. The man took up so much space on that horse, and Owen knew he must be related to those boys in the field who shot their BB gun all last summer; related to Jon, Troy, and July. He saw it then, how men like this could all be related to one another, a long lineage of men taking whatever was in front of them, of *boys being boys*. The long rifle poked out on both sides of Clyde's dad's hips. Clyde came over the hill on a second horse. The horses were the same size, but Clyde was dwarfed next to his father. When he saw Owen looking at him, he puffed up his chest, a cheap imitation of his father with his skinny arms and his oversized T-shirt. Clyde took his hand off the saddle and ran it over his buzzed hair. His father kept his eyes locked on Owen, like his son wasn't there. Owen did his best and looked Clyde's dad in his eyes, and then he turned around and walked back towards the house. Jeez Louise barked up a storm.

26

An early evening in May, they flipped the fire pit over and had their first fire of the year. Owen had grown accustomed to the fires in his life. The fire in the woodstove each morning and every night, the candles Tennessee lit atop her dresser, the circle they built around the pit in the summer. The flames danced up and over the rim of the bowl, and Owen held his fingers out to the fire. His palms grew hot. He spread his fingertips wide and leaned back. Tennessee and Bob each had a beer, and Bob rolled and smoked his cigarettes in quick succession. Soon the bats came out and ducked and flitted across the midnight-blue sky. They sat in silence for a while, a log popping every now and then.

Owen imagined what it would be like if Bob and Tennessee knew about Gail. Maybe she would talk then, be more than a rock in his chest, her lips sealed shut. He could have his T-shirt off. She could enjoy the flames, maybe even chat a bit with his uncle and cousin. She could be a smoker, too, if she wanted, and he imagined her with a bird-sized cigarette.

Bob got up and got another round of beers for him and Tennessee, but he said, "Two is enough," when he handed Tennessee hers.

She nodded.

Soon Bob got up and got another beer for himself. They threw another log on the fire. The stars stretched long and thin above them, and Bob grew weepy and leaned over the flames and pulled both of them in towards him. He had a hand on Owen's kneecap and the other arm around Tennessee's shoulders. "You're both such good kids," he said. "Just goddamn good kids."

He looked Owen in the eyes. "Your dad would have loved the shit out of you. If he knew you were here, he would have stuck around."

Owen wasn't sure why his dad would have stuck around, when even his mother, who knew him and said she loved him, had left him here next to the ocean. He wanted to ask Bob, but there was a glassiness in his uncle's eyes. It looked like they'd been emptied out, like he had disappeared into himself. Bob turned to Tennessee. "And Marie loved you so much." A frog was stuck in his throat, and he took a swig of beer to clear it. "It's just she couldn't be around me because I'm a fuckup." Tennessee looked straight ahead, her cheekbones high and mouth tight. Her eyes rolled so subtly that only Owen saw them. Bob pulled both of his hands back towards his body and held his palms in front of his face. He looked at his hands like they didn't belong to him, like he didn't know what they were doing there. Tennessee stood up and put her arms around his shoulders and squeezed him while he looked at the ground.

"There's something I have to tell you." She inhaled deeply. Clouds moved overhead and it felt like the roof of the sky was closing.

Her dad looked up at her. The fire shone orange on the side of his face. "What?"

"I'm gay."

Gail sat down in Owen's chest, a big plop down, and then quiet again, disappeared.

Bob looked at his hands again. "That's okay. It's okay. I wish it wasn't true, but it'll be okay."

"You wish it wasn't true?"

"It's just going to be hard. So, so hard. It won't be easy."

"Oh, you're old. It's different now. Everyone is gay these days."

"Yes," he said. "Everyone is gay these days." His face was somber. He wrapped his arm around his daughter's waist and put his other hand on Owen's knee. He looked deep into the fire. "Good kids," he mumbled to himself.

Tennessee went into the kitchen and brought two beers outside.

Owen thought she'd give one to Bob, but she handed it to Owen instead and kept the other for herself. She grinned and placed her index finger to her lips. He took a pull on the beer and placed it on the ground behind the chair where Bob couldn't see it. It didn't matter anyhow. Bob was somewhere else.

Owen finished the beer and Tennessee got him another one, and soon he just sat in the chair and drank his beer openly. Bob fell asleep sitting up. Gail felt the buzz from the beer because Owen passed it down to her. The beer tugged her out of her shell and pulled her out into his chest so he could feel her again, really feel her behind his ribs. He let her know what it was like to be fifteen and in the woods next to a fire. He was warmed by this secret that Tennessee and he were sharing. Owen could not remember a single time in his life when he'd felt so good, maybe watching *The Little Mermaid* on the big screen, the only time he'd been to a theater, or maybe the one time up in the tree watching the boys shoot their gun in the field, before the business with the fire and his lungs seizing up.

Gail whispered up to him in his chest, "How many punk rockers does it take to mow a lawn?" The sound of her voice startled him.

"How many?" he asked. Tennessee stood up and wandered to the edge of the woods where she pulled her jeans down to her ankles. Owen had been surprised the first time he'd seen his cousin pee in the woods, but he'd kept his mouth shut and now he was used to it. Tennessee peed outside whenever she felt like it, even when a bathroom was twenty feet away. Owen looked towards the fire.

Gail finished the joke. "Punk rockers don't mow lawns. They mow hawks."

Owen sputtered beer out his lips. Tennessee had her hands wrapped around a tree trunk and she leaned her bare ass way out, peeing on a fern. When she came back, Owen told her the joke and she erupted with laughter. The smell of pine smoke burned the inside of his nostrils.

"That's what I like about you, Cousin. You're funny," she said.

Owen got up and went into the bedroom to take a spurt of his inhaler.

27

There's something about clear, blue skies and the promise of summer that turns human beings into absolute animals. One day left at school. Tennessee had disappeared to god knows where. Owen walked home through the woods, alone.

The sun splintered through the trees. Birds chirped all around him. They yelled and screamed and sang and belched. The woods were never quiet because of the birds. Their songs drove Gail nuts and she did her best to ignore it. After her one joke the night Tennessee came out, Gail had returned to silence. The times they were out in the woods were the only time she had difficulty maintaining *Gail's vow of silence for an undetermined amount of time*. His ears buzzed after a day of school bells ringing, lockers slamming shut, and kids yelling at one another over the music that played from their cell phones in the hallways. It was chilly in the forest, the shadows from the trees stacked on top of one another. He tiptoed on rocks over the small stream that led to the inlet. His boots rustled through a fern and scuffed against the dirt.

He got to the fallen fir and he ducked under the large trunk, his backpack rubbed against the bark, and he rose up on the other side. He pushed the hair out of his eyes and found Jon, Troy, and July waiting for him. Owen placed a hand to his chest. All the birds stopped singing. The wind even stopped blowing.

Gail stomped her feet in his chest, "Run," she said. "Turn around and run." She was not so quiet, not so much a rock, thus ending *Gail's vow of silence for an undetermined amount of time* (time determined).

He wanted to run but he was sandwiched between the fallen tree and the boys. There was never anyone else in these woods. They must've followed him. *The Army of Acronyms is relentless.* Jon held a long stick and he flung it into the woods. It crashed through the branches some thirty feet out. Owen thought for a moment of Jeez Louise running after it.

The three boys all took a step closer to Owen in unison. "Turn around now," Gail whispered to Owen. "It's your only chance." He cleared his throat. Troy's mouth curled like he'd just taken a bite of sweet chocolate. The boys seemed at ease in the woods.

Owen turned around and grabbed the fallen tree trunk with both of his hands and swung beneath the tree. His hair brushed against the bark.

"Where you going?" Jon said. "We just want to talk."

Owen's feet landed on the other side of the trunk and he pulled himself out from under it. He took two steps before he was jerked back by his backpack. He turned around. Troy had grabbed ahold of it and his eyes shone. *The wrong kind of attention.* Gail curled her wings at her sides and tightened her stance. Jon and July walked around the side of the log. Troy stepped closer. He placed a hand on Owen's shoulder, and it was such a gentle gesture that Owen thought maybe they'd simply let him go home. All he wanted was to go home. Troy looked at him deeply. Like Owen, he also had small wisps of hair that grew on his upper lip. His eyes were dark brown, almost black. Owen had never stood so close to a boy like that. Any other situation and Gail would be yelling, *"BUMP-BADA-DUH! CHARGE!"* but she was busy stomping back and forth in his chest.

Troy shoved Owen, and he fell easily to the ground. The forest turned the sound back up again and the wind tore through the trees like a cracked whip. The water rushed to the Sound. It was loud, way too loud. The trees stretched high into the air above him. They looked like rows of spears and their tops swayed. For a minute, from this angle, it looked like it could still be a beautiful day. Owen remembered where he was, and he tried to pull himself up off the ground, but his head was downhill and his backpack was heavy. He couldn't get up.

Jon and July each stepped on Owen's wrists, gluing him to the ground. The blood rushed to his head and his sinuses tingled. Troy straddled him with a foot on each side. He leaned down and grabbed Owen's collar and picked his shoulders off the ground. Then he punched Owen in the nose. His nose knocked against his skull and blood poured out like a water faucet. Gail knocked around in his chest, trying to break free to let the boys have it. *Let me at 'em. Give them hell. Float like a butterfly and sting like a bee.*

Blood dripped down the back of Owen's throat and ran across his cheeks and into his hair. He tried to stand up again, mustered more strength, but Jon and July placed more pressure on his wrists. They must've weighed a thousand pounds each. Air sloshed around in his head like an ocean. Troy stomped on his stomach, and all the air left Owen's body. He gasped to save any of his breath but there was no use. It was all gone. The desert sands returned to his lungs.

This is death, he thought.

For a moment, Owen heard only the distant ocean's roar, its static buzz and hiss. He imagined the rhythm of it flooding the Sound, the waves pulling away from the coast of Asia and slamming against North America, and then sliding away from North America and roaring back towards Asia, a simple back-and-forth, a surging. Jon and July laughed openly above him. The ocean burst inside him. With each set of waves that struck the Washington coast, a spurt of blood gushed from his nose. It tasted like seawater.

He sought mercy in Jon and July. He thought they might take pity on him, maybe not let Troy kill him in the woods. They looked off in the distance, like they were oblivious to what was happening. Troy kicked his stomach methodically. The blows were so continuous and rhythmic, Owen no longer felt each individual kick but instead felt a nest of pain. He studied the blue swoosh on Jon's Nikes. Gail cowered in the far corner of his chest, huddled in a ball near his spine. He turned towards July's hiking boots. They were laced all the way to the top, the same way Owen wore his. July's socks poked out of the top of his boots, and the one closest to Owen's face had three dull yellow stripes running across it. There was no doubt.

They were the socks Owen had been searching for.

He wanted to scream at July. *WE ARE THE SAME. WE ARE TERRORS.* But July's eyes would not meet Owen's. Troy moved back and forth on each side, taking turns kicking every rib, climbing up Owen's side. His method was scientific. Each blow sent tremors of pain up Owen's body. Owen squirmed and writhed. His shirt had slid up and his belly hung out. Leaves and sticks cut into his back.

Troy's boot climbed Owen's rib cage, and when it reached the place where Gail lived, Owen shut his eyes, squeezed them shut. *Duck, Gail. Wrap yourself up tight. I die when you die.* He dripped the words down his throat. Blood gushed down his chin. He considered going limp, of lying on the forest floor and giving up. This was how it would end for him.

Gail sent words back up. *Careful. I die when you die.*

Troy's boot slammed against the walls of Gail's home and Owen felt the bone crack. He imagined the earthquake she was experiencing, her walls bending and caving in on her, the bone dust raining down from her ceiling.

28

In the end, it was not how Owen died. He wasn't sure what made Troy stop. At one point, Owen must have seemed like he was conceding to death, because July put a hand on Troy's shoulder, a gentle hand, and Troy stood up straight like he was waking up from a long nap. He bent down one more time, but he didn't hit Owen, he simply said, "Homo." The three boys left him there on the forest floor. His eyes couldn't focus on anything, but he saw July's dull, yellow-striped socks one more time as he walked past.

Owen lay there for some time. After a while, Gail stopped shaking and she lay there, too, quiet. Deep in the distance Jeez Louise barked her head off. It felt like there was sand in all of Owen's joints. His breaths were shallow. He needed his inhaler. The woods grew colder. The blood dried on his face and it felt like glue on his skin. He listened to the running water of the shallow creek.

A stick snapped. Then another. Footsteps. It would be Tennessee, finally walking home from the water to find him bloody on the ground. Owen couldn't gather the strength to sit up, so he kept his focus on the treetops. When it was Clyde who leaned over him and not Tennessee, Owen jumped back for fear that Clyde was also from the Army of Acronyms and was here to finish the job the boys had started.

Clyde put a hand out. "It's okay," he said. "I'm here to help."

He touched Owen's shoulder. Owen winced. Clyde smelled like dead grass and dirt. His face was in a shadow, but Owen could make out his dark blue eyes. Tears came to their corners, and they looked like two lakes, the water flooding the shoreline.

"Let's get you home." Clyde moved the hand that had been on Owen's shoulder and placed it under his neck. Together they picked Owen off the ground. Clyde walked behind Owen, his hands under Owen's armpits. They stumbled through the woods like a bloodied and beaten conga line, Clyde supporting Owen, letting Owen lean all the way back at times, nearly carrying him. Maybe Clyde wasn't so skinny after all.

They got to the house and Owen turned and faced Clyde. "Thank you," he said. "I could have stayed there forever."

"You had to get up at some point. You good?"

Owen nodded.

Clyde waved two fingers in a small wave and turned to walk home. His figure grew fuzzy in Owen's vision. Owen's head pounded, and so he turned towards the house.

Tennessee could be heard in the backyard, so he entered the house through the front door. The screen door creaked loudly. He booked it to the bathroom, locking the door behind him, safe again. His hands shook. He spit a mouthful of blood into the sink. His eyelids were swollen, and a blood blister spread across his left eye. Blood caked his entire face from his scalp down to his chin, and two lines diverged: the larger snaked down his chin and around the right side of his neck, and the other drew from his chin down his chest, pooling in his belly button. His wrists were sore, and he knew tomorrow would bring bracelets of bruises. At least one of his ribs was cracked, maybe more. He could see the break. It was one of the pale gray ribs that swam in open air, the middle one. It looked like a black hair was stuck to the bone, but he knew better.

He turned on the bath and ran the water warm but not hot. The water was loud and comforting, and it filled all the space left by his body's pain. He warmed a washrag and set to cleaning the blood from his face. When he tried to talk to Gail, she was too tucked tight inside herself, still unsure of whether it was safe or not. He was alone. He climbed into the tub and it soothed his muscles but irritated his ribs and his bruises. The scratches on his back stung. He soaked his body and let the pain leak into the water. If he didn't move a muscle everything felt okay, but as soon as he lifted a finger, the feeling of getting hit by a truck came back.

He racked his brain but he couldn't figure out why the boys had done it, no motive and no sense of reason. Of course, there was the time in the school hallway, but since then he'd kept his eyes down, had avoided staring. There was the word Troy had thrown at him before they left—*homo*—but that word didn't describe him. He was a *Terror*. He knew they were from the Army of Acronyms sent to harass him, scare him into turning himself in. How did they know he was a Terror? And why would July, a Terror, work for the Army of Acronyms? He thought of a scorpion stored away in July's belly. It was just his luck he'd discover the other Terror the same day that Terror beat the shit out of him. Owen's brain felt like mud. He drained the tub and climbed out.

He needed to wrap his chest. He found gauze under the sink but couldn't get it to stretch around his body. For the first time he felt like crying. Pressure built in his chest and spread across his shoulders.

Tennessee knocked on the door. "Owen, that you?"

He had two black eyes forming from the possibly broken nose. He had missed a spot of dried blood near his right ear. Despite his efforts, he was still a sight for sore eyes.

"It's me," he croaked. His rib pressed against his sternum.

"You okay?"

How to answer that question?

Gail spoke for the first time since the beating. "Let her in. We need her. We both need her."

He called out, "One sec," and pulled on his underwear and jeans. Brown streaks of forest floor ran down the backside of his pants. He cracked the door, hiding his body. Tennessee gasped at the sight of Owen's face.

She pushed hard against the door and slid into the room past Owen. "What the fuck? Who did this to you? What happened?" She smelled like dirt, having spent all afternoon in the garden.

Owen kept his back towards her, his arms wrapped tightly around his chest. "It's nothing. I just need help wrapping this around my chest. I think one of my ribs is broken." The gauze hung limply out of his right hand, coiled on the floor to his side. Tennessee leaked righteous anger. She would murder whoever did this, and so Owen decided not to tell her. He stared at the corner of the room, the toilet and the sink. Her voice echoed off the walls.

She placed a hand on his shoulder. She shook her head no, over and over again. "This is fucked," she said. "Why would someone *do* this?"

"Who knows?"

"MotherFUCKers," she yelled. Owen could feel the breath from her nostrils on his neck. She put a hand on each shoulder and started to spin him around.

"Wait," he said. "There's a thing."

She stopped spinning him. She reached back and turned the fan off, and the room fell empty without the white noise. He peeked at her in the mirror. Strands of her hair wisped along the long braid down her back. He kept his right hand over the hole in his chest, like he was reciting the pledge of allegiance. He studied her for a moment and tried to remember small details in case this was the last time he saw her. Perhaps she'd give him up. Perhaps he'd disgust her, and she and Bob would kick him out. Perhaps she'd see him as a Terror and kill him. A cluster of freckles had come out in the sun on each of her cheeks. Her dimples curved up in a continuous smile, and purple bags hung beneath her eyes. She stared at his shoulder and then caught his face in the mirror. He breathed in as deep as he could, a shallow, trembling breath.

"There's something in my chest, and no one has met her but my mom. Well, and a doctor in Ritzville. And a nurse. No one can know."

Tennessee cocked an eyebrow. She spun him around slowly. "Your asthma? It's a she?"

He stopped rotating for a moment. "It's not the asthma. Just promise me you won't give me up to the government and that you won't kill me when you find out. You can kick me out. Give me time to pack my things, but don't kill me." He was tired. His body hurt.

She let go of his shoulders and wrapped her arms around him. "You think that's a reaction I would have?" She squeezed him gently and then released him.

Gail nuzzled her beak against his lungs. "See, Owen, you're loved. She loves you. I love you. It's okay." She plopped down in his chest. All it took to end *Gail's vow of silence for an undetermined amount of time* was getting pummeled to the brink of death.

"Okay." He stared at the wall for a moment. The toilet clicked on and the tank filled for a few seconds before shutting off again. "Okay," he said. "There's a hole in my chest, but it's okay. It doesn't hurt."

"Did they do this to you? Did they stab you?"

"No, no, no. Not them. It's a hole that's been there since I was born, but that's not even all of it." He spun around the rest of the way so that he faced her, and his right hand fell to his side. It was only a moment, but he saw her eyes widen and then narrow, the same look of horror he'd seen in the doctor's office.

She put her index and middle finger to her bottom lip, held it there, and then reached towards his chest. "My god! Ouch." Water touched the corners of her eyes and he worried he would now have to comfort her.

"It doesn't hurt, but there's still another thing. The *she*." The kind of silence that stings the nostrils. The kind of tension you can walk through like a fog. "There's a bird that lives inside the hole."

Tennessee's eyes widened and then narrowed again. "What? How? What?" She shook her head back and forth and put her hands up in front of her. "Can I see?"

"Of course." He remembered to breathe.

She leaned down so his ribs were at eye level. Gail was curled up in a tight ball near his spine. Owen's legs were sore, and so he leaned against the counter. He shivered.

"I can't see it."

"Hold on." He placed his finger on the bottom rib and ran it along the bruised bone. His chest was tight with pain. "Come on, Gail. It's all right," he cooed. Gail stood up and took two small hops towards his finger.

Tennessee jumped back. "Oh my god."

"It's okay," he said. "You want to touch her?"

"Sure." There was hesitation in her voice. He knew she was disgusted but she tried her best to hide it. He was a monster. He would have to accept that no human would ever see his bare bones and all his organs and think he was beautiful. Some things just were. She stuck her index finger out and slowly brought it to his chest. She brushed the cracked bone and Owen winced. "Sorry." She brought the finger up again but didn't touch the bone. Her finger hovered outside the hole. Gail brought her wing up and slid it between the ribs so that it stuck straight out. Tennessee brushed her fingers along Gail's wingtip. "Fuck." Her eyes brightened at Gail's touch.

The aches settled back into Owen's bones.

Tennessee noticed and she took her hand away from Gail's wing and brushed a bruise beneath the hole in his chest. "Who did this to you?"

"I don't know."

She cocked an eyebrow. "Did they find out about her? Is that why they did this to you?"

"No. They never found out about Gail."

"Gail?"

"The bird." He nodded at his own chest in the mirror. "Her name is Gail." He shivered again.

Tennessee placed a hand on his bare shoulder. "Let's move you into the bedroom." She pushed him towards the bed. "I have so many questions."

He had run through thousands of scenarios wherein someone discovered Gail, but he was not prepared for questions.

Tennessee fed him aspirin and water. She put on her boots and left him sitting up against the wall in her bed.

Owen's brain was nothing but a misty fog. The day seemed like three weeks' worth of days wrapped into one. He couldn't believe it was the same day he'd been at school or in the bath or out in the woods. The pummeling.

Gail put a firm wing on his spine. "I'm not going to talk to Tennessee for a while," she said. "I think it's best. Baby steps."

"Yes, baby steps," he said. He worried that his cousin had been gone for too long and was off gathering the Army of Acronyms. But she returned a moment later with rosemary, lavender, and sweet grass from the garden. She tied the herbs up in a loose bundle and hung them over the bed. "To promote healing," she said. The teakettle whistled in the kitchen. She left. She slammed cabinets, and dishes clashed against the counter. She returned with the tea that tasted like musty mushrooms.

He sipped the tea. He held the cup and felt the warmth in his fingertips and palms. He pulled the smell into his nostrils and imagined the steam that smelled like dirt was reaching all parts of his insides.

Tennessee placed a hand on his forehead like she was checking his temperature, even though he certainly did not have a fever. He was sweaty. He waited for her to speak, but she said nothing. She cocked her head, opened her mouth, and closed it again.

She stared at her tea, so he spoke instead.

He spilled the beans. He told his cousin almost everything. He told her about the year before when the bird had flown inside the house and how it'd prompted him to start roaming and climbing trees back in Montana. He told her about never leaving the house before that. He even told her about his fear that he would never meet another human outside of his mother. Gail stayed quiet in his chest, listening like this was the first time she'd heard any of it. Ever the nervous braider, Tennessee braided and rebraided her hair while Owen talked. He told her about the asthma attack (of which she already knew plenty), and he told her about the doctor and the nurse. He constantly brought his fingers to his chest and repeated, "No one, never." Tennessee mirrored Owen, placing her own two fingers to her chest like they were taking an oath together. At one point, Bob came home, but Tennessee shut the door without a word and Owen picked up where he'd left off. Every secret he shared felt like he was unraveling a skein of secrets in his stomach. The yarn grew looser and looser, and he felt a weight lift. Soon it seemed like there was nothing left to tell.

But there was.

He never told her that Gail could talk and that she whispered up to him all day long. He didn't tell her about feeling the air and knowing how others felt instantly. He didn't talk about July. He never said *Terror*. He remained mum on others like him and the Army of Acronyms.

Afterwards, Tennessee set her tea on the floor, and then she leaned over and hugged him. She rubbed his back. Her hair was now in two perfect braids, not a strand misplaced. She gripped his bare shoulders and lifted herself back up. "I love you."

Gail was bursting in his chest. Bob was outside, drinking beer on the back porch and watching the sky unfold with stars, so they were practically alone.

"Gail wants to whistle," he said, and hearing that, Tennessee's eyes filled with excitement and he felt special instead of grotesque. It was strange sitting in a room with another human and his shirt off.

Gail whistled loudly. *Poe-tweet-tweet-poe-poe-poe-tweet-tweet-tweet-TWEET-TWEET-POE-TWEET-TWEET-TWEET-TWEET-poe-poe*. Tennessee shook her head in amazement. Gail's chirps were so loud that spit flew off her beak and landed right on his cracked rib.

"I think I need to wrap my chest," Owen said. "Can you help?"

Tennessee stood up and went into the bathroom to collect the gauze off the floor. He scooted up in bed and raised both his arms over his head. Slowly she wrapped the gauze around his body. It felt like the gauze was there to keep him together, to hold everything inside.

He slept like a rock for fourteen hours straight.

29

Tennessee said, "Healing is a flat spiral," and Owen guessed what she meant was you always got closer to feeling better, but sometimes it felt like you were right back where you started. Some days he felt better than others.

He was so grateful to have Gail back, squawking and telling him jokes. It seemed he kept wishing for his life to turn back to the way it had been. Like how once he learned what staying disappeared entailed, all he wanted was to return to the days where he watched soap operas and played migration in the living room of his mother's house, but it was too late then. Once Gail stopped talking, really shut herself up, all he wanted was for her to take up space inside him again, even if it meant it was harder to stay disappeared.

He was glad for Gail's company, but lying in bed all day was fucking boring. Nothing to do, he stared out the window and watched summer drip away. His cousin tried to keep him company, but he shooed her away after the second day. "It's summer," he said. "Enjoy it for the both of us." Her presence made him feel guilty, and all she wanted to do was ask questions about the bird in his chest anyways. He wanted peace. When he was left alone, his mind wandered through tangled scenarios of the Army of Acronyms pulling him from bed. At times, he thought if his mother were there, she would triple lock all the windows and doors, and afterwards, when she'd hug him, he'd know he was entirely safe. Tennessee came home at night smelling like saltwater and dry grass. She brought him trinkets from her explorations: a seashell once, small stones, and even a jar full of water and pebbles from the Sound. He placed the small jar on the windowsill. If he looked at it just right, he could zero in his vision so he was only looking at the jar, and then it was like he was at the ocean. He imagined the expanse.

"Pieces of magic," Gail reminded him every time his cousin brought him a gift, and she coughed up the pebble from the first time at the ocean.

Sometimes, he thought of Clyde picking him up and steering him home, but everything from that afternoon was too fuzzy to fully understand what was a dream and what had been real, and so he worried his memory was unreliable. He wondered why the boys had chosen him for the beating. He wondered what they saw that he couldn't.

Bob never called it a beating. He always referred to it as a fight, and he was quietly proud of Owen taking so many hits. *Boys will be boys.* His only advice was, "Next time pick someone smaller than you."

• • •

Sunny afternoon, late-July. Owen lay in Tennessee's bed and watched the leaves rustle in the wind. A seagull cawed. Gail was asleep. She was lethargic most days, barely able to open her eyes. His muscles were sore from rarely climbing out of bed. A creak developed in his fractured rib, and it whined every time he lifted his elbow. He was a rusty machine.

Tennessee sat on the floor by her small table near the closet. A scarf was spread out on the table and on top of the scarf were rocks, a couple twigs, three candles, and a beer bottle cap from the night her and Owen drank beer after she'd come out to Bob. She sat with her eyes closed. She breathed deeply. She shuffled her tarot deck but set the deck down without choosing a card. She turned around and faced Owen. "Is there something bothering you?" she said.

He'd learned that she could be like that sometimes, just saying exactly what she was thinking, asking exactly what she wanted to know.

"I just spent all of last year trying to float under the radar, to blend in, like a walking stick," he said. "I thought I was good at staying disappeared, but those boys still saw something in me that made me stick out. I can't place a finger on it. Why can't people leave me alone?"

She scooted forward on the floor, her legs crossed. The air moved around her and it knocked the candle flames around on the table behind her. "Wanting to be ignored is the best way to get noticed," she said. "A walking stick isn't always focused on staying disappeared. It just looks like a stick. It never stops being who it is. It is out loud with its walking-stick-ness. It's why punks get left alone." She tugged at the tear in her jeans and placed a thumb under the three chains she wore around her neck. "If you glow bright and stick yourself out there, then people figure there isn't much left of you to hide and so they leave you alone a little bit. They understand that there is nothing there for them. Now, that pisses other people off and then they are mad that you aren't like them, that you have the audacity to be different, to be wholly yourself, and that can bring other bits of trouble."

"Damned if you do. Damned if you don't."

"Sure, but at least then, you get to be who you are, even if it doesn't stop the stares. The stares stop bothering you and they stop landing on you once someone thinks they've figured you out a little bit."

Owen nodded. Gail stirred in his chest. They both felt that familiar feeling of being stuck in a room, in a house, and in a body. "I got to let people figure out parts of me," he said.

"Sure."

"How?"

"Don't think, just answer. What do you want to change?"

"I want to cut my hair." The words spilled out like a creek rolling over a log, falling over a ledge, off a waterfall.

She stood up and clapped her hands together. The clap echoed around the small room and the sound startled Gail. "That's what I'm talking about. That's easy."

She came over and grabbed his hands. "Get up. Let's do it."

All control left his body. He let himself be pulled from bed and into the bathroom. Before he knew it, the bathroom fan buzzed loudly and he sat in front of the mirror, the clippers alive in his cousin's hands. "How do you want it?"

"Different."

His hair was longer now, growing quicker than he'd expected and touching the middle of his ears.

Tennessee smiled widely. "I can do different." She brought the clippers to the left side of his head and buzzed a stripe of hair around his ear. The clippers made his skull hum, and the cut hair floated to the ground. She buzzed along the other ear. Then she buzzed a lane around each of those stripes. She kept going. When she was finished, both sides of his head had patches of hair clipped close to the scalp, while the hair on the top and in the back was left long and shaggy. It was a loose, feral Mohawk, not too long, but curls tickled the back of his neck, and the sides were tight to his ears.

"I like it," he said.

"I want to see," Gail whispered up to him, sending the words up his throat.

"I think it's time to unwrap the gauze," he said.

"Arms up."

He lifted both his arms up and his cousin walked circles around him, pulling the gauze away from his chest. The skin under the bandage was yellow and purple, like it had been pickled for two months, but his rib looked like a full rib. No crack. He put his arms down and his left rib creaked quietly again.

Gail leaned far forward, nearly sticking her head out between the top two ribs.

"She doesn't recognize you," Tennessee said.

He ran his fingers along the shaved sides and felt static along his arms. It was one of the first times he saw himself in the mirror.

• • •

That night he joined his uncle and cousin in the backyard for a fire. He was cautious at first, having not stepped outside in nearly two months. But it was like returning home after a long vacation. Things were just as he'd remembered them. Tennessee and Bob each got drunk, and typically the mood was easygoing, but this night Bob got serious. His eyes were glassy, but he wasn't somewhere else yet.

"I want things to be good for both of you at this house. I want you to be comfortable."

"I'm comfortable," Owen said. Ever since he'd told Tennessee about Gail, he'd felt his body soften into a sense of home. Tennessee nodded.

"It's just growing up, your mom"—he nodded towards Owen—"and I weren't allowed to be comfortable. Our mom, your grandma, tried to control every aspect of our lives. Our dad did what he could, but he drank too much gin to really make a difference." He rolled a cigarette and kept talking. "I don't want either of you to feel like you need to run away at seventeen. Everyone runs away at seventeen."

How old had Owen's mother been when she had him? Eighteen?

Bob lit his cigarette and looked into Owen's eyes. An owl hooted in the distance. "Your mom had it especially hard. I'm going to do what I can to avoid making the same mistakes my mom made." He took a pull on his cigarette and then stood up. He hovered between Tennessee and Owen, pulled them both in for a huddled hug. "I love both of you exactly as you are," he said.

Tennessee smiled at Owen over her dad's shoulder. "Thanks, Dad," she said, and Owen knew she meant it.

The night ended with Bob pulling Owen and Tennessee up and out of their chairs to show them how to properly throw a punch.

Bob stood with his feet hip-width apart and his fists at each side. "You rotate the wrist from up to down like this," and he slowly thrust his fist, turning the wrist down and throwing his knuckles in front of him in one fluid motion. "Now you try." The fire bounced light off his face and knuckles.

Owen and Tennessee each tried to throw slow punches, and he came around and corrected each of them. He patted Owen's right thigh. "The power from the throw has to come up from the ground through your back leg. Your whole body is behind the hit." Then he stood up straight and did it again but fast this time. "Like a one, two, three." Each punctuated by a punch. They stood in a circle around the fire and threw punches at shadows until sweat poured from their foreheads.

"Would you ever hit someone though?" Gail whispered up to Owen.

"Nice to know how, even if I never use it." Then he imagined a body on the other side of his fists, skin and bone that he'd knock into. His rib creaked with each left jab.

30

Owen could not figure out how time worked. No matter how hard he tried, he could not put a finger on the present, couldn't describe linear time in the right way. It seemed that life moved in moments and events. Catastrophic events, sure (think: forest fire, lungs ablaze, a doctor peering at Gail), but there were also events that shifted time for no apparent reason (this one: drive to the beach, howl at the moon, swallow a pebble). He floated through life in large swaths of time, unawares. After a summer of lying in bed, healing, resting, learning how to throw punches, getting back the bird in his chest, he woke up and realized he had time-traveled to the first day of school and he hadn't even planned what he would do when he saw the boys, saw July, the boy with the yellow-striped socks.

He stood a block away from the school, students swirling around him. It was early September and chilly warm. *Let them not kill me*, a prayer said to no one at all.

Tennessee walked two strides ahead of him, her chin up and hair piled high on her head. She was out loud with her walking-stick-ness. He channeled her.

Owen remembered that his power came from the ground through his rear leg. Rotate the wrist and put his body behind the punch. His shoulders were stiff and chest tight with anxiety. Earthquakes vibrated through his whole body. He prayed again. *Let them not kill me. Let them not kill me. Let them not kill me*, until it was a rhythm punched into the soles of his shoes. Gail stretched her wings long at her side. He wasn't sure what he'd do when confronted by the three boys. He rethought his plan to be fabulous, to live life loudly. He felt good, pants rolled up and his new flannel over one of Tennessee's old Smashing Pumpkins shirts. His hair was freshly shaved, buzzed down and clean on the sides, the Mohawk floppy and curls loose. He worried he looked *too good*.

The pavement was hard beneath his Converse. Before he knew it, he was inside and still alive. The ceiling seemed higher. His backpack cut into his shoulders. The students moved around him, completely unaware that he was there. Gail fluttered in his chest and it was nearly impossible to not feel her. *I have no bird in my chest*, he thought. He looked down at his body. His wrist floated in the air in front of his chest. He applied more pressure, more force to his hand. He ran his fingers through his hair, felt the Velcro static. He went to class.

Everyone had time warped over the summer. Ava, a vegan now, wore torn black jeans and a Minor Threat T-shirt, but no cape. Dean wore a jade crystal in his ear instead of the safety pin. Hair grew along his cheeks. Even Tennessee seemed taller, more in her body.

After lunch, Owen heard shouts and laughter in the hallway and he knew it was Troy. The voice was thick in the air, like throwing dirt clods. Owen could see over all the students, straight down the hallway to the staircase at the end. The sun cut a ray of light through the window that stretched the two stories of the stairwell. Troy chased somebody down the stairs.

"Poor sap," Gail whispered up to him.

Owen blinked twice. He wanted to go help whoever was being chased, but Gail put a wing to his left side. He put his thumb under the strap of his backpack. He turned around and went another way to class.

It was like that then, still head-down-barrel-through, but only during school when he was in the hallway or during gym and rarely outside of school. (He was still careful when he walked through the woods, his heart pounding every time he ducked under the fallen fir.) He learned to compartmentalize his fear for only when he really needed to head-down-barrel-through. Other times, at lunch with friends or down by the water with Tennessee, he was easy, more himself.

31

Tennessee got a part-time job at the feminist bookstore in Olympia, and so they threw a Halloween party to celebrate. They invited Dean and Ava. "Just the four of us," she told Owen, "small but fun." She gave her dad money and asked him to buy the beer.

Bob made her promise they'd be careful. Then he brought home three cases of Miller High Life and left for the night. He was going out more in general. There was a bar in town, a block over from the Albertsons, Cast and Characters. Even when he was home, he was often somewhere else, his eyes wet.

Owen and Tennessee went to Goodwill and flipped through racks of musty clothes, building costumes. In the end, Owen found a green velvet dress that stretched tight from his neck down to his ankles. At the ankles, it spread wide on the floor, a tail.

"Ariel," he said.

Tennessee went as Stevie Nicks, borrowing a black cape and floppy black hat from Ava. She found a tambourine at Goodwill.

Tennessee built a fire in the fire pit early in the evening. They dragged the CD player onto the porch. Tennessee loaned him a purple bra to wear over the dress where Ariel's seashells lived. She ran red lipstick across his lips.

He looked at himself in the mirror, smoothed the dress along his thighs. How could he send this to Gail? He passed her the sensation of never feeling at home until now.

Pavement played on the stereo and they were halfway through their first beers when Ava and Dean showed up. Both dressed from *Scooby-Doo*. Ava as Fred, a yellow wig and an orange scarf tucked into her white polo, and Dean as Daphne, complete with a long, orange wig and a purple sweater and skirt. The four of them stood around the fire and laughed.

"Jesus," Dean said.

"We're so fucking gay," Ava said.

"Hella gay," Tennessee said.

"Gay as the day is long," Dean said.

They drank beer and sat around the fire, each got excited about the music or about one another and it was easy, so easy. Gail was relaxed in Owen's chest and, at moments, he didn't think of her. Not that he ignored her and she was small, more like he was at ease and didn't have to actively ignore her. He was.

They talked about drugs they wanted to take. Even though he'd never thought much about it, Owen said he wanted to smoke weed.

"Weed's not a drug," Ava said. "It's a plant."

Tennessee said she would try coke once.

Dean wanted to try Blossoms Blossom. No one had heard of Blossoms Blossom before. Owen leaned over the fire, his beer hung loosely between his fingertips, swinging between his knees. The others leaned in towards Dean, too.

"It's a flower. It grows all around here, an old, old plant used by Indigenous people for thousands of years. It's psychedelic. You're supposed to live with the plant for a long time, and the plant glows with bright, neon colors. You ignore the colors and you let it glow until it stops glowing. Then you eat it, and it's supposed to be one of the most beautiful trips you can experience." He took a swig of his beer. "My cousin told me he felt death and birth all at once. He's different now, more himself. I've always wanted to try it."

Owen's heart pounded loud in his ears and he drank some beer to quiet it down.

"I'd try it." Tennessee shrugged.

"Hell, I'll try anything once," Ava said.

• • •

Later, the fire died down and the logs shrank into embers and coals. Dean spread them around with a stick and Ava poured her beer over the top of them. The air smelled like baked bread.

They hiked into the woods, each with a full beer in their hands. Owen had lost count of how many he'd had. His head was loose on his shoulders. He couldn't take full strides in the velvet dress, so he walked short steps, waddling behind everyone. Since the pummeling, he hated being out here. He wouldn't do it alone for fear the three boys were waiting for him, that the Army of Acronyms was around the corner. Ava's hand appeared out of the darkness. He gripped it loosely. They didn't turn at the creek, but they hiked deep into the woods, walking towards Clyde's property. Owen was lost, but he trusted that the others knew where they were going, and he kept his fingers wrapped around Ava's palm. Gail was quiet in his chest, swaying to a song in her head. Ava reached towards him at one point and pulled him towards her. She drew him so close he could smell the plastic scent of her wig. Sticks snapped under their feet.

The four of them stopped and Owen leaned against a tree, felt its trunk under him. He took a swig of his beer. "Do we need more?" Gail whispered up to him. He wasn't sure. Why not?

Owen looked around and realized he didn't know where his cousin or Dean went. He tried to look over Ava's shoulder, but it was pitch-black behind her, like there was nothing but her and him and the tree he leaned against. He tried to watch Ava, but she swayed and it gave him motion sickness; there were two of her. Her wig was turned to the side and wisps of her black hair poked out from under the blond.

A hand on his shoulder. "You're hot," Ava said to him.

Owen shook his head, thinking she was saying he was warm.

She put a hand on his head and touched the shaved sides. "Ariel," she said, "a mermaid." She pressed herself against him. Everything was tight in his dress and it felt like he was suffocating. She put her hand on his hip and he felt the ground through her, felt an anchor to her body. She kissed him. The lipstick had dried out his lips and she tasted like bad beer and potato chips, but there was the flavor of sweet candy under it all.

He'd never been held or kissed like that before, couldn't even fathom it because of the bird in his chest, and so he let himself be kissed. He leaned against the tree. The bark dug into the dress and into his ass, and she pressed against him harder and he thought he might fall over. He put a hand to the tree on his side and pushed back against her. None of it made sense. They were all gay, gay, gay, gay, gay. Here he was though, tight in his dress, Gail close to shouting, "*BUMP-BADA-DUH! CHARGE!*" but staying quiet, only thinking it to herself.

He felt bile in his stomach and acid in the back of his mouth. Ava's hands were everywhere now, along his sides and thighs and his shoulders, and she kissed his neck and put hands on his hips. His head swirled. He let his beer drop and fall onto the ground behind him, rolling away. He put his other hand on the tree now, focusing on not falling over and staying upright. Where was everyone? He'd spent so many days on the bathroom counter wondering what this kind of attention would feel like, but he'd always dreamt of faceless bodies and trees and oceans, never an actual human with a warm body and spirit. Ava's hand was on his left thigh and the other was between his shoulders. Her hand fiddled along his back. Her hand was cold on his back. The night air stung his shoulder blades. The dress was not so tight. The purple bra hung loose at his elbows. The dress puffed in front of him.

Ava had unzipped the dress.

She tugged at it and tried to pull it forward, tried to peek at his chest. He pressed himself off the log and stood up, anything to block her from seeing the hole in his chest. A twig snagged the dress right at his asshole and it kept him from standing all the way up. Ava thought he was trying to facilitate the removal of his dress. She tugged at the top of it more. Gail curled tight in his chest. Like always, she became a rock near his spine.

He pressed away from Ava. Her hands left the dress alone and they climbed down his ass and felt both of his cheeks firm in her palms. She was unstoppable. She kissed his lips, smearing his lipstick and slobbering on his upper lip. She bit the bottom lip and pulled it away from his face. She turned him around and he leaned over the tree, both hands on the trunk. She kissed his back and his shoulder blades. He swayed between wanting it to stop and never wanting it to end. He felt both simultaneously.

She slipped her hands along his thighs and in and out of the legs of his underwear. She pressed hard against his dick over his underwear. Her left hand went exploring along his belly and then his sternum. She slipped her hand under the waist of his underwear and wrapped it around his penis. She pressed her ear against his shoulder like she was listening to all his organs. Her left hand kept climbing and when it pinched his right nipple, he nearly forgot everything he was supposed to be hiding. Gail knocked on his spine, a soft tapping to remind him she was there.

He opened his eyes. He realized where he was. He was leaning over the fallen fir, the one where he'd met the boys that sunny afternoon. The last place he wanted to be. He couldn't help it, though, because he was coming inside of his long velvet dress. He pressed himself up, shaking. Tears came to his eyes and he couldn't say anything, cat got his tongue. He was full of the impossible surprise that someone would want to be with him in this way, that a real human could listen to his body and give it affection when he'd barely learned how to give it to himself. He shook his head back and forth.

Ava pulled her hand out of his underwear and placed it on his shoulder like a mother. He reached up and grabbed her left hand just before it slipped into the space where there was no skin, just ribs and a bird. He pressed it down to his belly. She pulled her hand out from under the dress. She zipped it up.

He felt in the present, like all the beer had left his body at once. His eyes adjusted to the dark. The sobs were quiet at first, but his knees felt weak and he had to lean far forward against the tree.

He thought of the boys and how some humans could be absolute animals, and others could unzip your dress and caress and hold you afterwards. She rubbed circles between his shoulders. The tears came from the back of his throat. He rubbed his face against the tree and the bark scratched his cheeks. He pulled himself up, embarrassed and confused. His left rib creaked. Then he leaned over the fallen fir one more time, the tree pressing against his stomach, and he vomited.

Ava watched Owen throw up and it brought salt from her belly and she threw up next to him. Gail dry heaved in his chest. Owen felt better afterwards, expelling everything from his system.

"Maybe I'll be a new man after this," he whispered down to Gail, rubbing circles on Ava's back while she threw up on the forest floor.

Gail nuzzled her beak along his rib. He felt water return to his eyes, but he held back the tears.

Later, the four of them met up and hiked back through the woods. Dean threw up near the garden. "Y'all are lightweights," Tennessee said. "I can hold my beer."

They went to bed when they got back. Owen and Dean on the bed. Tennessee and Ava on the floor. When Dean and Ava were asleep, Owen heard Tennessee get up and cough and throw up in the bathroom.

The next day, Tennessee told Owen that she had made out with Dean in the dark woods.

"It was pitch-black out. He looked like Daphne," she explained, "and Daphne is queer canon. Besides, we were all drunk."

They tidied up the back porch, picking up beer bottles and feeling like death. Ava and Dean were gone. Owen did not tell her about him and Ava.

32

It was mid-November when Owen got a letter from his mother. He set everything down on the kitchen counter and went right into the bathroom to open it. It was a yellow envelope, battered by the weather. He pulled his gloves off so he could tear the envelope open. He thought maybe it said she missed him.

It said she wasn't at the old house at all anymore, but she couldn't say where she was living, a repetition of what she'd said on her phone call the previous year. She did say she missed him. The sentence was squeezed in between all the other sentences that felt like business—ways for him to remain incognito and updates as to how she was ensuring his safety. She was careful not to mention why he should stay hidden. (She had a sharp paranoia that *they* were reading her mail.) She ended by saying he was smart and she knew he was almost completely disappeared, but he shouldn't get comfortable. She signed the letter: *Love, Mom.*

There was another piece of paper in the envelope. He walked out of the bathroom and into the bedroom. He threw his jacket on the bed. The second note was a thin piece of office paper folded in half. It was a printout from a forum on a Pacific Northwest Doctors and Nurses Community Group (the battalion known as PNWDNCG in the Army of Acronyms). A doctor detailed a boy he'd seen a year earlier who'd come in after a severe asthma attack. He described Owen to a T. He said he knew the boy was a Terror. He described how he finally had a Terror within his grasp, but the mother had rushed him out before he could examine him. The doctor wondered if anyone had heard reports of Terrors. Did anyone know where they could find this boy? Several posters called him crazy. *Conspiracy theories*, they said. Someone said that Terrors were everywhere. *No way to know how many walk among us.*

Gail started rambling nonstop about how it was going to be okay. She said they would keep surviving, that he was doing great and it was nothing to be worried about. They knew the doctor was after them, so the letter didn't change anything. Last time, she refused to talk for six months. Now she wouldn't shut up.

He walked outside and the air was cold and full of water again. Gail kept chatting and he tuned her out. She was spiraling. (He wasn't sure what to call what he was doing.) His eyes stung. It seemed he was spending so much of his time wanting to cry.

He wasn't sure where he was going but he walked into the woods, skipped right over the creek, and kept moving. It was his first time alone in the woods since the boys, but the letter had ripped the fear open. He'd tried living cautiously and what had it gotten him? A creaky rib. A crooked nose. Anxiety and a whole lot of loneliness. He ducked under the fallen fir and came up on the other side and stopped. He felt someone next to him. He put a hand to his heart and Gail talked faster.

"SHHH," he said out loud, and then, "Quiet, girl." He felt movement in the trees and he started to panic. This was a mistake. All the bad shit happened in these woods. He was close to Clyde's property, but Jeez Louise wasn't barking, must not have been outside. He looked around and saw nothing but trees and ferns. He thought maybe it was the calm before the storm, like how the wind had stopped the day he'd run into the boys out here. He looked past the fence. It was the part with all the rotting wood leaning hard against the electric wire.

Clyde sat on his horse on the other side of the fence. The horse made him eight feet tall, sitting down. He was in dirty brown pants and a muddy rain jacket. His hair was buzzed short, the straight-boy uniform, but Clyde didn't seem like the *boys will be boys* type. Clyde looked almost identical to how he had the day he'd helped Owen home, maybe broader shoulders and more hair on his upper lip. He met Owen's eyes. Owen stood still. Water dripped through the trees. Clyde put his finger to his lips and smiled. He pointed towards the road. Owen turned and looked in the direction of his pointer finger. He didn't see shit. He looked harder. He looked so hard, everything grew fuzzy. He blinked a couple of times. Then he saw her.

A doe stood ten feet away, looking right back at him. Her eyes were big, the size of tennis balls. Her front right hoof was in the air, her wrist limp like Owen's. The three of them stood like that for who knows how long. Each one of them watched the other, waiting for one of them to move, and no one actually moving. Owen thought maybe he could stand like that forever. He could study her coat, a million different shades of brown and rust. Her white tail flicked softly towards the water.

She turned away from Owen and looked up towards Clyde and his horse. He leaned forward and put a hand to his horse's side, begging her to stay still without saying anything. It was a soft gesture, like the ruffling of hair or a hand on a shoulder. The deer looked past Clyde up the hill. It put all four hooves on the ground and then took off towards the road just as Jeez Louise came running down the hill, barking her head off. The deer crashed through the woods, flattening all the ferns and bouncing over fallen trees.

Clyde's horse started walking back and forth, relieved to be able to finally move again. "Damn, dog," Clyde yelled. He reached over to a tree and ripped a branch off and threw it towards the water. The dog ran after the stick. Clyde waved quickly at Owen and turned his horse around and went towards his house. The rifle on the back of the saddle swayed left to right.

Seeing the quiet doe in the woods had undone bits of the anxiety the letter had laid in Owen, but it was too short, over too quickly. He tried to cling to the feeling he'd had when everything had stopped and the world seemed okay, but it was gone, having run off with the deer.

Owen watched the space where Clyde and his horse had been, a man-sized hole, but something different from the space-taking lineage. Owen couldn't explain it, but there was something gentle and quiet there.

33

It was around this time that everything started to get real messed up. Bob rambled more than usual. He sat near the fire and he smoked cigarettes, and he talked on and on about how Tennessee was at the age when she would be running away.

"We all run away at seventeen," he said in between inhales of his cigarette. Gail shifted her weight from side to side in Owen's chest, unsettled. Bob pointed at Owen. "Your mother ran away when she had you. I ran away to here and then had Tennessee a few years later. Everyone runs away at seventeen." Tennessee walked in through the back door and went into her room. Bob gestured at the shut door. "See? Running away."

Even after Owen went to bed, he heard Bob murmuring about how you didn't need to leave a place to run away, and what was he going to do once she was gone. Tennessee slept soundly on the floor. Probably rolling her eyes in her dreams.

School was messed up, too. Whatever happened between Dean and Tennessee had gotten between them, and Tennessee had dropped the idea of saying exactly how she felt, electing to keep quiet instead. Dean didn't sit next to them at lunch anymore. A few times, when Owen and Tennessee walked to class, he'd pop out of nowhere, eyes and cheeks red with tears. He asked to talk to Tennessee alone. Tennessee would just say no, she was heading to class. Her nails left red crescent moons on Owen's biceps, she squeezed him so hard.

It had been months since Owen had seen Jon, Troy, or July at school, but that made him even more nervous. The doctor had already resorted to random online message boards, trying anything he could to find him. Maybe he'd get ahold of July. Maybe the Army of Acronyms was already in contact with the boys and they were in hiding, waiting until Owen's guard was completely let down. He needed to puff on his inhaler often.

The only thing that wasn't messed up was Owen and Ava's friendship. He wasn't sure how to be around her after the time in the woods, but it only lasted a week or so before he realized Ava was pretending like everything was normal and so should he. And not long after, Ava brought it up anyways. She pulled him aside at school between classes one day. She placed her hand on his shoulder like she had that night, gentle, like she was really trying to feel his body through his shoulder. The river of students walked behind her, all heading to class.

"I hope things are okay between us. Did I mess things up?"

He looked into her eyes. He looked so hard he could see himself in them. He was a scrawny kid with fucked-up hair. He should be so lucky to have been touched by her. He nodded.

"Things are great," he said. Gail put her wing heavy on his spine. "And I was drunk. I'm sorry."

"I think we were both too drunk for what happened. You shouldn't be sorry. I'm sorry. It was my idea."

He was quiet for a moment. The other students brushed across his backpack.

"It's okay," he said finally. "But we're just friends, right?"

She stuck her hand out. "Friends for sure," and they shook on it.

She reached her arms around him and pulled him in for a hug. "I'm sorry if I made you uncomfortable," she said, her mouth near his ear.

• • •

Soon, Owen was more used to things being messed up than he was to things being normal. He spent the days walking to the shore by himself. He felt the deep water's pull, and though he didn't feel safer, it felt like coming home. He sat next to the big log and imagined the doctor stealing him away, the usual Army of Acronyms daymares, and there was a bit of comfort to it. Something in the tortured scenes wherein he and Gail were on exam tables, being cut up and torn apart, reminded him that some things never change even when the world got messed up. The Army of Acronyms would always be after him. His was a fear he could rely on. He thought if he ever saw the Army of Acronyms approaching, he'd wade into the Sound forever, give in to the pull he felt next to the water. A few times, he'd get up from his log and Clyde's dad would be standing under the trees, his hat sitting on his eyebrows. He watched Owen with a bit of disgust in his cheeks. Owen ignored it, walking quickly back to the house, but while he walked away, he felt the presence of Clyde's father behind him, his eyes piercing the heavily wooded forest.

At night, Owen sat in bed and put on a CD, plugging in his headphones because his cousin was never in the mood for music anymore. He listened to music and imagined his mother listening to the same song, twirling on wine or maybe smoking by the window, the stereo turned on low while she explained how the world was to Owen.

Listening to music was like masturbation for Owen. For a moment, everything lined up and felt clicked into where it was supposed to be. Each anxiety in its compartment. Every bit of longing for his mother tucked tight into his memories.

Everything simply *was*.

Owen sat with his shirt off, and it seemed Tennessee was completely used to Gail. Gail didn't say a peep, only chirped from time to time, but no speaking. Tennessee shuffled her tarot cards and moved the rocks around on her table. She lit candles and knelt with her eyes closed. He was never sure exactly what she was doing. Running away, maybe. He slid the window open. The wind chimes knocked against each other over the Dirty Projectors on his headphones. He wondered if the wind was long enough to be blowing in Montana at the same time it was blowing in the Puget Sound. He wondered if his mom felt the same wind.

34

One night, middle of April, Owen had only been asleep for an hour or two when Tennessee shook his shoulders softly and he woke up in a flash. She put a finger to her lips and handed him some clothes and his boots. Gail yawned and stretched long in his chest. He got dressed in the dark bedroom. After he laced up his boots, Tennessee put a hand on the laces and motioned for him to follow her. His uncle's snores shook the wood-paneled walls. When they stepped outside, Tennessee motioned for them to push the car out of the driveway. The gravel crunched under the wheels and their boots. They jogged alongside the hatchback and leapt in at the end of the driveway. The Rabbit's motor roared alive at the bottom of the hill.

She turned the radio on and up loud. Thom Yorke belted, *"This is what you'll get when you mess with us."* Tennessee rolled her window down and pulled an American Spirit out of the yellow box.

The moon was big in the sky, illuminating much of the road. Even the old highway was lit up. "Look at that moon. So beautiful, it's fucking stupid." Tennessee blew smoke out of her mouth. "Ridiculous."

It was a Wednesday and they both had school in the morning, but no part of the trip felt connected to their everyday lives. There was no one else on the road, like maybe they were the only ones awake in the whole world. Tomorrow was impossibly far away and yesterday had been left behind. Owen thought he could live in this in-between space forever. He didn't even care to ask where they were going, and his cousin wasn't telling. He wondered if they were running away. Tennessee was seventeen. Maybe she was taking him with her. He was okay with the idea.

It was one a.m. when they pulled off the old road and got out next to the beach. Their feet slid in the loose sand and they hiked over the dunes. The short hills were covered in beach grass and foxtails. Down on the beach, there was a group of people standing next to a large cliff-side. There were small patches of light coming off the wall, like lightning bugs. He thought his eyes were playing tricks on him, so Owen stared harder at the lights. The longer he stared, the harder it was for him to determine if the light was really there or simply imagined. The ocean was a soft static roar, not as loud as it had been last time. The big waves crashed over each other. *The boy born during the flood* standing next to America's cunt. The beginning of the world.

Tennessee slumped her backpack off her shoulder. She led the way to the people milling about by the cliff. They got to the group and Tennessee introduced herself and Owen. She gave everyone a hug. Owen shook hands with everyone. Megan, a woman who wore a leopard-print tank top under a cheetah-print scarf. Her pants were zebra-striped. The moonlight bounced off the waves and lit a halo around her red frizzled hair. Freckles spotted her cheeks. Lou, a white boy with suspenders and a button-up shirt like he sold newspapers on street corners. Comet stood next to Lou. He had dark skin, dark like the ocean when it drank up all the night's sky, and he was beautiful. Owen had never met a boy so beautiful. His hair was short, and the top was bleached blond. He had a gold ring in his left nostril. He looked Owen in the eyes when they shook hands, just like how Owen tried to do when he was trying to see someone. Comet's handshake was firm but gentle.

Tennessee and Megan met online three months earlier. They had been chatting about Blossoms Blossom for months. "Had the idea after our Halloween party," Tennessee said. "Don't worry, you're getting one, too." Owen felt panic rise in his belly. *Life and death at the same time.* Tennessee nudged him in the ribs. "Consider it a late birthday present for you and an early present to myself."

Comet unloaded harnesses and ropes from a duffel bag and started tying knots and fastening clips. They laughed and moved about effortlessly. They told inside jokes. Tennessee leaned in towards Owen, "These are our people."

Our people.

He smiled softly but remembered that none of these people carried an animal inside their body. Tennessee pulled two mason jars out of her backpack and handed them to Comet.

One by one, Comet and Megan scaled the rock wall. They climbed up slowly and diligently, placing great thought into each step. They dragged rope up with them and fastened it to the wall every few feet. Owen grew light-headed. He thought it could be the lack of sleep or maybe the moon making him crazy. It felt like witchcraft. He wasn't sure how long they were on the cliffside, climbing to different sections of the wall and stopping to put flowers in mason jars. Slowly, they came down the way they had gone up, a VHS tape rewinding and playing a movie in reverse.

Comet gave the mason jars to Tennessee. He clapped his hands to his chest and bowed slightly. She held the mason jars up to the moonlight and handed one to Owen. "This one is totally you." Inside each of the jars was a small flower bud, maybe an inch in length. The middle of the bud gave off a small glow, almost undetectable. Owen was surprised he'd been able to spot them from so far away. His flower glowed purple. Tennessee's was orange.

"You're right," Comet said. He pointed at Tennessee's jar. "That one's you, and that one is definitely his." He placed a hand on Owen's arm. Light-headed again. Electricity. Gail moved around in Owen's chest and he was worried she would knock around like she used to, bump into his lungs and stomp on his heart. He swallowed his excitement, and Comet left to climb back up the wall again.

Owen plopped down next to Tennessee and he fell into the metronome rhythm of the water. He held his jar up to the moonlight again and watched the ocean through the glass. Each wave lapped the shore, and when he looked through the jar, the foam turned pink and spread across the sand like fingers spread wide. Tennessee pulled out a cigarette and lit it and then placed her hand over his jar. "You have to pretend the colors aren't there. That's the deal. Ignore it." He set the jar in the sand and felt its glow next to him.

Megan walked over and sat next to Tennessee on the ground. She stretched her index and middle fingers out, the international symbol of asking for a drag. Tennessee slid her lit cigarette between them. Megan took a puff. She explained the steps to taking care of the flowers. "Always enough saltwater, some sun but not too much. Patience is key. Wait, wait, wait. When you think it's time, wait longer." She took another drag from Tennessee's cigarette. "And keep it hidden. Closets are good as long as you take it out for some sun. And if you get caught, you didn't get it from us, you don't even know who we are."

Tennessee raised an eyebrow. "Who?"

"Exactly." Megan passed the cigarette back to her.

Owen dug his fingertips deep into the sand and it was cold. He closed his eyes and imagined his fingers reaching down deep into the earth and spreading like veins beneath the continental plates. He could cause earthquakes by shaking his arms and disturbing the major faults. Buildings would fall like sandcastles.

When he opened his eyes, Megan was hunched over his cousin. She gave her a friendly kiss on the lips and then stood up. Tennessee blushed. Owen averted his eyes, sure he was not supposed to see that kiss, too tender to be witnessed. Megan offered Tennessee and Owen each a hand.

"You guys ever go to the Fort?"

"The Fort?" Tennessee asked.

"Yeah, punk shows on this island in this old fort. It's close to where y'all live."

Tennessee stood with her eyes wide. She could only nod up and down.

Megan shook Owen's hand once more, and he was looser this time, easier. She walked down the beach, and the ocean reached out to her ankles with every wave.

They bent down and gathered their mason jars and placed them in the backpack, then walked back to the car.

35

The flowers sat in the mason jars at the bottom of the closet in the bedroom. Every afternoon after school, they pulled the jars out and placed them on the windowsill. The sunlight leaked through the glass and pebbles of light reflected off the floor and the walls. Orange and purple wafted out of the buds. The light pooled in the bottom of the jars like it was affected by gravity. Each day they ignored the glowing and placed the jars back in the closet before Bob came home.

The light from the flowers did something to Owen, changed him chemically, or he thought it could have been the arm touch by Comet. Whatever it was it made him feel drunk at times. Sometimes it made him forget about the Army of Acronyms and missing his mother. Other times it made him *only* think of the Army of Acronyms, of men like Clyde's dad, and of the boys in the woods.

The kiss between Tennessee and Megan lingered in his brain for weeks. What would it be like to receive a kiss like that, not like the hard, messy, sour kisses he'd gotten from Ava in the woods, but something kinder?

36

One afternoon, Owen walked down to the Sound and found the beach covered in blobs, hundreds of them. They were clear sacs with small orange and red rocks inside. He put a hand to his chest in awe. He poked one with a stick, and it moved like jelly: jellyfish. He recalled a nature special he'd watched on jellyfish. The creatures had bounced a waltz underwater, gliding in the ocean. On the beach, however, they were without movement, their clear sacs displaying only the drab sand. They stretched from the dead tree all the way down to where the cliff jutted into the ocean.

Further up the beach a little ways, Clyde walked along the jellyfish. He bent down and picked them up from time to time. He held them in front of his face like he was examining a clear, amorphous pancake. Then he flung each like a Frisbee into the water. Owen knew Clyde was dangerous, like his dad, a man who took up space. The Army of Acronyms incarnate. It didn't make sense on paper, but similar to the pull he felt to the ocean, Owen felt a pull to Clyde, like a loose rope connected the two boys, but Clyde was a hick who up until a few months ago wore the cheesiest Christian T-shirts. He was quiet, with shoulders hunched so far forward he was in danger of tipping over. Owen wasn't even sure what kind of music he listened to.

Owen walked towards him anyways. He wasn't sure what he would say to him. His feet moved without his permission. All he could think about was Clyde placing a soft hand on his horse's side, that tender gesture. He reminded himself that Clyde had taken him home after the pummeling; in a way, he had taken care of Owen. A seagull picked at kelp near the trees.

Clyde watched him approaching and stood up straight, hands on hips, elbows bent. When Owen reached him, he pointed at the jelly-fish on the ground. "Jellyfish," he said. "If you don't touch the tenta-cles, they won't sting you." He bent down and flung another into the ocean. It landed with a thud in the shallow water. "Wash your hands afterwards." Clyde's voice was low, and it struck Owen's sternum.

The wrong kind of attention.

"They can sting?" Owen said.

"Oh yeah. Big time. Try it." He motioned to the piles of jellyfish around them. "Worth it though. They'll die on the beach like this. Only way they can survive is by getting them back in the water."

"There's too many. We won't be able to get them all back in." Owen reached down and touched the slimy skin.

"Tell that to this guy," Clyde said. He held one up in front of Owen's face and then flung it into the water. His movements were quick and heavy.

Owen laughed at Clyde's corniness, his sentimentality. Owen picked up a jellyfish and threw it into the Sound. It landed with a loud plop. *What a story*, he thought. Wait until Tennessee heard about him and the Christian boy flinging jellyfish into the water, saving them one at a time. They worked side by side, tossing the jellyfish into the sea. The tide came in and so they moved back towards the woods and threw in the jellyfish further up the shore. Clyde picked up each jellyfish with a huff. When he flung it into the water, his back muscles tensed up and flexed beneath his thin T-shirt, thick farm boy muscles. He definitely wasn't so skinny anymore; it was hard for Owen not to stare. They shared the silence of the work. Owen didn't talk to Clyde, afraid he would ruin the whole thing, whatever strange thing this was, touching slimy creatures. "Boy stuff," Gail said, speaking the words right into Owen's throat.

The beach was almost cleared of jellyfish when the day grew cold and dark. Gulls had stopped their squawking, and the seals their barking.

Clyde's father came out of the woods. Clyde waved absentmindedly at Owen and followed his father. And all Owen could think was that something about the two men seemed odd, like they were two different creatures, like there was no way they were related.

Owen wiped his nose and a burning spread across his nostrils. He went to the water and washed his hands off. The air grew cold, and he pulled the edges of his sweatshirt tighter around his body. The waves crept up the sides of his boots. He splashed water on his nose, and the sting of the jellyfish venom was replaced with the sting of saltwater.

37

Graduation drew close for Tennessee and it was all she talked about. She talked to Megan online every night, and the two moved quickly, becoming girlfriends nearly instantly after the beach kiss. Bob was out most nights at Cast and Characters, and when he was home, he was silent. He was preemptive with Tennessee's running away. Nothing to run away from if he wasn't around. Owen was left alone with Gail.

He was on the bed, lying on his back. He reached up and ran his fingers along the bundle of herbs that hung above the bed. He brought his fingers to his nose and smelled the lavender and sweet grass, rubbing his fingers on his belly.

BUMP-BADA-DUH! CHARGE!

He went into the bathroom, pulled down his pants, and jumped up onto the counter, his ass on the cold countertop. It was easy now. He grabbed his dick and he thought of the jellyfish, and his nostrils stung. He brought his heels up on top of the counter, splaying his knees out wide. His fingers found his mouth. He ran his hand down the backs of his thighs until he found his asshole. He closed his eyes and imagined lying in piles of jellyfish, of their venom stinging his body. When he was finished, he went into the bedroom. He felt a little bit of shame, like after every time he masturbated. He also felt the bits of himself scattered around the room.

For some reason, he missed his mother the hardest afterwards. He opened the drawer with his plaid shirts and found the letter his mom had sent six months earlier. He reread it and thought about the doctor and nurse chasing after him. He saw his mother in his mind, asleep on the couch, arm hanging over the side, and a cup of coffee on the floor. He tapped each of the dotted *i*'s with his finger. It was validating to hold the piece of paper in his hands and know in his heart how dangerous the world could be. He wondered if July had to deal with anything like this, or if he was better at staying disappeared.

"Nothing you can do about it but live your life," Gail reminded him.

He nodded and fixed his hair and put on his best-looking outfit (green flannel on top of the Radiohead shirt, and the leather necklace with the rose quartz tied in front). He walked back and forth in the bedroom like it was a runway. Gail put her wings on her sides and puffed out her chest.

Tennessee came into the living room from work. He shoved the letter back into the drawer. His cousin opened the fridge. The woodstove squeaked and thudded, and she threw in wood and flicked the lighter and the door creaked shut. The flue opened and a rush of air could be heard in the stovepipe. It was nearly summer, so a fire inside was odd, but Tennessee and her dad had taken to having fires even when it was warm so they could smoke indoors, blowing the cigarette smoke up the chimney.

He collected himself and calmed his nerves. He went into the living room. She sat in front of the stove and unwound her braid, pulling the ropes of hair apart. She smiled and handed her beer to Owen. He took a swig. She pulled out her cigarettes and lit one and blew the smoke up the woodstove. He reached his hand out in front of his cousin, his index and middle fingers pulled apart, his attempt at asking for a drag. Tennessee cocked her eyebrow and slid the cigarette between his two fingers. "Your lungs," she said.

He put his hand out and stopped her. The cigarette fit perfectly in his fingers. He brought it to his lips. The smoke was harsh and tasted like dirt and vanilla, and immediately his head felt vacant, light. He felt fabulous, very cosmopolitan. He did it once more. He tasted the stale smoke in his mouth. He thought of his mother. He thought of his family going back hundreds of years, inhaling the same type of smoke. Smoking as a way to feel more human. He passed the cigarette back to his cousin. "Our little secret." He sat down next to her.

"No one, never," and Tennessee tapped her chest with her two fingers.

He coughed, and spittle hung from his lips. He wiped his mouth with the back of his hand. "Why do you smoke American Spirits? Why not rollies like your dad? Why not Marlboros?" He wasn't sure why, but he always thought if he smoked, it'd be Marlboros, like his mom.

"All those other cigarettes have all sorts of shit in them. Rat poison and whatnot. These are organic, just tobacco." She held the yellow box out in front of her. "Rollies don't have filters and are harder on your lungs. Rollies are what the hipster kids who don't give a fuck about dying early smoke. Marlboros are for white trash who think they're cowboys. Camels are for cowboys who think they're white trash. Parliaments are for hipster kids who *do* give a fuck about dying early."

He nodded.

The heat from the stove was bright, and Owen scooted away from the fire. Tennessee locked her eyes onto a log. "Do you remember when we came to visit you when our grandparents died? You were a kid, a baby."

He couldn't remember a time when anyone was over at his home in Montana. It was always his mom, the bird, and him: a trio. "In Montana?"

"Yeah, we stayed with you. My dad and your mom got wasted and swung around dancing in the living room all night. That was the first time I'd seen my dad cry. My mom had just left, and both his parents had died. Now he cries nearly every night." Tennessee took a drag on her cigarette.

Owen didn't know how to respond, so he offered only silence.

Tennessee continued, "I wonder what happened to them when they were growing up. Our parents, I mean."

"What do you mean what happened?"

"My dad always talks about how his mom was hard on them, hard on your mom especially, but he never says *how* she was hard. And in the end, Grandma dies because she's sick, and then Grandpa two days later in a car crash. It had to have wrecked them both. The night we got to Montana for the funerals, my dad and your mom bitched and moaned about their parents and they cried. They were drunk as skunks. They kept saying 'poor dad' over and over again, like a scratched CD. You were quiet. Can't believe you had a bird in your chest, and you knew not to show her off."

Pockets of the funeral came to Owen, but there was too much distance and it felt like a dream. His last hurrah must have been around that time. Something about how both parents dying so close together was sure to make the world's dangers that much more present for his mom. How would he have reacted if his mother died like that? He tried to imagine what his mother was like when she was his age. Did she listen to music? Have friends? Had she ever worked anywhere but the diner? He couldn't even imagine his mom then, the one who kept him safe in the house.

"My mom was clear that no one could know," Owen said. They both tapped their chests in unison.

"I spent most of the time in the corner reading, but one time my dad and your mom went out to smoke and I got up and went over to my dad's drink on the table. I think it was gin. I took a sip. My first ever taste of alcohol." She looked down at the beer in her hand, took a drink. She puffed on her cigarette. "You came over and I gave you a drink, too. You were probably only three or four. It was our secret."

"I don't remember any of that."

Gail nudged his ribs. "I remember," she whispered up to him.

"I bet Gail remembers," he said.

"Do java finches have great memories?"

He nodded.

"It just seems we've always had secrets that are just ours. I don't think we should keep secrets from each other. No more secrets." She offered him the cigarette.

Owen took a pull on it and passed it back to her. His stomach rumbled. A log popped in the stove. He sat up and put his hands under his thighs. "I don't want secrets," he said. He thought about the bundle of secrets he still kept in his belly: the Army of Acronyms, something different inside him—*the bird can talk.*

Tennessee stamped the cigarette out in the ashtray and went into the kitchen and then into her bedroom. She returned a second later with a kitchen knife and a chunk of rose quartz. "Pinky out." He put his finger out and she placed hers next to his, so the tips were just touching. She took the kitchen knife and dug the blade into Owen's fingertip. The knife was dull, and he had to push against the blade to break the skin. She did the same to hers. Then she kissed the rose quartz and placed it against his lips. He kissed it. They locked their pinkies around each other. They held the rose quartz above the fingers and let the few drops of blood mix. "No secrets," his cousin said, holding his gaze.

"No secrets," he agreed.

"Megan and I had sex."

"SEX sex?"

"Yep." Tennessee flipped the pack of cigarettes up in the air. A smile curled on her lips. "I think I'm in love. She's perfect."

The right kind of attention.

"What about you? Any secrets?"

"Gail can talk." A bit of the skein unraveled. He whispered down to Gail, "Say something."

He lifted his T-shirt over his head. Gail hopped forward so her beak was right up against his rib. Her breath tickled the bone. "Nice to meet you, Tennessee."

Tennessee held her breath and placed her hand to her chest. She leaned back. "Holy shit. How'd you teach her to say that?"

Owen laughed. "She's not a parrot."

Tennessee sat still, a statue, mouth agape.

He wiped the blood from his pinky on his jeans. "Tell me more about Megan."

But Tennessee bent down over his chest and stared at Gail. She didn't want to talk about her girlfriend. All she wanted was to see the bird who talked. He felt a little like the circus freaks who used to tour the country. Slowly Tennessee formed questions longer than *What?*

and *How?* Gail answered Tennessee's questions: *What's it like in there? Do you ever wonder what it's like to fly?* (*Oh, you know, dark and warm, cozy. Owen is a good host.* And *doesn't everyone who cannot, wonder what it's like to fly?*)

They showed off parlor tricks. Gail told a nasty joke about Jesus being hung like this, and she spread her wings wide (insinuating his large *you-know-what*). Owen opened his mouth and Gail shouted words up his throat so that her voice echoed out of Owen's mouth, like a bird calling from deep in a well. She spit up the pebble and swallowed it again. They shared emotions and feelings so intertwined that Owen wasn't sure which were his and which were the bird's, although this was more difficult to demonstrate to his cousin.

Tennessee hugged him afterwards. "Must be nice," she said, "never being alone."

He smiled. "Nice is one way to put it."

Later they lay in their respective beds (Owen on the mattress, Tennessee on the floor; Tennessee had given the bed to Owen permanently now, claiming the floor was better for her back). Owen felt Tennessee smiling widely. She drifted off to sleep, murmuring about a talking bird. Bob came home a few minutes later, a woman with him. Their voices were hushed, like teenagers sneaking around in the night. Small rays of purple and orange light wafted under the closet door. Owen ignored them. He fell asleep to Bob and the woman smoking and giggling on the back porch.

38

Owen stood on the empty beach and scanned the water for seals. His eyes lost focus, turned fuzzy. Sharing one of his secrets with Tennessee had made him brazen, made him want to share Gail with the world, stand up on the desk in history class and shout, "There is a place in my chest where there is no skin, just bones and a bird who is a chatty Cathy," but of course he didn't do this, never could, so instead he said the words out loud now on the empty beach. He spoke them so quietly that no one could have heard them even if they were right in front of him, but he said them anyways, spoke them to the waves. He released them.

He plopped down hard on the ground. The sand was cold between his fingertips. It was a Wednesday afternoon. Tennessee was off at work or hiding somewhere with Megan. His cousin didn't bring him around so much anymore.

Owen let his mind wander. He thought of Tennessee and Megan, how difficult it would be to find someone like Tennessee had. He wanted to be felt up without worry, wanted to kiss without danger of Gail causing too much of a ruckus, and maybe someday, he wanted to have sex with someone, shirts off, but it seemed impossible. He thought of all the possibilities of sex with everyone he was attracted to (everyone really). Comet and his gold ring. Clyde and his small waves, mouthing *hello*. Ava and the way she rubbed circles on his back.

"How do you guys do it?" he whispered down to Gail. "How do you get someone to love you?"

"I'm a bird," she said. "It's different for me."

"How so? We're all just animals."

"Well, I don't know for sure, since I don't meet a whole lot of other birds in here." She tapped the walls of his chest. "But going off what I suspect."

"What you feel in your bones."

"Yes, what I feel in my bones. I meet another bird like me, and we dance for a minute. He clicks on a branch above me. I click beneath him, soft clicks to let him know I'm interested. Deliberate clicks, though, so they can't be taken for anything else but a click that says, *YOU, I am interested in YOU.* Then maybe I spin around a little bit. Show it off." She puffed her feathers out in his chest and stuck her ass in the air. She spun around a couple of times. She smacked her beak together in a *click*. Owen felt her then.

He felt her spinning and trying to get someone's attention. He felt her deep desire to be seen as beautiful and healthy and lovely. She spun around again. "Maybe he starts singing to me. He whistles a tune that tells me I am right for him, and I know it's time. I click a couple more times, definitive yeses, and then I hop next to him." Gail was excited now. She spun around faster in his chest, and it was like that first day in the locker room when every boy felt like a possibility. Owen put a hand to his chest and closed his eyes. He lifted his arms over his head, trying to get his breath back. Gail continued. "Then we peck at each other and lock eyes. Then it's love, right then, when we lock eyes and are done pecking and are still there. I mate for life." She collapsed on the floor of his chest.

Owen stood up and walked towards the house, dizzy. His feet slipped in the sand. The desert sands dusted the edges of his lungs and he hurried back through the woods. He tried to keep an even pace, to remind himself that if he went too fast, his lungs would get worse. He thought of spinning around Clyde and he walked faster. Gail sat on her rump, oblivious, dizzy with spinning. He walked right past Bob, who was watering the garden.

Once in the room, he dug through piles of clothes in the closet. The flowers sat on the floor and the room was bright with light. It was so thick he had to swim through it until he found his backpack. He unzipped the front pouch and pulled out his inhaler. One puff and then another. It was a lot, this feeling of love, of mating for life.

39

Owen was on the back porch alone. The moon was full in the sky. It was that time when the moon was bursting and making everyone crazy, even Gail was crazy in his chest, nearly as crazy as she had been the week earlier when she'd shown him her mating dance.

It was almost eleven o'clock at night when the landline rang. No one called him and he was enjoying the crisp air, so he let the phone keep ringing. A big mama raccoon walked out from the trees, followed by her three babies. The mama scanned the clearing and the three cubs ran across, the coast clear. The phone stopped ringing. Owen settled back into the cheap plastic patio chair.

The phone rang again. Everyone in the house ignored it, so he got up to answer.

It was his mom. A year and a half and here she was, calling out of the blue in the middle of the night. He sat at the island.

Her breath was heavy in his ear. "Oh, Owen, Owen, Owen, Owen. Oh, Owen, I can't believe it's you. Oh, Owen, I thought you were dead." She shuddered, and he knew her whole body was shaking. Her hand must've been over her mouth.

"I'm here, Mom. It's okay. I'm here. I'm alive."

"It's just, I saw him. He found me. He came into the diner. I don't know if he was just hungry or if he tracked me down, but he found me. I made Elayne wait on him and I ran out the back door, but we made eye contact. We made *eye contact*, Owen."

"Who, Mom?"

"*Him.* The doctor."

He rubbed his wrists and thought of the doctor's eyes glowing with desperation. "Okay," he said. "Okay, okay, okay. That doesn't mean he knows where I am. It just means he knows where you are."

"Yes, yes, yes. You were always so smart. You taught yourself to read, you know."

"The TV taught me."

"Are you safe?"

"I'm careful. I listen to Gail. I don't make a stink. I blend in." He ran his hand along the shaved sides of his hair and looked down at his torn jeans. "No one notices me." On cue, his left rib creaked, and he leaned forward onto the counter.

"What's your plan if they find you?" She was calmer now, probably leaning against the phone booth.

"I don't know. It depends on where I am. Either run or fight or give up, depending." He wanted to talk about something else, to lie on the couch and watch reruns while she drank wine.

"Owen, no matter what, if they ever find you, I will be there, I will break you free. I will give up everything to keep you from becoming a lab rat."

"I know, Mom. Thank you."

"I should go. Phone could be tapped. Do you need anything?"

"You can't talk?" His voice had settled into its raspy tenor for months, but it cracked now, split in two.

"Can't risk it. Say hi to Tennessee and Bob." The receiver clicked in his ear and he set the phone down.

The kind of silence that hangs thick in the air.

He went into the bedroom and found Tennessee kneeling in front of her table. She moved rocks and candles around, placing them in one order and then another. Gail ran her wing along his side. She plopped down in his chest. He dug his inhaler out of his backpack and took a puff.

"Telemarketer?" Tennessee asked.

"My mom." He sat down on the edge of the bed.

Tennessee spun around and sat cross-legged on the floor. "Are you okay?"

He leaned forward and put his hands on his thighs. He imagined his breath reaching the base of his spine. "She called to tell me that the doctor found her. He came into her work." He imagined the space behind his eyelids and his eyes fluttered.

"The doctor from when you came out here?"

"The doctor from when I came out here." His cheeks were hot.

"What can we do?" Her eyes were wet.

"Nothing. It's fine. It'll be another two years before he finds this house, and I'll be gone by then."

"You'll be gone by then?"

The sentence had fallen out of his mouth, wholly formed, just *plop*, but now that he'd said it, it was so obvious. "I'll be seventeen next year," he said. *Everyone runs away at seventeen.*

Gail lay down on her back. "That's right. We'll get the hell outta dodge," she whispered. That bird always wanted to migrate.

Tennessee got up and went to her dresser. She pulled down a small black rock and handed it to Owen. "Obsidian soaks up bad energy."

He ran his finger along the rock's sharp edges. It cut dully into the pad of his thumb. "My mom went around the house and put up all sorts of things to protect us. Acorns on the windowsills. A broom above the front door. A glass of water on the refrigerator. She even painted the porch blue."

"Did it make a difference?"

He shrugged.

"Sometimes it's about the comfort it brings us and less about the actual impact. Like right now, there's not much to do, so it feels good to do something, anything really. Your mom felt helpless."

He remembered her voice on the phone. Yes, helpless. He held the rock up and watched the light bounce off the black, disappear into it.

"Let's do a thing." His cousin held her hand out. He gripped it loosely and they went into the kitchen. She pulled down a box of salt and two bowls. She filled each of the bowls with salt, the piles of crystals like sand dunes.

She handed him a bowl. "A ring of salt around the house to protect you."

They walked outside. The air was muggy and there was the hint of a rainstorm coming. "You walk this way"—she pointed to the left—"and I'll walk this way, and we'll meet back here." She pointed at the ground. "Think about who should be let in, and who you need protection from." She pinched the salt with her fingers and dropped it onto the ground, walking away from him around the house. He did the same.

He thought about the people he wanted to let in: Comet, his mother, his uncle, Tennessee, Ava, and Megan. Clyde.

He thought of the things he most certainly did not want near the house: the Army of the Acronyms, the doctor, the nurse, any doctor or nurse, Jon, Troy, Clyde's dad.

Tennessee passed him and they continued on, walking away from each other. He dropped more salt. They were laying an electric fence around the house.

He reached the front of the house and his cousin placed her bowl inside his. She put her hand on his arm. "See?" she said. "Now it feels like we did something."

But Owen's breath was still uneven, and when he closed his eyes, he saw the doctor. They went inside and Tennessee grabbed them each a beer before moving onto the back porch. They sat down, held eye contact, clinked their beers, and touched the bottles to their knees before taking a drink. The beer helped with Owen's uneasiness. He looked out over the backyard, but he couldn't see the ring of salt they'd left on the ground. It felt like they'd done nothing. Gail wasn't any help. She paced back and forth in his chest, running through every scenario wherein they had been captured and she somehow saved the day.

The wind blew softly, and trees swayed. Tennessee cleared her throat. "You know we're family, right?"

He nodded. "Cousins."

"Not just that. I will always look out for you."

"I know. And you too." He thought maybe she meant she would protect him from the doctor, keep him safe from the Army of Acronyms.

She took a breath, readied herself. "I'm moving out after I graduate. Megan and I are looking at places."

Tennessee had her own skein of secrets. He remembered their promise. The blood on the rose quartz. "Oh," he said.

"At least you'll get your own room," she said. "And it's going to be in Olympia, a quick bus ride away."

He'd never ridden the bus before. "Don't do that. I don't need consoling. I'm happy for you."

"I know. I'm just saying. It will be better for both of us."

He sipped his beer, nodded, and tried not to cry. Everyone ran away at seventeen. Everyone disappeared eventually.

40

Ten days later it was June and the air was still cold. School had been out for one week. Nearly all of Tennessee's belongings were packed in boxes. When she told Bob she was moving out, she fired off a laundry list of reasons why it was better, just like she had with Owen, including it would be one less mouth to feed, the bit about Owen getting his own room, and Bob wouldn't be scared to bring his girlfriend around the house anymore. The last bit stung Bob and he mumbled his response. Owen had heard the woman's voice several more times after that first night, always after Tennessee had fallen asleep. Once, he'd even gotten up to get a glass of water, hoping to catch her, but when he came into the living room, she was gone, a ghost.

At first Bob denied it. "Girlfriend? Girlfriend? I don't have time to have a girlfriend." Then, without prompting, he changed his tone. "I mean, I have a friend I've been seeing, but it's casual. It's nothing you need to move out for." And finally, "You don't have to move out," he pleaded. "Just stay a little bit longer."

But Tennessee's mind was made up. She was buying a car so they wouldn't have to share the Rabbit, and then it was sayonara.

Since then, Bob had gone out nearly every night, drinking at the bar to avoid having to see his only daughter pack her things. Owen took a similar approach, walking down to the water nearly every day. It felt good to feel the pull of the saltwater, like the ocean wanted him. He thought about his mom, worried about her while he threw rocks and watched seals. Sometimes it felt like his mother took the threats he faced more seriously than he did. Gail did her best to tell jokes, but they came out uninspired, tired.

What do you call a cow with no legs?

Ground beef.

But tonight was different. Tonight, Owen and Tennessee were going to the Fort. They drove down the highway with the windows down.

"The Fort is a space for anyone who's ever felt outcast," Tennessee explained, her cigarette stabbing the air with each word. "There are punk kids and queer kids and white kids and Mexican kids and Black kids and genderqueers and anarchists and communists and dorks: a smorgasbord of teenage fuckery." She pulled over onto the side of the highway, handing him a flashlight.

They climbed out of the car. Owen shined his flashlight at his cousin. He had convinced her to wear her hair down long and big, a supermodel in the spotlight. She put a hand in front of her face, shielding her eyes. He focused his flashlight back at the ground. She'd shaved the sides of his head and painted his nails orange. They hiked down an overgrown path to the water. A few minutes into the walk, Tennessee leaned over and put a hand on his flashlight. "Shut it off."

They were flung into darkness, so much darkness it hurt. He closed his eyes for a half second, speeding up his process of imagining roots digging deep into the earth. The world was only mildly brighter when he opened his eyes. The soft tumble of the Sound could be heard. Out here it sounded less like an ocean and more like a creek. The grass brushed against their bodies and their footsteps kept a steady beat until they reached the clearing next to the water. The beach was like the beach at home, but out here the water was quiet with the soft roll of a river.

Ava, Lou, Comet, and Megan leaned against a dead tree, twice the size of the dead log on the beach at Bob's. Megan yelped when she recognized Tennessee and Owen. She set into a sprint to meet them. She and Tennessee hugged. Tennessee settled her head on Megan's shoulders. They pulled apart. Soft kiss, and they each took a step back.

Megan turned towards Owen. "Nice to see you again," and she hugged him tightly.

It felt strange to be remembered.

Comet was in a T-shirt and shorts. His hair was black now, shorter. He had two gold hoops in each ear. He leaned over and hugged Owen. No electricity this time. Owen hugged Lou, who was in suspenders and dark red lipstick. And of course, Ava. Ava with a big hug, rubbing circles on his back. Ava in all black, always all black.

They all walked down the beach together. Tennessee held Megan's hand. Lou smoked cloves, and the whole beach smelled like incense. Comet walked near Owen, but a step ahead of him, and Owen had to walk quickly to keep up.

Ava grabbed Owen's arm and nestled her head on his shoulder. "Look." She pointed up at the sky. The stars were a blanket, and the moon just a sliver. "It's Jupiter."

A light brighter than the other stars, hanging just above the horizon.

They reached a short dock that stretched out into the water. The boards creaked beneath their feet and the dock swayed in the water, rocking side to side. At its end, Lou hopped into a small aluminum boat and pulled it alongside the dock. He held it close so everyone could ease into it. Owen was the last one in.

It took Lou a couple tries to get the motor running. The air smelled like gasoline, and everyone stayed quiet.

Once they were on the water, Owen fell into the rhythm of the Sound and his stomach settled. Comet sat next to him, and Owen felt heat coming off his body.

He pulled his jacket tighter around his chin. Gail bounced around in his chest. "This is it," she said. "This is living. These are the types of things birds dream of."

Ava unscrewed a flask from her bag and passed it to Owen. "Vodka."

He nodded and took a small sip. It tasted like kerosene. He passed it to Comet, and when he did, their fingertips touched. Everyone passed the flask around. Owen's knuckles grew stiff in the cold, so he curled his fingers into a fist. The boat skidded on the surface of the water and it carved two waves that rolled all the way onto the shore behind them. It was like when Owen ran his hand along the surface of the water in the bathtub.

Lou pulled the boat up onto the shore on the other side of the water. It was a long strip of land covered in rocks with grass poking up here and there. Voices drifted through the woods. They hiked up the small hill and into the dark. Owen felt uneasy, but everyone was smoking and laughing and so he drank a little more vodka to settle down. The voices got louder, and it was like a net of sound was being cast across the forest. Gail sat with her ear pressed against the hole in his chest. She shared the air with him, and it was easy and lovely, and Owen had not felt air like that in a long time, maybe ever. They arrived at a short concrete building with no real doors or windows, just a bunch of door-sized holes, and not much of a roof, either. A fire burned in a small barrel in the middle of the paved path. People were scattered about, mostly teenagers. They wore leather jackets and denim vests and plain hoodies and flannels and T-shirts and dresses. Their clothes were dotted with metal-studded pyramids, their pants rolled up to show boots and Converse. Next to the fire, a boy with pink hair made out with a guy with a Mohawk, not loose like Owen's, but tall and hard like concrete.

It seemed that the night was full of one thousand possibilities and that the Army of Acronyms would never find him, a ring of salt around the Fort. The hurricane of anxiety eased in his chest for the first time since his mother had called.

As soon as they arrived, Comet weaved through the crowd, laughing and hugging nearly everybody, truly the life of the party. Owen thought he was a little like Gail in the way he wanted to make everyone laugh. Owen wanted some of that, the joy in being friends with everyone, the opposite of staying disappeared. Tennessee let go of Megan's hand and leaned over and put her mouth right next to Owen's ear. "Welcome to the Fort. These are our people." Then she tapped her chest with her two fingers.

Our people.

A loud screech came from inside the building. Someone cheered.

A snare drum popped a couple of times. People put out half-smoked cigarettes and moved inside. Tennessee pulled Owen into the building. They were two steps from the doorway when the air exploded with sound. Guitar and drums and a loud voice reverberated through the crumbling fort's walls.

They stepped over bits of trash and walked through the maze of hallways. The only lights in the whole damn place were the strands of Christmas lights. There was something about being inside the old military fort, seeing it rotted and decayed and taken over by all these punks and queers. Something that gave Owen some hope, like if this building could be overtaken, maybe others could, too. They reached a room in the center, where a large banner with **THE STINKERZ** scrawled across it in spray paint hung behind a band: three teenage boys in dirty jeans and soft eyes. Ava bobbed her head back and forth. She passed Owen the flask, and he choked down more gasoline. The whole room shook with the sound, and then it was quiet, just a guitar ringing out, and like that, the song was over.

Each song only lasted a minute or so, but during that minute, everyone ran into the middle of the room and flailed their bodies and banged their heads and shook their hair out. The guitarist bounced up and down in front of the microphone. The drummer tore his shirt off two songs into the set. Owen ran into the center of the room. It was bodies jammed against bodies. Beer sloshed onto his boots. Someone popped him in the nose with their elbow, and the familiar head rush of a bloody nose came, but blood never dripped. Sweat was airborne. Gail bounced around in his chest. She twirled with her wings out and flapped them up and down, and Owen swore he lifted off the ground. He was floating there in the middle of the room, but when he looked down, his feet were planted firmly on the concrete floor. Someone knocked into his spine. The whole room was bodies and sound and sweat and beer, and it was fucking stupid how beautiful it was.

Afterwards, Tennessee dragged Owen back outside with her and Megan and they shared a cigarette. "Just wait," Megan said. Her fingers ran through Tennessee's loose hair. "Broomstix are the shit."

If the Stinkerz were raw, distorted punk, like kerosene in a flask, then Broomstix were punk rock rolled up in a joint and passed around the room. Two women, one behind a keyboard and the other behind a small drum set, played music that everyone had to lean in to hear. Everyone sat cross-legged on the cold concrete floor. The sweat dried and cooled. The songs built up and released energy in a more tender way, like they were emptying hearts out. In the middle of their set, when everyone was hushed, the singer announced that they were standing on the land of the Squaxin Island Tribe. "We are on stolen land," she said. Another instance of the lineage of men who took up space, but Owen thought this proclamation was trying to counteract that, undo it somehow.

Megan and Tennessee sat in front of him. They leaned into each other; their bodies pressed against one another. Gail leaned against his spine, hard. Once, Tennessee reached behind her and placed her hand on the floor. Owen grabbed it with his hand and squeezed her fingers tightly. She pulled her hand back up to her lap, and she turned around and smiled.

Owen wanted to get up and go look for Comet, but Gail stopped him. "Just take this in. Don't change a thing," she whispered up to him.

41

The next morning, an ocean crashed inside Owen's skull, so he stayed under the covers, ignoring all signs of an outside world progressing without him. It was nearly four in the afternoon when he roused himself out of bed. The room was nearly empty. Tennessee had moved everything but his dresser, the bed, the lamp on the floor, and his collection of rocks and the Mason jar of water from the Sound that sat on the windowsill. The only poster left on the wall was the one detailing the lifespan of the Douglas-fir that hung near the closet. He found a note on the dresser.

Didn't want to wake your hungover ass up. We got the keys today. You slept like you were dead. I found this on the beach the other day and it reminded me of Gail's rock. Will you give it to her? See you real soon.

Next to the letter was a small BB pellet. He held it up in front of him. It was then that he noticed there was only one color swirling around the room. Purple light everywhere. Tennessee had taken her flower. He lifted his T-shirt and raised the BB to his ribs, his finger pinching the pellet near his heart. He bit his lip. He passed Gail the pellet through his ribs. "Here," he said. "She's gone. Put this next to the rock." He sat down on the floor, up against the bed, and tears came to his eyes.

Gail cried to herself in his chest.

42

Owen could not get used to sleeping alone. It had been four days since Tennessee had moved out. He turned the radio on low, so it was a soft hum near the window, but it didn't help. He was used to the rhythm of his cousin's breathing while she slept. He was used to her presence. The room felt big and empty without her and her things. He and Gail couldn't fill all the space of the bedroom. He lay in bed, tossing and turning and willing himself to sleep.

Earlier in the day, Tennessee had come over to grab the last of her toiletries. She'd hugged him and apologized for not calling, insisting it was because she was in "love jail." It was her first time at the house since she'd moved out. She asked if Owen had met Bob's girlfriend yet, and when he told her no, he hadn't, she said, "Looks like the ring of salt is working," and then she left, leaving him alone. He and Bob had barely talked since she'd left, and all the hope he'd felt at the Fort had fallen away so the world felt flat and dried-up.

Now Gail was fast asleep in his chest, taking no time at all to adjust to being the only ones in the room. She snored loudly under the covers, with tiny bird whistles after every snore.

He closed his eyes and focused his breath and reached deep down into himself so that he could feel what Gail was feeling. Sometimes he could get whiffs of her dreams when he focused everything on the task. She was always flying, never anything else.

Recently he'd started to think differently about how he and Gail shared the air. He thought maybe everyone shared the air with everyone else, but it was more intense for him because of Gail. When he stood next to someone who was sad, he felt sad, too. An hour after Tennessee had left that day, he and Bob had gone to the grocery store to pick up some food, but less food than usual since it was just the two of them now. They were silent the entire trip. They communicated in the grocery store by holding up cans of green beans or a round watermelon and the other nodding in agreement. The grocery cart's wheels rattled on the asphalt while they walked to the car, the cart only containing two paper bags of food. A man paced back and forth near the Rabbit, blabbing to himself about which radio station he preferred. His voice rose and fell depending on nothing at all. They walked past him, and Owen felt anxious and happy and mad. Emotions so intertwined he couldn't tell which were his and which were the world's.

Now time had gotten so far away from him that morning light trickled in through the window and it felt like he had time-traveled. He wasn't sure if he'd fallen asleep. He closed his eyes tight and he thought of him and Comet walking through the woods together. He showed Comet each of the plants Tennessee had taught him. Owen wanted to impress Comet, like an older brother. He thought of Clyde and his gentle gestures, a hand on his horse, saving the jellyfish, one at a time. But every time he thought of Clyde, it was a jumble of emotions, like: *evangelical blowhard* and *not our people*, but also helping Owen home, a beaten and bloodied conga line. And instantly Clyde's father appeared, and then it was the cyclone of the Army of Acronyms. He redirected his thoughts and imagined he and Ava perusing records and picking out music together. He remembered the time in the woods. It felt odd to think of such a good friend like that. He shifted onto his left side and his rib creaked. His brain was working without him, moving too fast to keep up.

He heard Bob get up and shuffle into the kitchen. He put the kettle on for coffee. He turned the radio on, and a British news anchor recounted the world's news. Owen thought he heard the quietness of someone else's voice, someone trying not to be heard. He couldn't tell if it was Bob's girlfriend or if four nights of no sleep were catching up to him.

* * *

Gail was sick of Owen the Mope by the next morning. "Time to get up," she said. "Up and at 'em. Up! Up! Up!" She stomped around in his chest and waved her wings furiously up towards the ceiling like she could use the power of telekinesis to levitate his body up and out of bed. It was noon.

The wall loomed empty above him. He stared at the ceiling and found images in the spackle: Marilyn Monroe, a cartoon dog, a rocket ship. The air was warm and buzzed outside the window, and the sun burned his hand that rested near the glass.

"Coooooome onnnnnnn." Gail's voice stretched in his chest.

He shoved the covers off the bed and got his right leg off the mattress. He let it hang there, his toes brushing the carpet. Finally, he mustered his energy and pushed himself up. He pulled on a loose T-shirt and some cutoffs and went into the living room, where he made coffee and picked up after his and Bob's meal from the night before. The air in the room was hot and stale. He went back into the bedroom and opened the closet and picked up the Blossoms Blossom. Streaks of purple wafted up towards him. It never got old watching the color swirl around itself, but he always only looked for a second. He placed the jar on the windowsill for some sun. He ignored it.

He took his cup of coffee and went outside.

It was cool in the woods. The shadows from the trees were stacked on top of each other. Sunlight leaked in here or there, but mostly it was dark. He felt the danger he always felt in the woods, like he could face off with the Army of Acronyms at any moment. There was a bit of comfort in this danger, and he was pleased he still worried for his life. He'd started to feel like maybe he didn't care anymore. The creek rippled along the forest floor. He leaned against a pine and felt its bark through his T-shirt.

"It'll be okay," Gail whispered up to him. "We will get through this like we always do. Tennessee's not gone forever. She's—"

He shushed her. "Jesus. I just want some peace and quiet."

Everything was silent again. The creek trickled and a woodpecker banged high in a tree. He squatted down and took a sip of his coffee. There was a scurry out of the corner of his eyes near the creek, and so he stayed still and waited for it again. A salamander crawled out of the water and onto a rock to sunbathe.

Owen wobbled along the creek bed towards the water. When he dipped out from the brush and came onto the shore, the sun was bright and it surprised him. The Sound seemed extra loud. It felt like he was waking up from a nap. He took another drink of his coffee. He closed his eyes and orange spots filled his vision. He sucked in the saline air. There was a sadness in it, and he wondered again if things besides him and Gail could share emotions through the air. Maybe it was his own sadness.

He opened his eyes and stretched his limbs long around him. Gail did the same in his chest, her first movement since he'd shushed her in the woods. He realized he wasn't alone on the beach; his arms snapped reflexively back to his sides. Clyde leaned against the dead tree. He sat in the sand with his knees sticking straight up, so that he sat in the fetal position, a tall boy all wrapped up in a ball. Owen felt the pull to the water and the pull to Clyde, each playing tug of war for his attention, calling his name.

Owen cleared his throat, shoved his hand in his pocket. "Easy," Gail started, but he shushed her again. He felt the sadness come back like a wave and wondered if he should put a hand on Clyde's back to let him know he was there. The longer Clyde went without noticing him, the more awkward Owen felt, but he couldn't do anything but stand there and stare at him. The waves tumbled on the sand. Clyde's rounded spine stuck up through his shirt like a prehistoric lizard's armor, those farm boy muscles. He slowly rocked back and forth; the dead tree rocked with him.

Owen couldn't take it any longer and he cleared his throat, louder this time.

Clyde's eyes whipped open. They were red, his cheeks raw. He sat up straight. "Hey." He scrambled to stand up.

"You okay?"

"I'm fine." Clyde looked around, peered behind Owen, trying to assess whether they were alone or not. He rubbed his eyes with the back of his hand. "It's nice down here. Nice to be next to the water."

Owen stepped closer. "Yeah."

The wind blew hard against Owen's hair and he brushed it from his eyes.

"I should go." Clyde looked up towards his house. "Give you your alone time."

"I don't need alone time." Owen wanted Clyde to stay. He didn't know why, but he did. He really looked at Clyde and reached deep into the air to try to feel what he was feeling. Clyde's eyes were a pale blue, and Owen thought he could see a whole ocean in there. His chin and cheeks were lined with small pockmarks from old acne and the habit of shaving every day. How could it be that Owen was the same age as this boy who felt decades beyond him?

"I should go before my dad sees us talking." Clyde's eyes darted towards the woods.

"What? Why?" Clyde's dad flashed in Owen's mind, the brim of his hat sitting low on his eyebrows, his flannel shirt tucked tight into his pants and his iron belt buckle the size of a saucer.

The Army of Acronyms is relentless.

"He doesn't want me talking to you. He's a thief of joy." Clyde's fingers lifted in a low wave, barely perceptible. He mouthed *goodbye* to Owen and walked into the woods.

Gail shook her feathers out in Owen's chest. He realized he'd been holding his breath. The trees moved around Clyde and then the branches swept back around him like they were closing in. Clyde walked towards the right, the direction of his home, surrounded by that buzzing electric fence. Jeez Louise started barking up a storm when he'd disappeared from Owen's view.

Owen threw his head back and put away the rest of his coffee. He let the mug hang loosely and swing at his side while he walked back through the woods.

"That was weird," Gail said. "Him alone on the beach. His dad not wanting you two talking."

Owen stopped walking. He put his hand to his chest and felt his heart beating through his shirt. "What do you think he meant by *thief of joy?*"

"That was weird, too."

Owen wondered if thieves of joy could be related to the Army of Acronyms. Maybe they were a faction or a company. He thought it could just be another name for the same thing. Men angry at something that had nothing to do with them. As always, he thought of the doctor.

When he came to the garden, he took a right and walked towards the road. He wasn't sure where he was going, but he didn't want to go home yet. He set the coffee mug on the front porch, stopped at the garage, and looked at his mom's station wagon. Its once-red paint now looked burnt and faded. The body was boxy and bloated. He ran his hand along the dusty back window, and it felt like sand against his palm. He climbed into the backseat. He closed his eyes and inhaled deeply. It smelled like old cigarettes and mildew. The glass wind chimes on the back porch clinked together, the sound wandering in through the cracked window. He remembered the old bottle tree from the front yard at his mom's house. He ran his hand along the damp, sticky bench seat. He opened his eyes. He could almost see his mother in the driver's seat, could almost hear the sound of her turning the crank to roll the window down and lighting her cigarette with her other hand while stopped at a red light. Gail plopped down in his chest and he felt her weight on his stomach. He missed his mom so goddamn much. He missed Tennessee, too, but not like he missed his mama. His longing for his mother rose and fell with time like the tide, and it seemed it was high tide. He lay his head down on the seat and wrapped his arms around his knees like Clyde had. He let the car hold him until he fell asleep for the first real time in five days.

Owen woke up a few hours later, rested but confused as to where he was. He sat up with a start, and slowly the scene pieced itself together. The light had shifted from the orange glow to a cooler blue in the garage. There were ants in his pants from where the seat belt buckle cut into his left butt cheek. The door creaked and popped open. He slid out between the door and the stacks of boxes.

He stepped out into the evening air. The driveway was still empty. He picked up his coffee mug off the front porch and went inside to take the flower off the windowsill and get some dinner started for Bob and himself. There was a silence in the house while Owen moved around, picking up dirty mugs and tossing empty beer bottles, so he turned the radio on low while he worked. It was tuned to public radio, and two older men discussed the *state of the world*. "It's all up," one of the men said, "violence against women and Black folks and queer folks and trans folks. We are witnessing a backlash." Owen stood in the living room, a dirty towel draped over his arm.

"Turn this shit off," Gail said.

Owen walked over and stood next to the radio on the sill. He always heard the commentators as background noise, but he had never actually listened to the words they were saying.

The other man spoke now. "But many are arguing that these communities have always faced this amount of violence. It is only now that they are receiving the attention they deserve—"

The Army of Acronyms is relentless.

Owen shut it off. The silence came down like a sledgehammer. He went to the back porch and brought in the CD player and set it on the floor near the couch. He put on LCD Soundsystem. The room filled with sound again, joyous and raucous sound.

He spun around and picked up everything he and his uncle had strewn about, their sadness having exploded across the room. He washed the dishes. Gail whistled along with the music. He remembered the nights when his mom came home from work and put on some coffee. When she turned the radio on and they spun around the room, it felt good to take up all that space.

A car crunched onto the driveway. He turned the stereo down but not off. He heard one door, then a second open and close. It had grown dark outside, and the wind rattled the tomato cages outside the kitchen window. He wondered if it was not the Rabbit that had pulled in but someone else instead. The doctor? *A thief of joy?* (Whatever that was.) He thought of what the news commentator had said, and something stirred inside him. He could not move.

There were hushed voices in the driveway. He heard each footstep on the gravel to the front door, but when they reached the door they stopped, and the door didn't open. Gail shook in his chest, also unsure of what to do.

Finally, the screen door creaked open, followed by the front door, and Bob called out. "Owen? Owen, I'm home. There's someone I want you to meet." It turned out either the ring of salt had a set time limit before it wore off or it could not withstand the power of someone really wanting someone else to come inside.

Natalie was a good foot shorter than Bob. She had long, blond hair, but her eyebrows were dark brown and two perfectly sculpted crescent moons. She wore a blue plaid shirt over a Melvins T-shirt and dark jeans. She stretched her hand towards Owen. "Natalie," she said. There was chipped teal nail polish on four of her five nails.

Gail pushed Owen forward, pressing against his bare rib. "Move, you dummy. Shake her hand. And close your mouth."

Owen shut his mouth and stretched his hand forward. "Owen," he said. "It's a pleasure."

Her brightly painted red lips parted to show her white and slightly crooked top row of teeth in a smile. The next song came on and she put a hand to her chest. "I love this album." She sighed like she was remembering something from a long time ago. She looked Owen in the eyes. "You and I," she said, "we're going to get along."

Owen felt a warmth from her, and then instantly felt he was betraying his cousin. He ignored it, and the three of them worked to make dinner. They baked wings and tossed a salad. Bob grabbed Owen a beer from the fridge when they were ready to sit down. "To celebrate," he explained. They sat in the backyard, no fire, but the three of them with their plates of food on their laps. Natalie worked at Albertsons with Bob, but in the produce department. They'd known each other for over ten years. No kids. She liked a lot of the same music as Owen, but older mostly. Sonic Youth. Nirvana. Fugazi.

Later she grabbed everyone's plates and took them into the kitchen to wash. She insisted that Owen and Bob stay seated. Bob rolled a cigarette and lit it. Owen sipped on his second beer. The blanket of stars had unfolded above them, and the bats had mostly disappeared, save for one or two that still stumbled in the sky.

Bob inhaled. He blew the smoke out of his mouth hard. "What do you think?" He looked off towards the water. The light from the porch struck him so that Owen only saw his right ear and the outline of his nose.

"She seems nice."

"She is."

"Has Tennessee met her yet?"

Bob took a drink of his beer. "Not yet." He sucked in a drag of his cigarette. "Let's keep this between us. I want to introduce her when Tennessee is ready, more settled. She can be—" He tapped his fingers on his knee, conjuring up the right set of words to describe his daughter. "She can be a tough nut to crack. Baby steps."

"Baby steps." Owen sipped his beer and felt the carbonation against his upper lip. He wondered what Tennessee was doing. He still felt fuzzy from the nap in the station wagon earlier. Crickets chirped, and the air was nothing but two boys drinking next to each other. He felt like maybe this was family, just being quiet together, despite the Army of Acronyms, despite an absent mother or daughter, despite the world, just quiet.

Natalie came out a second later with another beer for herself and Bob. "Tell me about you." She tapped Owen's knee with her beer and leaned in to hear his answer.

"What's to say?" he said. "Bob's my uncle. I'm from Montana." It took everything for him not to mention the bird in his chest. For some reason, the day had made him more tender and open, and he felt safe next to Bob's girlfriend, someone he barely knew. He felt he was betraying his cousin again, so he reigned it in. "Not much to say."

She nodded. "That's okay."

His skull buzzed with the beer. He took one last drink and stood up, announcing it was his bedtime. When Owen turned towards the house to go inside, Natalie reached over and grabbed Bob's hand.

Everything felt wrong in the bedroom. The room was nearly empty, with piles of dirty laundry in the corners. And Owen still felt like he couldn't fill the room, like it was way too big for him. He gathered up his blankets and pillow and went out the front door. He dragged everything over the gravel and into the garage and laid out a bed on the backseat of the wagon. It was cramped, but it felt like his. Gail was asleep in no time. He watched the red fabric hanging loosely from the ceiling until he fell asleep.

43

Slowly, Owen moved items from the bedroom out into the car. He moved the bundle of herbs from above the bed. He moved the mason jar of water from the Sound and the rocks that sat on the windowsill. One day, he pulled down the green velvet dress from when he was Ariel. He hung the dress over the driver's side window like it was a curtain. He set the flower in the very back of the wagon where it got a good amount of sun during the day, and then he set it under the seat each night. The car filled with the musty purple glow. Soon the car no longer smelled like stale cigarettes or mildew. It smelled like lavender and sweet grass from the herbs, but also like the compost pile from Owen's armpits. He took a pinch of tobacco from his uncle's pouch and lit it like incense in the ashtray. The car filled with tobacco smoke, and the next day it smelled stale and he remembered his mother.

The ring of salt he and Tennessee had laid had burned patches of the lawn, so two lines of dead grass and dirt zigzagged around the house. Despite the ring of salt, Owen didn't feel safe in the house like he used to, something about his cousin leaving, something about the big open room and being all alone with only the bird in his chest. Owen felt safe in the station wagon. He imagined the extra work it would take the Army of Acronyms to find him hidden in the backseat. They'd show up to the house in the middle of the night to steal him away, only to find an empty bed and piles of clothes he no longer wore. They'd think he was a Houdini.

He spent the next few weeks wandering down to the beach or along the edges of the property. A part of him wanted to catch sight of Clyde again. The pull towards Clyde had gotten more intense lately, and the loose rope, not so loose, but the beach was always empty, so he settled onto the sand to look out over the water. He tried to focus on the pull he felt next to the deep water, but after a few minutes he got bored and would wander into the woods again. He walked along the electric fence, but here, Clyde didn't appear. Always it was Jeez Louise barking her head off. Her barking sent Gail into a frantic state, and so he picked up a stick and chucked it into the woods, sending the dog bounding after it. Owen wondered if Clyde had left. His mom had left. Tennessee had left. Everyone was always leaving. And someday Owen would leave, too.

44

Boat ride over the chilly water. Fire outside of the stout cement building: the Fort.

"It's beautiful," Tennessee said.

"What is?" Owen asked, drunk. Pairs of people stood around him. Gail was plopped down in his chest. Ava on his left and Comet to the right. They stood in a circle around the fire.

"That we have something like this. Something entirely dictated by nature. Shows at the Fort are on weekends and it has to be high tide. Everything else is based around that—the bands that play, the people who show up—everything coincides with the tidal chart. And today is that day. Look at this weather. It's magic." The night sky was deep blue above them, no clouds, really just spectacular.

In low tide, the water pulled away and was too shallow to take a boat to the Fort, so shallow that the dock and Lou's aluminum boat sat on the ground. At highest tide, the boat, the dock, everything rose fourteen feet off the ground in the water and then it was easy to take a boat to the island. They only had eight hours or so before it all sank back down again.

Megan stood behind Tennessee, her arms wrapped around her waist, head on her shoulder. "Maybe someday we'll flood the Sound and then we can have shows every weekend."

"Such hubris." Tennessee's teeth shone white in the fire when she laughed. She smoked cigarette after cigarette like her dad, a quick succession of prayers.

Ava passed around a small bottle of peppermint liqueur that glowed bright green and tasted like Listerine. Owen passed the bottle to Comet and Comet threw his arm around Owen's shoulders. He felt Comet's arms through the thick denim jacket. Owen's whole body buzzed.

Later, Owen stood next to the fire alone, too drunk too fast. Music shook the building and the ground.

"Take it easy," Gail whispered up to him.

But he didn't want easy. He wanted *different*. He wanted change. Really, what Owen wanted was the freedom of possibility he'd felt at the Fort two months earlier. He wanted to feel like the Army of Acronyms could be destroyed or at least be avoided. He went inside.

Music loud in his ears, so loud it felt like it came from inside him. His hands flew up into the air with every beat of the snare drum. His head shook with the bass's thud. He was overcome by the Holy Spirit of Motherfuckers and Misfits.

Praise Sid Vicious.

All praises sung to the holy Kim Deal.

God is a woman, and she listens to punk rock.

The set was soon over, and then Owen was back outside. More artificial green, artificial peppermint booze. More begging for something to change.

The night passed quickly like a chaotic movie montage. Owen outside, quiet. Schnapps. One blink. Two. Then Owen inside, thrashing into anyone who'd let him. Gail thrashed, too, having given up any semblance of bringing sense to Owen. He didn't think about the doctor or Comet or his cousin or his mother or Clyde's *thief of joy* or even Gail. He was simply a spirit swirling and gurgling in a room full of bass and screams and energy. Bodies pressed against his so tight he couldn't breathe. His lungs were the desert sands, but he stayed in the middle of the unrelenting pit. He let his lungs wear themselves out, stumbled over to the door, his hands on his knees, panting.

The night air was cold on his skin, sweat turned to ice water. It was the space between the second and third band. Megan, Tennessee, and Ava crowded around him.

Tennessee rubbed his back. "Did you bring your inhaler?"

"I'm fine." His lungs stung deep in his chest. He focused on his breathing, slow and deliberate. Ava passed him a bottle. "What's in this one?"

"Water."

It seemed the Fort had shrunk, more people and less space. The walls felt closer, everyone packed in like sardines. Gail pressed her wings wide against his ribs, and Owen felt her bursting inside him.

The peppermint booze had subsided just enough to let his brain think. He knew how to make things different and how to get the kernel of possibility to unfurl. He needed to kiss someone. Kiss someone like Bob kissed Natalie or how Megan kissed Tennessee. All this love was what was making him crazy. Love for everyone with no concentration, no focus. He just had to pick someone. Ava? Too much of a friend. July? Too dangerous and not here. Clyde? Not here. Comet? It had to be Comet. Why not? Hadn't there been electricity once? Certainly he could find it again. Didn't he feel something like love for Comet?

Gail immediately dissented. He didn't even get the chance to share the idea with her before she knew. Their emotions were so intertwined. "Bad idea," she said. "You're drunk. Too drunk. Too fast. Not the way to do it, bud."

Owen looked around and realized he didn't recognize a single person. He made his way through the hive of bodies, but everyone mistook his attempt to leave as playful mosh pit shoves and so they shoved him back and he had to work twice as hard to climb out. The music thudded outside. The concrete building thumped and the ground shook. A fire still burned weakly in the barrel near the entrance. He found Comet arguing with a white woman with matted hair down to her waist.

Comet leaned against the Fort, shaking his head back and forth. He yelled something to the woman, but Owen couldn't get close enough to hear, and the music was so loud, everyone making too much noise outside.

The woman leaned in, saying something, close to stomping her foot.

Clyde picked at his nose ring, spinning the jewelry in his nostril. Owen realized he was staring from six feet away. There was no way to slip between the two and get Comet alone. Anyways, Comet looked agitated, like kissing Owen was probably the last thing on his mind. Owen placed a hand on the edge of the building. The concrete was warm to the touch. He felt a tug on his sleeve, and he jerked around. Ava motioned for him to join her and Tennessee. She passed him the bottle. "Those two have been arguing for an hour. He's got it."

Owen nodded and took a swig. He leaned against the Fort. His head felt like it was full of helium, like it could float away at any moment. Gail sat down in his chest. "What's the rush, honey?" He hated it when she called him "honey" like he was some child, and she was his mother. They were nearly the same age. He tried to pass her the sensation of standing next to Comet and feeling the electricity zap his arms, of his skin buzzing, but the booze had deadened everything. He could only pass her a gentle swaying and music pulsing in his skull.

He waved his hand in the direction of his cousin and friends, and then stumbled a few feet away from the building and off into the woods. They were only thirty miles away from the house, but the woods felt so different out here. The air was drier and saltier. There were fewer ferns and less greenery and more dead sticks and old logs.

"No Jeez Louise to chase them away," Gail joked.

He leaned against a tree and steadied himself. The Fort seemed far away now, and it felt like he was alone even though he was only twenty or thirty feet away from everyone. Sweat pooled in the small of his back and in the backs of his cheeks, and before he knew it, he vomited neon green onto the forest floor, something radioactive.

"Good thing you weren't kissing Comet," Gail said.

He wiped his mouth with the back of his hand and stumbled back to the show. When he returned, everyone was standing in a circle near the fire, including Comet. The woman was gone.

Tennessee tapped Owen's shoulder. "We're ready to go. Come on. Come to our apartment with us. I'll give you the tour."

45

I t was two a.m. when they pulled into the parking lot. The yellow apartment building paled in the moonlight, and two brick chimneys loomed like dark pillars. Megan and Tennessee's apartment was in the back corner of the complex.

Megan turned on a lamp. A laptop and a stereo sat on a wire rack to the right of the room. On the left was a beaten-down tan couch and a long coffee table. Owen didn't recognize any of the posters on the wall: one, a group of animals marching in the streets carrying protest signs, and another **HELLA GAY** at the top of tiny sketches of Prince, George Michael, Ellen DeGeneres, Gertrude Stein, and C-3PO. An ashtray sat on the floor next to the sliding glass door that opened up to a concrete patio. The carpet was littered with stacks of books and notebooks and piles of CDs.

Tennessee brought out blankets and pillows, and they built a small nest in the living room. The blankets were smooth, and Owen slipped his socks off so he could feel the cool fabric against his bare skin. Tennessee put on music, and the room was bright and loud with sound. Ava brought Owen a glass of water and sat next to him on the floor. Comet and Lou sat on the couch just to their left, and Megan and Tennessee sat next to the patio door. They slid the door open. The breeze felt nice in the stale room. The floor was a tangle of limbs, and everyone was so alive, even more so than at the Fort, laughing with their mouths open and teeth shining. He felt too much love then, and it made him crazy again. He still wanted to kiss Comet, hold hands with Ava, cuddle with Lou. He kept his hands folded in his lap. Ava played with his toes, pulling at them under the blanket.

Comet relayed the argument he'd had with the woman about how white people with "dreadlocked" hair was problematic. Everyone understood except for Owen, who wasn't sure what the big deal was.

"Our culture has been stolen time and time again by white folks," Comet said. "Our fashion. Our music. Our art. Our hairstyles. She thinks we're the same because she is a woman and I am Black."

Owen felt the bristles of carpet under his palms. "But women are treated like shit, too. Isn't it kinda all the same?" He thought about the men on the radio.

"No," Comet said. And he looked Owen deep in the eyes like he was trying to figure him out, see whose side he was on. Owen tried to only pass him love because he didn't know what else to do. The conversation stuck in his chest. He wanted to yell that he was on the same side as them, his friends, but he couldn't, and so he listened.

"Race means different things to the world than gender," Megan said.

"Race is more important in the world, especially this country, but women still suffer," Comet said.

"We all suffer," Tennessee said. "Queers, Black folks, women. We just suffer in different ways and to different depths."

"I don't get to hide my Blackness," Comet said, "but I also don't have to suffer as a woman. It's tricky. There are different layers and levels to privilege."

Owen had the privilege of staying disappeared.

"Long story short," Ava said. "If you're white, you don't get to have dreadlocks."

"I think I get it," Owen said. He thought about what it would mean to move through the world with no animal in your chest but with something you could not hide instead, to wear a thing you could not practice away in a bathroom mirror, that you could not wrap up tight with your other secrets in your belly, but he also wondered what it meant to hide a secret for a lifetime, to pretend to be something else. "I'm sorry," he said. "That woman sucks."

"Now you get it," Comet said. Everyone laughed. "But really, though. Sometimes we just need someone else to say that person sucks. It's so easy to feel crazy all the time, like am I the only one who sees that they treat me this way?"

• • •

Later it was just Owen and Comet in the living room. Ava and Lou had gone home. Tennessee and Megan were in the bedroom. They sat up listening to music, not saying a word. Comet was quieter than usual, not trying to make Owen laugh, just thinking. Owen thought about the time Gail had done her mating dance in his chest. He sent telepathic clicks to Comet, spun around in his mind. He built up the energy in the room, spread it out wide. Comet sipped a beer and stared out the patio door.

Owen leaned his elbow onto the couch. "Can I sit up here?"

Comet turned around, surprised Owen had spoken after being silent for so long. "Of course." He slid over to make room.

Owen climbed up onto the lumpy couch. He drummed his fingers on his knees, softly thudding with Morrissey's *Viva Hate*. Gail was a rock in his chest, mortified beyond belief, having never been in a scenario where she wanted to kiss the boy next to her. Owen was alone. He would do it, though. Make things different. Time moved slowly, but Owen was aware of its passage.

Magic was always gone in the morning.

A car alarm went off in the distance, and it shook Owen and reminded him that the world still spun, and that billions of people were getting on with their day, and so he should, too. He let his pinky finger fall right next to Comet's so that they were almost touching. He could have kept his hand there forever, millimeters away. He relaxed his hand completely and it fell on top of Comet's. Comet continued to stare forward like their hands weren't touching, like there weren't currents flying between them. Owen leaned forward, moving in for the kiss. He channeled tenderness and quiet.

Inches from Comet's face, and Comet turned away, inhaled deeply. "I should go home," he said. He placed a hand on Owen's knee and stood up. The sunrise was just beginning to brush the edges of the sky outside. Owen felt the weight of his body on the couch. He had a flash of the time with Ava in the woods. She'd known what she wanted. Hadn't she convinced him to want it, too? But the CD was ending, and Comet stood at the door, his hand on the knob. The silence was insurmountable. Owen swallowed air and said goodbye.

Comet left.

46

Owen's heartache had a smell to it, so the station wagon smelled like yogurt and tangy fruit. The smell grew over the days until one night, Owen woke up and thought he might retch. Gail dry heaved in his chest, so he cranked down both of the windows in the back of the wagon. The summer air swirled outside, knocking tree branches around, but the garage was still and stiff. A mustiness rolled off the old boxes and mixed with his sour heartbreak smell.

At first Gail tried all her tricks for cheering him up, and then one day she stopped. No jokes. No running her wing down his spine. No fluttering her wings. She let him be sad.

The morning after he'd been woken up by the smell of his heartbreak, he hiked down to the water. He leaned against the rotting log and stared up the beach. The pull to the water was intense, but his heartbreak made him too lazy to act on it. The sun burned the corners of his eyes.

Gail spoke, and her words shook him a little, dislodged the heartbreak in his chest, and moved it around so it wasn't stale.

"Do you think maybe you were too drunk to kiss Comet?"

The soft bark rubbed against his back while he thought. "No," he said.

"Are you sure? I was still drunk, which means you were probably drunk, too."

He thought harder. He lifted his palm and let the sand sift through his fingers.

"Okay," he said. "Sure, I was drunk, but I don't think I was too drunk. Plus, people make out when they're drunk all the time."

"Sure," Gail said. "But I don't think you even wanted to make out with Comet. I think he was there, and you wanted to make out with *someone*. Think about your time with Ava. You can hardly remember it. It's pockets of events. Wouldn't it be nice if you could remember a make-out session?"

Owen thought maybe that would be nice. "Doesn't change right now. Right now, I am sad and embarrassed."

Gail told him she didn't think there was anything to be embarrassed about. "Just do it different next time," she said.

Realistically though, Owen wondered if there would be a next time. He couldn't fathom trying something like that again, drunk or otherwise.

• • •

The next day, Natalie smoked her Camels on the back patio. She was over all the time. She helped herself to food and coffee and beer. Now she listened to music on the CD player with her elbow propped up on her knee, hunched over her phone. Owen slid halfway off the couch so only his mid-back and shoulders were supported, staring at the ceiling. The fan whirred near the back door. He craned his neck to look outside and he knew, felt in the air and in his bones, that Natalie was about to cry. He sat up, but not too quickly. She had set her phone down. She looked far off into the distance and he thought maybe there was something she was looking at, but he couldn't see anything.

"Maybe she's watching the wind," Gail whispered up to him.

"You're so obsessed with the wind." He pushed himself off the couch and went outside. He opened the door and it creaked on its hinges. Natalie just kept staring out at nothing, still on the verge of crying. The music on the CD player was quiet, acoustic guitar and a boy's voice that cut over the simple plucking. Owen sat across the porch from her at her side. He figured they could let their sadness swirl together back here. What's that about misery loving company?

He wanted to ask her why she wanted to cry but couldn't find a tactful way to bring it up.

"Just sit here and be open," Gail said.

The singer sang about wild sage in a field, and Owen could smell the herb, and he recalled his mother painting sage smoke in the corners of their home. Soon he wanted to cry, too.

When the song ended, Natalie turned towards him. "Morning," she said.

He nodded.

"Do you like the Mountain Goats?" She paused. "I mean, it doesn't matter because I'm not changing it, but do you like them?"

"I've never heard them."

"Really?"

Natalie lit another cigarette. "You know when you have your heart broken and you can only listen to one album or even one song while you heal, and then that CD is just forever connected to months of heart-break?" She took a drag and nodded towards the stereo. "Dan," she said.

Owen leaned forward.

"What am I talking about?" she said. "You're too young to have had your heart broken."

"I've had my heart broken," he said.

"Not in a real way though, in a puppy love sort of way maybe."

"I haven't talked to my mom in over three months."

"Oh." She took a long drag on her cigarette. "I'm sorry," she said. "That is heartbreaking. What album do you connect to your mom-heartbreak?"

He thought for a second. Every time he listened to music, he thought of his mom coming home and swirling drunk with him in the living room. Both of them always in their underwear, Gail squawking and having a riot. It was one of the reasons he loved music so much. Even this Mountain Goats album he'd never heard before reminded him of his mother, but really the one that made him miss her the most was *Bitte Orca* by Dirty Projectors, not because they listened to it together, but because he always thought she would like it if she could hear it. "*Bitte Orca*," he said.

"Your mom's got wild taste."

"I don't think she's ever heard it, but I think she would like it if I played it for her." He took a sip of coffee. "Is your heart broken now?"

"No, now I listen to the CD anytime I want to feel sad. It's like flipping a switch."

Owen couldn't imagine *wanting* to feel sad.

Natalie stubbed out her cigarette and went inside. He listened to her rummaging around in Bob's bedroom and then in the kitchen. She popped back outside in a green bikini top and cutoffs with a tote bag bursting at her hip. She shut off the CD player, no more sad music. "It's nice out," she said. "Walk down to the beach with me."

"Always."

She placed her giant alien-eyed sunglasses on him, and together they hiked through the woods and down to the beach. The sunglasses turned everything pale blue.

The sun was bright on the beach. Natalie laid out two towels next to each other. She sat on one and patted the other. She applied sunscreen and rubbed the bright blue lotion into her shoulders and face and belly. She passed Owen the bottle and he rubbed some on his arms, face, and legs. The lotion was cold.

He had never thought to lie out in the sun on the beach, and now he felt like a fool. How good the sun felt on his skin and face. He sank into the towel and the sand shifted beneath his body. It radiated heat. He closed his eyes and saw orbs of orange and swirls of purple when he did. The waves were a soft thrumming on the shore. Seagulls yelled in the distance. He wondered what Comet was doing. Was he thinking about Owen's foolish attempt to kiss him? Owen would be forever embarrassed every time he heard Morrissey's *Viva Hate*. Maybe Comet was mocking Owen to his friends. Or maybe, and this was the most likely scenario, he was simply going to disappear, and Owen would never see him again.

He opened his eyes and the world was off-kilter, turned on its side.

He felt dizzy. He propped himself up with his elbow and scanned the landscape. There was nothing but strings of kelp and the sun.

Natalie opened her eyes and sat up. "What are you looking at?"

He turned towards her. "Nothing." Her belly was already turning pink in the sun.

The nice thing about heartbreak was it meant that he didn't care about the Army of Acronyms or being discovered as a Terror. In fact, it took a lot of discipline and willpower to not simply lift up his shirt now and show Natalie, to let Gail drink in all of the landscape, the Sound, and the ridge of hills that lay on the other side of the water. He felt guilt in wanting to tell Natalie about Gail, like he was betraying Tennessee, maybe even betraying his mother, the only two people in the world who knew his secret, the bird in his chest. But since everyone disappeared, didn't it make sense to embrace who was in front of him? It was just him, Gail, Natalie, and Bob. He hadn't spoken to Tennessee in a week. He thought maybe he'd never see Comet again. He worried that he was nearing another phase in his life where he wished he could go back to the time previous. The way he'd wished he could go back to being a boy and a bird locked away in a house, or how he'd wished Gail would say something, *anything* when she was practicing *Gail's vow of silence for an undetermined amount of time.* Now, he wanted to be living with Tennessee again and to go back to before he'd tried to kiss Comet, when they were just two friends trying to understand each other. Maybe that's what Natalie was doing when she listened to music that reminded her of her heartbreak, traveling to another time in the past. She had propped her head up on the tote bag. Her eyes were closed. Her beer sat next to her in the sand, her hand draped around the bottle. Owen recalled his mother asleep on the couch, her hand draped over the side, lingering towards her half-drunk cup of coffee on the floor. It seemed there was so much sadness wrapped up in looking back, all the loss and distance. He wondered if his mom felt sadness when she looked back, if she felt pain in remembering when they'd lived together, before the mess with the forest fire and the doctor. He wondered for the first time if she missed his dad or if he never came up, and she saw him as someone who had entirely disappeared. Maybe she was happier now, living with her friend Elayne. When

Owen looked towards the future, he saw nothing. It was blank. He considered again telling Natalie about Gail, of lifting up his shirt and sharing that part of himself with her, but then he thought about the Army of Acronyms and how dangerous something like that could be. He'd gotten lucky when he'd shown Tennessee. He couldn't be sure of that luck again.

47

Owen woke up one morning and the world was water. Rain fell for days at a time. It fell so hard streaks of mud ran along the back porch. Grayness descended over the landscape. Grass and leaves and trees burst with water. It ran through the forest floor. The Sound rose so high that the fallen log was almost always covered in water. The bucket was back in the living room, collecting water from the leaky roof. The garage was cold, so he brought out another blanket and only unrolled the windows to air out the car.

He felt the rain in his bones, and it felt like home, like his natural state. The boy born in the middle of the flood, at the exact moment the water spilled onto the streets. His mother's Pisces fish. A lifetime of luck.

Owen hadn't talked to Tennessee since the night he'd tried to kiss Comet. It meant he didn't have to feel so bad about liking her dad's girlfriend, but not seeing Tennessee or any of his other friends dug a trench of loneliness in his gut. He ignored it. He learned that if he let every single feeling pass him by, if he let it all roll by like water off a duck's back, then he could avoid feeling hurt. It meant he didn't feel the deep joy of the bath or the pleasure of his first cup of coffee in the morning or the chill of the rain seeping under his skin, but the tradeoff was worth it.

Numbness > Sadness.

His daymares grew in vividness and frequency. The doctor catching up to him seemed inevitable. Gail did her best to redirect his angst. She pushed him to take longer walks near the water, even when it rained cats and dogs, knowing that simply standing next to the Sound put him at ease. She encouraged him to put on music to avoid being alone with his loneliness.

Bob and Natalie were home together all the time. Owen often walked in on them curled up on the couch, Natalie's feet slipped under Bob's legs. They drank beer and listened to music. Bob didn't turn the news on anymore. Owen sat next to the woodstove and felt the heat from the fire. On paper, it seemed that even without Tennessee, Owen should have been happy. He thought all the elements were there: a warm house, school hallways that were fairly safe, and a family structure that looked like all the good ones on TV. But he couldn't escape the cloak of apathy that fell over him without his friends.

He still couldn't sleep in the bedroom. By now it had grown into something entirely too large to tackle. His shoulders could not relax in the company of Natalie and Bob like they could around Tennessee. Something about his cousin knowing the bird in his chest, parts of him disappeared in the house with her gone.

School was quiet. As a junior, Owen watched the new batch of bullies move in and swarm the younger students. He saw their awkwardness as a stage he was happy to have left behind. He kept his head down and barreled through. He had felt too exposed eating lunch on the floor in front of the trophy case without Tennessee and Ava, so he'd wandered until he found a stairwell tucked in the left corner of the school. He ate lunch on the landing, and sometimes Clyde sat at the top of the stairs, quietly chewing on his ham sandwich and crunching on his stinky sour cream-and-cheddar potato chips. The pull to Clyde had ebbed, but it was still there, tugging Owen upwards, towards him. They rarely made eye contact, but whenever they did, Clyde raised his hand in a small wave, and Owen nodded in reply.

• • •

Slowly Gail regained her gumption and told more jokes.

Two nuns drove down a road in Italy. Wow, I've never come this way before, said one. It's the cobblestone road, said the other.

A research team of scientists sent out a survey of ten puns to answer the question of whether a pun could elicit a laugh. They found that no pun in ten did.

Owen sat on the couch on a Friday night and Gail told him joke after joke. The jokes washed over him. He was alone and had pulled a beer from the fridge, so he was light with carbonation and alcohol. (His first sip of alcohol since the radioactive goo at the Fort.) Gail laughed after every joke harder than he did. Soon they were a pile of laughter on the couch, Owen and Gail all mushed up as one. Tears ran down his cheeks and his throat caught with laughter. Gail shook on the floor of his chest, her wings wrapped tightly around her body. It felt good to feel something.

What's the difference between an Ohio Greyhound stop and a crab with a boob job?

Owen lost it at the image of a crab with a boob job. He convulsed on the sofa and kicked his feet against the table. His lungs were the desert sands and crabs in bikinis waddled in his mind.

One's a crusty bus station and the other's a busty crustacean.

Dead. He was dead with laughter.

When Bob and Natalie came home an hour later, the beer had turned sour in his gut and Gail had run out of jokes. Owen sat on the couch, sad and listless again, hungover from laughing so much. Owen was deep in an anxious spiral when they walked in. He'd peeked out the window ten minutes before and thought he saw headlights coming up the road, but they never passed the driveway. He thought it could be the doctor pulling over onto the side of the road, waiting for him to leave the house. Bob and Natalie talked in hushed tones and giggled, and Owen felt like a stranger, like he wasn't in the room with them.

He remembered the night he and Tennessee had sat by the fire and he'd tried her cigarette. Blood on a knife. Rose quartz. A kiss. A promise to always be truthful. He felt guilt stir up in him again. It mixed with the sour beer and turned in his belly. It had been seventy-two days since they last spoke.

He called her the next morning to ask if he could come over.

• • •

Owen and Tennessee were silent in the car for nearly the entire drive to her apartment. No one had been home when she'd picked him up, and he was grateful for that. He wanted her to find out about Natalie on his terms, ideally much later in the evening. He ran over different ways to tell his cousin that her dad was still seeing someone and that she practically lived there, and then, depending on how she took that news, he'd tell her that he liked Bob's girlfriend and sometimes they had fun together.

"She'll understand," Gail whispered up to him. "She loves you. You've done nothing wrong."

He scoffed at Gail, dripped the eye roll down his throat. "I kept it from her," he reminded her. "We promised."

Tennessee put the car in park. The night had grown dark quickly and rain drummed on the windshield, the water running races down the glass.

She put a hand on the wheel and turned towards him. "Megan is inside. Can I see Gail for a second? It might be our only chance."

He looked around. A streetlamp stood two parking spaces over and it shined right into the car, lighting up the interior. The car was wedged between two trucks on either side. "It's too dangerous. I don't want to lift my shirt up here."

"Okay, I get it." She leaned far forward and put her mouth just an inch above his chest. "Hello, Gail. I miss you. I hope my cousin is being nice to you. Can I get a whistle?"

Gail whistled a *tweet-TWEET-poe-poe-poe-poe-poe-poe-poe-poe-poe-poe*. The air fluttered in his chest, just above the space where his heart was.

Megan was sitting on the couch when they walked in. She sprang up and wrapped her arms around Owen and squeezed him tightly. She rubbed the space between his shoulder blades up and down. Tennessee walked past them and into the bedroom where she rummaged around for a few minutes. Megan invited him to sit, and he sat on the floor, leaning against the couch. She put on music and grabbed him a beer.

Tennessee emerged a moment later with armfuls of blankets and pillows and a small velvet pouch that nearly matched the green velvet dress he'd worn as Ariel the Halloween the year previous. "Let's get comfy," she said. "I have a surprise for you, Owen." She spread the blankets on the floor and the couch and walked around turning some lights off and other lamps on until the room hummed with a yellow glow. A string of multicolored Christmas lights wrapped around the room at the ceiling. Owen held his breath. His cousin clearly knew about Natalie and was about to spring it on him. How had she found out? It felt like such an obvious trap, and he was an idiot for not seeing it. He prepared himself to be bombarded by Tennessee and then to never see her again. He wondered if Megan was in on it.

Finally, Tennessee stood in the middle of the room. "Tonight, we're going to get stoned." She grinned from ear to ear. Owen remembered to breathe. She sat down cross-legged across from him and dug a pipe and some weed out of her velvet pouch. "Do you still want to try it? Have you still never done it?"

He nodded. "I've never done it."

The glass was cold in his hands. He brought the pipe to his lips. Tennessee scooted behind him and placed her arms around him. She placed his fingers in the right place on the glass pipe and showed him how to hold it so.

"Like this." She lit the flower and he breathed in deeply. The first hit was quick and hard, and he coughed to high heaven. The second hit was easier. He felt the carpet bristle against his palms, could feel every fiber of it. He leaned his head against the couch, and the up-holstery scratched the buzzed hair on the side of his head. He forgot about his beer. They passed the pipe around, and it wasn't long before Owen felt like he was underwater, like the air was water and here he was, breathing under it. He was high.

· · ·

Owen was cocooned under blankets. Only his head poked out from the covers. It was late, late, late in the evening, too late for them to be up. Owen felt tears coming to his face. His whole being felt pent up in his body. It was the first comfort he'd felt in two months.

Tennessee and Megan talked about multiverse theory and they traded different ideas for what it could mean. Tennessee held her hand above the coffee table. "See, in one universe I slapped the table now"— her hand still hovering—"but in another universe I slapped it now." She waited a beat and then finally slapped the table.

"Sure, but that's boring compared to the drastic realities that could be existing alongside our universe. Worlds where dinosaurs were never wiped out or where America is a socialist utopia."

"One where America doesn't even exist."

Owen wondered if there was a universe where he had found love. Maybe Comet loved him back in another dimension. Maybe there was a universe where Owen and Clyde sat next to each other on the beach, watching the tide pull in and out, giving in to the loose rope between them. Maybe he and Ava were happy in another dimension. Maybe there was a world where there were only boys with birds in their chests and he could walk around freely, where no doctor could reach him.

Gail was exhausted in his chest, tired of reassuring him for months, and now that she was stoned, all she wanted was rest.

"Do you think there is a universe where someone loves me?" he blurted.

Tennessee and Megan turned back to him in shock. He hadn't said a word in twenty minutes.

"I think this is that universe," Tennessee said. She placed her hand on his knee and looked at him deeply. Her eyes were red blisters. "I love you."

"Me too," Megan said.

"Not like that," he said. "I mean the other way."

"It happens when you're not looking for it," Megan said. "You have to love yourself, to live with yourself and not seek it out and it'll find you."

He sat up. "I'm not looking for it."

"It's a slow burn," Tennessee said. "It's not like getting hit by lightning. It's like being poisoned. Slow and steady and then BAM, you wake up and you're dead, but instead of being dead, you're in love."

"You will find the right person someday." Megan smiled lazily, her eyes glossy.

He thought about Natalie and how happy she and Bob were. "Tennessee," he said. "There's something I have to tell you."

"Of course," she said. "Anything."

He looked into her dark green eyes, the color of washed-up algae, and he tried to remember what they looked like just in case this was the last time he saw her. "The ring of salt is broken," he said.

She waited a moment. She blinked. "Oh, that? I figured. My dad dating the same woman?"

"I think so. She is over all the time, practically lives there." He was cautious in telling her, gauging her response with every bit of information he divulged.

"Tell me about her." She seemed enthusiastic, as though she really did care about her father's girlfriend.

"She's nice. She works with him at the grocery store. They've known each other a long time."

Tennessee's face sunk. "Natalie," she said.

"Yes," Owen said, surprised she was able to guess the woman. "You know her?"

She shook her head back and forth. "Goddammit. He promised. That motherFUCKer. Un-fucking-believable." Megan reached out to console her, but Tennessee shook her touch off. "No. This is not okay." Her face turned bright red and she squeezed her eyes shut. "I can't believe this. I can't believe it. No, no, no, no—no!" She slammed her fist against the carpet. Her shoulders shook and then her back shook and soon her whole body was shaking with sobs.

Owen felt like he was watching her from another place, on television or through a telescope. Gail sat up in his chest. "You have to do something," she said. "Anything." He reached forward and placed his hand on her knee, a mirror of what she'd done moments earlier for him. There was no change in her body, so he let it rest there. The vibrations of her sobs convulsed under his palm.

Strings of slobber clung to the back of her hand. She brushed the hair out of her wet face. A yell jumped out of her throat. Her body returned to sobbing and there was a thick sadness in the air, and now it felt like mud instead of water.

"Who is she?" Owen finally asked. Tennessee had been so easy before. Everything had been so easy before.

"She's a homewrecker," Tennessee said. "She's why my mom left."

"Oh, honey," Megan said.

Tennessee shook her head back and forth. "He cheated on my mom with her, and that's why she left. Later, when I was older and knew what happened, I made him promise not to do it ever again." She sucked in air and bit her lip. Soberness washed over her face. "I'll fucking kill him." She slammed her hand against the couch. "He's dead."

Owen didn't know how to say he liked Natalie and that Tennessee's mom had been gone for twelve years and had not once come back to visit. Their moms were similar in that way. He didn't mention that Bob had asked him to keep his secret.

"Humans are far too much," Gail whispered up to him.

"Not a great time for your take," he whispered down to her.

Tennessee caught his eye and he wondered if she could tell he was dripping words down to Gail. Maybe his eyes had lit up briefly. He had some tells.

Eventually Tennessee and Megan went to bed and Owen lay in the living room alone with Gail. He could hear Tennessee talking to Megan in the bedroom. Her voice rose and fell as she got excited and then calmed down. He tried to parse out his feelings but he was still high and so he sometimes forgot he was supposed to be sorting out the mess with sharing his uncle's secret, and his mind wandered. He wondered if Tennessee would ever talk to him again, and then he thought of Comet and how he may never see him again because of the way their hands had touched, and then he thought of wearing gloves to keep from touching hands with a boy and ruining their friendship, and then he wondered what Mickey Mouse's gloves would look like on a human, like how big would they actually be? Here, he reminded himself to think of the situation at hand, and so he wondered if Bob would kick him out. And around and around it went.

He was sober but still cloudy in the morning. Tennessee's eyes were red, and her cheeks puffed out. Everything was dry, like she'd cried every ounce of water out the night before. She drove him home in her soft pants and T-shirt. The only time she spoke was when he reached for the door handle and she stopped him and asked for a whistle from Gail. She whistled *poe-TWEET-TOE-TWEEEEEEET*, long and breathless out of his chest, and Tennessee's lips curled on the outer ridge, a smile. She said she needed time. Owen stood in the driveway, his cousin backing the car up slowly towards the road, and big drops of rain crashing on his head.

48

Owen told his uncle on the back porch that evening. Natalie was still at work and so it was only the two of them. Swallows swooped in the trees in the early evening.

"You did what?"

"I told her," Owen said. He leaned onto his knees and looked out across the clearing. It was the first clear evening in a few months and so the November air was crisp. He pulled his sweater tight around his shoulders.

"I thought you promised to let me tell her?" Bob set his beer down on the ground and stood up. He paced back and forth. His hands were meaty and he reached into his tobacco pouch and quickly rolled a cigarette, his nervous tic akin to twiddling his thumbs.

"A hundred and twenty-four days. You had one hundred and twenty-four days to tell her. I couldn't keep it any longer."

"Jesus, you couldn't give me a heads-up?" Bob lit his cigarette. He bent down in front of Owen so their eyes met. Owen expected him to be mad, but there was pleading in his face. Small black hairs dotted his cheeks above his beard where he shaved, shaping the beard tight to his chin. The air was dark behind his head. "I just needed time to tell her. I didn't know how to tell her." He stood up straight and turned around, puffing on his cigarette. "It's just, Natalie is different. I love her, and I thought Tennessee would understand if I could tell her the right way, but I couldn't figure out how to tell her. I needed more time." He turned back towards Owen.

"A hundred and twenty-four days," Owen repeated.

"You know," Bob said, "men aren't supposed to do this to each other. We're supposed to have each other's backs. We're supposed to look out for each other. I thought you had my back." He shook his head back and forth, smoked more of his cigarette.

Owen shivered. He was half boy, half bird. Even now, with Bob ranting and feeling betrayed, his heart and mind went to his cousin. Gail sighed heavily in his chest. "At some point," she whispered up to him, "everyone will move past this. This family is a flock."

"I'm not great at being a man," Owen said.

"Maybe it was unfair to ask you to keep the secret. I should've been the one to tell my daughter, though." Night had swept across the yard. A breeze pulled through the trees. A frog croaked and crickets chirped, and Owen thought he could hear the gentle pulling of the water in the Sound over his uncle's smoking.

49

Owen prepared to grieve the loss of his family, to accept the fact that it would always be him and just the bird forever and ever, amen. He lay in the backseat of the wagon. The flower in the jar sat on his chest, rising and falling with each breath, teetering this way and that. Rain drizzled just outside the garage. He remembered everything Bob and Tennessee had done for him, all the ways he'd grown since he'd met them. It was more of a celebration of life than it was a funeral, but still he mourned. Gail wouldn't believe it. "It's in the air," she said. "It's in my bones. It's not over yet."

"You don't know how it is with humans," Owen said. "Betrayal is real and strong and true, and it's what I have done."

"Drama queen," Gail said, rolling her eyes in his chest. "Too many soaps."

The purple light wafted off the flower and filled the car's cabin. Owen cracked a window and it slipped out, unfolding into the open air. He shut his eyes and thought of it as his offering to his family past. Maybe it was time to think about running away more seriously. He knew he couldn't just yet. He was only sixteen, but he made his plan right then. In the next year, when he was seventeen, he would run away by wading into the ocean to live with the mermaids. He'd finally give in fully to the pull of the water, fully morph into his mother's Pisces fish. He thought seriously of the practicality of it. It would be cold at first, but he'd get used to the water's temperature. The discomfort would only last a few minutes.

Once Owen made up his mind about running away, he grew reckless.

The next day at school, he sat on the landing eating lunch like every other day. Clyde sat at the top of the stairs, dirty Carhartts and a baseball cap, worn unironically. Owen finished his sandwich and moved on to his HoHos. He unwrapped the package. He stood up. His finger and thumb mashed the cake and he tried to slide it out of the tight plastic, but he only mashed it more. He took the stairs one at a time. He reached deep down and felt the air, and Gail passed him nothing but bated breath. His stupid heart was beating hard in his chest. He needed his inhaler. Clyde looked up from his sandwich and watched Owen approach. He chewed once, twice, and then swallowed the bit of ham sandwich.

Not our people.

But in a few months, Owen would walk into the ocean, carry rocks in his pockets à la Virginia Woolf if he had to. What'd he have to lose? He thought of saving jellyfish one by one. Approaching Clyde felt like when he gave in to the pull of the water and climbed into the bath. He thought about Clyde's thick farm boy muscles. His hands dirty with work. Finally, Owen got the cake out of the packaging. The frosting was smashed, and bits of white crème seeped out the side. He held the smooshed cake in front of him. "HoHo?"

Clyde nodded and took the cake. "Thanks."

Owen let the corners of his lips curl up. Clyde looked freaked out, his left eyebrow raised and a smirk, like he'd never seen a HoHo before, like maybe he'd never really seen Owen before. Owen knew that wasn't true, though. Clyde might be different, but there were parts of him that carried the long lineage of men taking up space. Parts that pretended they weren't looking at the queer boy who lived next door. Owen left him on the stairs like that, dumbfounded with a smashed treat.

• • •

The next day Owen sat at his usual place on the landing between the two floors. Clyde walked down the stairs and met him there in the middle. He pointed at the wall next to Owen. "May I?"

"Of course." Owen scooted over a tad, even though there was plenty of room, simply a gesture.

He sat down next to Owen. Owen often didn't notice how much Gail constantly moved around in his chest. He only noticed the stark difference when she stopped, didn't flutter her wings or sigh heavily or scratch her ass. She sat completely still now. Clyde sat still, too, staring ahead at the stairs, which weren't interesting, and so he must have been thinking hard about something. Owen thought he didn't look like he was thinking about anything in particular. Owen held his breath. His heart beat all the way up in his skull, pounding his eardrums. He reached into his paper sack and it rustled loudly in the stairwell. He pulled out his sandwich and started eating. After a while, Clyde ate, too.

And so it was like that, Clyde eating next to Owen some days. Sometimes Owen ate alone. Sometimes Owen didn't go to school at all. He found he could simply skip class and no one seemed to notice, and if he was wading into the ocean before senior year, what did it matter anyway? But the days he cut class were boring. He'd sit in the wagon and stare at nothing. He'd take a bath. He'd masturbate. So mostly he went to class and sat in the stairwell in between A block and B block, and Clyde ate next to him. Owen still felt a danger in sitting next to Clyde, and he knew Clyde could have ties to the Army of Acronyms, but they never really talked, save for one or two words of offering.

"Chip?"

"HoHo?"

"Cookie?"

But still, it was different than when Owen was silent with Tennessee or Bob or Natalie. There was something that hung in the air around them that neither he nor Gail could place. It was like waiting.

50

Tennessee finally called the day before winter break. It had only been twenty-six days, but it felt longer than the seventy-two days before that. She claimed she would have called sooner but she wasn't ready to talk to her dad just yet.

"You need a cell phone," she said.

"Why?"

"So I can call you and only you and I don't need to worry about my dad picking up. Plus, you're sixteen. Who doesn't have a phone at sixteen?"

"With what money?"

"Megan's gone for a bit and I have the place to myself. Come stay with me. It'll be just the three of us," she joked.

Owen lingered on the thought that his cousin wanted him around. "You're not mad?"

"Oh no. I'm still upset, but we have to move past it at some point, and really, it's not your fault."

The next day he packed a week's worth of clothes into his duffel bag. He set the flower in the trunk of the wagon. He slung the bag over his shoulder, drew the hood of the raincoat over his head, and he set out in the rain towards the road. He walked down the hill that was like a roller coaster in a car and found it boring on foot. He held his breath for the entirety of Clyde's property, not realizing it until he reached the other side. Soon he reached the T. To the right lay the high school and to the left was the road to Olympia. He crossed the street and waited for the bus.

He'd written down the exact directions Tennessee had given him, his first time on a bus. It was only five o'clock but already the sky had darkened. Gail bounced around. "I got this," she said. "It'll be a good use of my navigational skills. Haven't used those in a while."

The bus sighed to a stop. It leaned towards the ground in front of him, bowing a welcome. The door was a sideways mouth opening up to a portal of fluorescent light and gray-skinned humans. Once Owen sat down, he felt more comfortable.

When Owen got to her apartment, Tennessee closed the door behind him and spun him around in a hug. He grew dizzy for a moment. His cousin left him on the couch to fetch beers and put on music.

She returned and handed him a beer. She sat down in front of him on the floor. "Megan's gone and we have the place to ourselves. Let Gail out."

Owen unbuttoned his shirt and pulled the left side over so it hung just to the left of the hole in his chest. They sat quietly for a moment, the silence punctuated by Björk turned on too low and the sipping of their beers. Everyone waited for someone else to speak, and when someone did speak, it was all three of them at once, asking about the others' week. They laughed. Soon the beer facilitated comfort, and the comfort made conversation easy.

They tiptoed around Tennessee's dad and Natalie.

They were in Tennessee's bare apartment, but it felt like the old nights they used to spend in the bedroom. They drew tarot cards. (Owen learned he was depressed but that he needed to see what he had, not what he didn't, and only then would he be able to celebrate with his community. Tennessee could not see the oppression that was right in front of her, a horned goat with two strings tied loosely around her ankles.) Even Gail drew a card. (She got the Hermit, and this sent Owen and Tennessee into a fit of laughter, but Gail did not find it funny.) At one point, Tennessee pulled down the bottle of Old Crow. They coughed down a shot each and then put it back.

"No one deserves this," Tennessee said.

"It tastes like death," Owen agreed.

They drank more beer. Tennessee put on Quasi and Hazel and Car Seat Headrest. They talked about nonsense: Tennessee's idea for a movie that took place in another dimension where most people were gay, and so straight teenagers had to learn how to come out to their parents. Gail had an idea for a restaurant where the servers were toddlers and the manager was a golden retriever. All of it was nearly too sweet for Owen, magnified by the prospect that when he ran away and disappeared, he would be leaving Tennessee behind. They shared stupid stories, and before long, it was three o'clock in the morning and Tennessee was wrapping a comforter around Owen and setting a glass of water on the floor before she went to bed.

The next morning Tennessee left a note that she was at work and that Owen should help himself, really make himself at home. He got up and stretched long. He slipped off his shirt. Wearing only his boxers, he walked around the apartment for an hour with his bare skin meeting the air and his knobby knees punctuating each step. Gail whistled a soft tune for nearly the entire time.

"This," she said. "Imagine if we had our own place and this was a reality. The two of us out in the open, just feeling the rough carpet beneath our feet. The world is so bright."

"Won't happen," Owen said. "We only have a few months left. Not enough time."

Gail slumped her shoulders in his chest.

When Tennessee got home a few hours later, she turned on the water and ground coffee. It was six p.m. The air was big and bright, like the night was water in a coffee mug that ran right to the top. Tennessee explained it was a full moon and she wanted to do a ritual with him.

"Something to help release everything that needs releasing," she said.

An hour later, they were in raincoats and boots, walking along the wet pavement. The night air was warm for December. It smelled like rain on dry dirt. They walked through the city streets. There were no bats or crickets, only the sound of rain hitting the trees. Owen couldn't even feel the pull of the Sound. There were streetlamps and cars passing by every couple of seconds, their tires blowing mist onto the sidewalk. And the moon. It was an orange globe mid-high in the sky. Clouds passed in front of it.

"Look at how stupid that beautiful fucking moon is," Owen said.

Tennessee howled quietly so only they could hear it. Gail howled in response. A couple of blocks later they reached a small park next to the water. There was a group of teenagers skateboarding in circles on the wet pavement next to an SUV. There were two minivans parked on either side of the lot. They passed near one and inside were mountains of things: blankets and clothes and boxes. Someone was asleep in the backseat, which was reclined all the way down.

The moon was so bright the whole park was lit up, Owen could almost make out the green of the grass. Tennessee unloaded her bag. She laid out a small blanket. She placed crystals the size of her fists at each of the four corners. She handed Owen a small bowl of salt and they walked around the blanket, casting a circle of salt around them.

Tennessee pulled out a bundle of dried rosemary. "From your house," she said. She lit the herbs, and the air filled with the smell of fire and dried plants.

Owen worried that someone would see them and the small fire, and they'd get in trouble. Trouble led to cops, and *cops are worse than doctors*. Gail urged him to relax, to ease into the night. He let his shoulders soften. He shut his eyes and breathed the smoke in through his nostrils. Tennessee stood up and walked around with the burning herbs, walking a circle around Owen. Then she snuffed the plants out and sat back down. She gripped Owen's hands. She closed her eyes.

"Tonight, we honor the moon at its fullest. Big and bright, it re-flects the sun back at us. We can see all that she shows us." His cousin opened her eyes and let go of his hands. She handed him a piece of paper and a pencil. "Write down everything you want to let go of."

He and Gail dripped words back and forth to each other, slowly building a list of everything they could leave behind:

Sadness
Scaredy-catted-ness
Moping around

Comet on the couch
Hoping Mom comes back
Not whistling everyday
Skipping breakfast

He wanted to write *the Army of Acronyms*, but he knew he couldn't let go of that fear. It kept him safe.

Tennessee wrote on her piece of paper, too. Afterwards they folded them up into squares. She set a small metal bowl down in front of them. "Thank the moon," his cousin said.

Owen closed his eyes. "Thank you," he whispered. The moon reflected back at him in the water, rippling a *you're welcome*.

Tennessee held her paper in front of her. "This used to be a part of me." She pointed at Owen's paper. "That was a part of you and Gail. But these things don't serve us anymore. Goodbye," she whispered to her piece of paper.

"Goodbye," Owen whispered. She held her lighter out and they lit both pieces of paper on fire and set them in the metal bowl. The paper burned up quickly and within seconds it was nothing but a pile of ash. The air smelled of smoke. They stood up. Owen's legs were dead asleep, and he had to slap his right thigh to wake it up, all tingles and shakes. He followed his cousin to the edge of the water where they dumped the ashes. There was a herd of seals asleep on the dock, stacked on top of each other, dog piles. Owen and Tennessee walked back and gathered their things. The teenagers had packed up their skateboards and left the lot, and there were only the two minivans, each with a person asleep for the night inside. On the walk home, Owen's back felt longer, and the moonlight buzzed on the hairs on the back of his neck.

51

After winter break, Owen walked tall in the school hallways. He told himself that since he'd laid out his plan for running away via sinking under the sea, he could set it aside, maybe enjoy his last six months. He took letting go of scaredy-catted-ness seriously, and he buzzed the sides of his hair down tight to the scalp each week and his loose Mohawk grew curlier. Brown dots that looked like coffee grounds sprinkled along his chin and cheeks. He started shaving three times a week.

The biggest change came during lunch.

It was the middle of January and the stairwell at school was a pale gray. This time of year, it felt like the whole state of Washington had been sucked of any happiness, all of it out the window in exchange for buckets of rain and unending cloud.

Owen and Clyde sat next to each other at lunch, not talking too much but a little here and there. It was a lot of Owen saying a sentence and Clyde responding with one word or two at first, but the sentences grew slowly and surely until one day, they were two boys talking.

He learned a bit about Clyde every week. Little things: Clyde mucked stalls on the weekend. He watched *SNL* every Saturday. (Owen didn't know anyone who still watched *SNL*.) His favorite thing to do was ride his horse around his property, let her run fast and hard.

Everything Owen shared was surface level, like when he ran his hand along the top of the bathwater. Nothing deeper. Nothing like

I have a bird who lives inside my chest. I am a Terror. In fact, it was mostly Clyde who shared, while Owen listened closely.

Once, Clyde came to school with small dabs of concealer around his right eye, his eyelids puffy and a bandage stretched tight across his eyebrow. Clyde sat on the landing. Owen could see the swollen eyes from the bottom of the stairs, two black eyes covered in light tan paint.

Clyde sat on the ground and Owen walked up the stairs towards him. Clyde turned towards Owen and the fluorescent light gleamed off the peach concealer. Without thinking, Owen took his thumb and brushed Clyde's right cheek, a reflex.

"You okay?" he asked.

"Yeah," Clyde said. "I don't want to talk about it."

Owen remembered how important it felt not to talk about his own pummeling with anyone.

"Of course," Owen said, and he sat down to eat his lunch quietly.

After that day though, Clyde talked more about his dad, how he kept the house on tight lockdown and how Clyde felt like he could never do enough to make him happy, so he was considering not caring anymore. Owen knew a lot about not caring anymore. Once he'd decided to wade into the ocean in a few months, it made caring what others thought that much more difficult.

A few weeks later, Gail thought Owen should share more of himself with Clyde. Owen sat alone, waiting for Clyde.

"Like what?" Owen asked. "You want me to tell him I have a bird in my chest and my mom abandoned me out here because a network of scientists, lawyers, doctors, and cops are trying to capture me for experiments?"

"No," Gail whispered up to him. "Don't be an asshole. Tell him something regular."

Clyde entered on the second floor and sat next to Owen on the landing. They rummaged through their lunch sacks, each pulling out a sandwich.

"Start small, with something specific," Gail whispered up to him. The words echoed in his throat.

Owen thought for a second. He said, "You like music?" Then realized it was a stupid question, like asking if someone liked television or food, but Clyde shrugged like maybe he *didn't* like music.

Owen continued, "For me, right now it's a lot of Angel Olsen, but I've also been into the Eels and the Mountain Goats lately." He laughed. "Mostly sad music, I guess."

"I don't know who any of those people are."

"What? I mean, okay. That's okay. You might like them though. Who do you listen to?"

"I don't really listen to my own music. Hard to in my house."

The next day Owen brought in the Discman and the small speaker Natalie had gotten him for Christmas that he used for listening to music in the wagon. He put on Angel Olsen first and then the Mountain Goats. The two boys sat there saying nothing, listening to small plucks of guitar and the way the voices floated like waves on a shore. Afterwards, Clyde was unimpressed. "It's okay, I guess. It's just a little slow and sounds like music my dad listens to."

The next day Owen brought in the Pixies and David Bowie. Clyde perked up. "I haven't heard anything like this," he said two songs into *Surfer Rosa*. The guitars and drums scratched over the small speaker, but the energy was there. A smile touched the corners of Clyde's mouth.

After that it was Prince and Car Seat Headrest and Dirty Projectors and Quasi and Sleater-Kinney. Each one brought life to Clyde's eyes and opened him up little by little. Owen felt a sense of pride in introducing Clyde to new music, and part of him wished he could go back to when he was hearing all these bands for the first time so they could experience it together. He wondered if the music cracked Clyde open like it had when he'd listened to it for the first time, but he never asked.

Really, a lot of their friendship grew in the silence. It was like the day of beached jellyfish all over again, two boys working at a task alongside each other, eating lunch while music crackled in the echoey stairwell, finding comfort in quiet and the other's company.

One day Clyde told Owen he was saving up money to run away to San Francisco as soon as he could.

Everyone runs away at seventeen.

"Why San Francisco? It's so far."

"There are only free people in San Francisco, and nothing's too far from my dad."

Gail perked up in Owen's chest, always fluttering her wings at the mention of migration.

"It's like another world there, another dimension, and it's just full of the wildest people. I've only been once when I was twelve, but even just walking around for one day, I knew I would live and die in that city."

"I've never been."

Clyde whipped his backpack around and flipped open his binder, pulling out a small postcard. "I've had this since our trip." He handed a glossy postcard to Owen, an image of the Golden Gate Bridge poking its head out of a thick blanket of fog. "I know it's cheesy," Clyde said. "Golden Gate Bridge and all, pretty touristy, but I always remind myself what's on the other side of the bridge, the city I need to get to."

But Owen thought immediately about jumping off that bridge. He couldn't help it. He thought maybe the best way to give himself completely to water was not to slowly wade in and let it consume him, but to plunge from a great height, a sacrifice of sorts. He handed the postcard back to Clyde, getting rid of the image as fast as he could.

52

Tennessee agreed to have dinner with her dad, Natalie, and Owen, but only because it was Owen's birthday and she was a good feminist and wouldn't blame Natalie for her father's fuckups.

They were only fifteen minutes late, and Tennessee was only mildly annoyed. Bob and Natalie were nervous: Bob because he wanted to get in the good graces of his daughter after having screwed up so badly; and Natalie, because this was her first time meeting Tennessee and because she and Bob were "in it for the long haul," as she kept saying. Bob wore his red flannel shirt tucked into a new pair of jeans and Natalie was in a bright floral dress, a collage of peonies. Owen felt severely underdressed in his plain T-shirt and old jeans. Bob and Natalie were so nervous they nearly forgot about Owen. He was simply grateful everyone was in the same room, no one disappeared.

The five of them sat around the island, each with a full beer raised with nothing to cheers. Bob had a small smile and cleared his throat like he was about to pick something to cheers to, but then he swept his hand towards Natalie, indicating she should say something. Tennessee rolled her eyes and glanced over at Megan. Owen's arm grew tired from holding the beer in the air for so long.

It was Megan who broke the silence. "To Owen," she said. She looked him in the eyes. "Happy birthday."

Everyone shook out of their stupor, like they had all been napping at the kitchen counter. "Yes," they all said. "To Owen." They clinked their beers together, tapped them on the counter, and each made eye contact before taking a drink.

Natalie made it her mission to keep the conversation going. She asked Owen to list off what he had accomplished over the past year.

Surviving school. Riding the bus.

And then she asked him what he hoped to accomplish over the next year.

Survive school. Get a job.

He didn't say anything on planning to wade into the ocean and give in to the lifelong pull of the deep waters. He didn't want to frighten anyone.

Bob interjected that Owen would be running away this year. "I hope it's only in the physical sense. I hope we get to remain friends," he said.

This made Owen feel worse, but he kept it to himself, nodding at his uncle.

Natalie asked Tennessee a barrage of questions. She asked her who her favorite band was and how she liked living on her own and if she liked school or if she was happy it was over and how she liked Olympia, and didn't it seem like she had the best group of friends? Then Natalie reminisced about her own group of friends.

Owen thought the two of them had more in common than Tennessee would like to admit; after all, Owen liked Natalie, so why wouldn't Tennessee?

By the end, Owen had forgotten it was his birthday. Gail ran her wing down his spine just like he liked, though. "Happy birthday to us," she whispered. "This is going better than I imagined."

"If everyone makes it out alive, it will be better than I imagined," Owen whispered back down to her.

After dinner, the five of them sat in the living room and smoked a joint Natalie had brought. Owen sat on the floor near the couch. Tennessee and Megan sat above him, and Bob and Natalie sat near the woodstove. They passed the joint around, and music and smoke filled the room. It was silly to Owen, these five people all together in a room. He was stoned, and so his brain wandered down random walkways and paths. He thought of how random life seemed to be, the people he met or the places he went. Everything seemed dictated by an outer force.

"Like a gust of wind," Gail pined, "aiding a flock of birds migrating south."

Owen knew he'd wait until summer to run away. He'd see how his lunches with Clyde turned out. Relish feeling safe in a house with a family for a few more months before he disappeared forever.

53

Owen wandered through the woods with his coffee the next day. He'd woken up close to noon and shuffled outside after finding an empty house. It wasn't late enough in the year for the air to buzz yet, and it was the time of winter when even though the sun was bright in the sky, the woods were cold and water still leaked from everything. He walked down to the beach. He kicked at kelp. A boat horn sounded off in the water. Seagulls picked at broken shells in the sand.

If Owen walked far down the beach, away from the log, he reached a place where, when the tide was out, the water splashed up onto the large rocks and there was no sand. There were only rocks that sat above the water and beneath the steep cliffside.

It was a long walk, so he was happy to have poured himself such a large cup of coffee. He found Clyde sitting alone on the rocks, invisible from the beach. Quite unusual for someone to be here in a spot Owen considered so well hidden.

"Good morning," Owen said. It must have been one in the afternoon.

Clyde nearly fell off the rock and slipped into the water. He turned around laughing, red in the face. "Jesus," he said. "You scared me."

Owen sat next to him on a rock a little lower and in front of his. The rock poked into his ass and it was only a few seconds before he had to readjust to stop the tingles spreading down his thighs. Clyde shivered. Owen had the urge to wrap his arms around him and warm him up, a reflex. Owen stuck his hands in his armpits to keep them out of trouble.

"I've never seen anyone out here," Owen said, "and I come out here all the time."

"Same."

They didn't say anything for a while, and it was awkward in a way it never was during lunch. At school they were faced with the task of eating and there was the inevitable ring of the bell, placing a time limit on their interactions. Out here they were faced with an infinite amount of time and nothing to keep their hands busy.

Owen stared out over the gray water. "Sometimes I dream about walking underwater and living with the mermaids." It felt good to tell someone else about his plan.

"There's no such thing as mermaids."

"You can't prove that."

"That's only because you can't prove something nonexistent. You can only prove something true."

"Is San Francisco next to the ocean?"

"Yeah, it's surrounded by water. Remember the bridge? Water nearly on all sides."

Owen remembered the bridge. "So, there are beaches there?"

"Yeah, duh. It's California. There are beaches everywhere in California."

Gail did the thing she did when she was bored, where she just started yammering on in Owen's chest about this and that, just observations she made about life and how humans were. Owen did his best to both listen to her and tune her out simultaneously.

"Where do you go when you get like that?" Clyde leaned forward so he was in front of Owen looking back.

"Get like what?"

"You disappear sometimes. Just for a second, but it seems like you go somewhere else in your head." Clyde's eyes were a pale gray like the water.

"Just thinking," he said to Clyde. He dripped words down his throat to Gail. "Can you keep it down?"

She was silent.

And then: magic.

Clyde leaned back. His arms fell at his sides and his right hand fell on top of Owen's left wrist. Owen didn't move his hand. He let Clyde's hand rest there, and the water slipped between the rocks and foam spread across the beach. Owen looked out at the boats on the water and the land on the other side and he felt the sun on his face, but all his energy was focused on the hand resting on his wrist. It seemed like even astronauts in space could see Clyde's hand on Owen's wrist. He imagined a boardroom with a slide pulled up of the two of them nearly holding hands, a long conference table surrounded by men in suits wondering *what it meant*. There was no way it wouldn't be in newspapers all over the world tomorrow. So different from when he had placed his hand on Comet's on the couch, maybe because they both wanted it. Who knows?

Owen downloaded the scene as best he could: the fishy smell like clams in the air, the wind touching the edge of his nostrils, the chill in Clyde's fingertips on the underside of his wrist, and the seagull that screamed while gliding just above the water.

And then it was over. Clyde cleared his throat. "I need to head back. More work to do." He stood up. "Can you stay behind for a second? If my dad is waiting for me, there'll be hell to pay if he sees we were sitting together. Sorry, I feel like I talk about my dad too much." Clyde towered over Owen, his shadow caressing Owen's face.

"You can talk about your dad. I get it," Owen said.

Clyde waved his little wave with two fingers and disappeared around the side of the cliff.

"Oh my god," Gail said. "You heart is pounding so loud. My heart is pounding so loud. What was that? Is Clyde into you? That was something. I can't believe that happened. I guess happy birthday to you."

Owen laughed and brushed the hair out of his eyes. All he could say was yes.

He wobbled along the rocks until his feet found the sand again.

"You know," Gail whispered up to him, "a boy could really disappear in San Francisco. It could be the ultimate place to run away."

"Anywhere but San Francisco," Owen whispered back down to her. He couldn't imagine driving over the Golden Gate Bridge and *not* plunging into the ocean. The urge would be too strong, and he would be too weak to resist it. The thought terrified him.

54

The sun poked its little head out more and more and so it was warmer in the wagon. One night, Owen slept with the window rolled down. The energy of the season burst around him. He lay in the back of the wagon each night and listened to the crickets and an owl hooting. Gail called out, *"BUMP-BADA-DUH! CHARGE!"* and he laughed and pulled his pants down to his ankles. He put a hand behind his head and masturbated, and all the forest sang out in the dark night around him.

• • •

Everything seemed so settled to Owen that he thought he might never get a panicked phone call from his mother again. The longer she went without calling, the better he felt. He imagined the doctor fading into a distant memory. Nurse Olivia dissolved completely until she was a faded apparition, à la Casper the Friendly Ghost.

He started to think that the Army of Acronyms had been entirely made up by his mother, one of her delusions.

Gail disagreed. "Even if they are not exactly named the Army of Acronyms, there is a collective group, a powerful group, that is dangerous. It always goes like this: Times are easy, and then the threat becomes real again. Then it fades away. The danger is still there, though, even if it's not present. Something is coming. I know you feel it."

He could feel it. Sometimes when he was downtown there were herds of men moving together like one creature, unbreakable in their defense. The air smelled like a fight, the souring of moods. *Boys will be boys*. He saw it around him at school, too. Boys growing up the same way, like that time in the woods. Boys growing up and turning everything bitter, wanting everything one way or no way at all.

But still, the threat of the doctor faded, and the Army of Acronyms grew more abstract.

55

He and Clyde didn't brush hands again, but they sat closer on the stairwell at lunch. Most people would not have been able to notice the closed gap of an inch between their shoulders, but Owen noticed, and he knew Clyde noticed, too. One afternoon Mr. Thurman passed them on the stairwell and Clyde scooted away from Owen ever so slightly. Why would he scoot away if he hadn't been sitting closer?

It was slow, but Owen realized one day that lunch with Clyde had become his favorite time of day. Owen felt the presence of Clyde's hand on his wrist for weeks like a phantom limb, his body carrying the memory. He loved watching Clyde get excited about the world. Owen thought he was naïve to be so excited, but it was nice to see his hope all the same.

Since lunch with Clyde had become Owen's favorite part of the day, it made complete sense to him that they would skip class together. It was a logical step, a way to stretch out the lunch break. He proposed it to Clyde and Clyde didn't hesitate to say yes. They stood near the trophy case. They turned in unison towards the front doors and walked outside into the bright, brilliant sun.

They arrived at the T and waited for the next bus. "First stop is coffee," Owen said. He was full on the idea of showing Clyde around to his favorite places in Olympia.

The bus squeaked and squealed to a stop. They sat next to each other but not too close on the ride downtown.

The inside of the café was bursting with activity, all men in suits making their way around one another without making eye contact. "Careful," Gail whispered. "Really not our people. Army of Acronyms."

Owen scoffed, but he put his hands in his pockets and watched his elbows. He walked up to the counter and ordered two cappuccinos.

They retreated upstairs and sat across from each other. Their knees swung wildly under the table and sometimes they bumped into each other and then they stopped swinging so wildly, but before long they forgot, and their knees found each other again.

"One more year and I'll have enough to move to California. What about you? Still considering?" Clyde sipped his cappuccino.

"Maybe," Owen lied. "I need a job. It's so far." He ran his finger along the books on the shelf.

"Can't get far enough away."

They finished their coffee and left to wander through downtown. They passed the tennis shoe tree and the record store. They stopped into the bakery and each had a free slice of bread topped with butter and honey. There were humans everywhere, all packed together, but sometimes it felt like no one could see them, like they'd disappeared in plain sight.

They wandered into a Rite-Aid. The air conditioner was on high and the store was tall and cold. Three men stood behind the pharmacy counter handing out prescriptions. Their starched white lab coats were enough to stir Owen into a panic, but he tried to remind himself the doctor was gone now and had lost his trail. They walked down the aisles and Owen remembered walking through the grocery store with his mother, months before his last hurrah, when she still thought it was safe for him to be out in the world.

They ended up in the makeup aisle. Clyde perused the nail polish and the eye shadow. He opened tubes of lipstick and showed each color to Owen. Orange. Pink. Dark pink. Dark red. Red. Brown. Pale Pink. Clyde picked up the orange tube and ran a stripe on the back of his hand. He held it out in front of him. He put the tube of lipstick in his pocket and they walked towards the exit. *Cops are worse than doctors.*

A horn blared on the street. A man crossed the street slowly, pushing a shopping cart full of empty cans and bottles. The car veered into the next lane and sped off.

"Easier to steal than to buy," Clyde said.

"I didn't know you liked makeup."

"I haven't worn it until now. Thought I'd try it out. Channel some Bowie." They crossed the street and stopped in front of the furniture store. Clyde looked at his reflection in the window. It was three in the afternoon. School was letting out. He pulled out the tube of lipstick and ran it along his lips. He painted two layers until his lips were bright orange. They looked like a hot sun sinking beneath the deep blue ocean of his eyes. He puckered his lips and turned to Owen.

Owen wanted to tell him everything then. He wanted to explain why he couldn't be the type to steal a tube of lipstick and then wear it in broad daylight. He wanted to tell him about Gail and how he loved her, and he knew there were others, but no one could be trusted. He wanted to talk about the Army of Acronyms and how his mother only called to tell him crazy things. He wanted to tell him about Comet and how Comet had broken his heart and how everything smelled like sour yogurt afterwards. He wanted to tell Clyde that he knew if he ever went to San Francisco it would be to throw himself off the Golden Gate Bridge, because he would never be strong enough to live in a city like that, to wear lipstick like this.

He kissed him instead. Broad daylight in front of the antiques store in downtown Olympia. He thought of everything he wanted to say, and he kissed him. He tasted the sweet, candy taste of lipstick, the same taste he'd felt on Ava's lips that night in the woods. Clyde's lips curled in a smile and Owen felt so loved then, knew he could say anything. He pulled away and looked at Clyde.

"I guess I've wanted to do that for a minute. Sorry." Owen looked down at the sidewalk.

Clyde tapped a finger against Owen's palm. "No sorries. I've wanted that since the jellyfish." And Clyde kissed Owen this time, really pressed his lips against Owen's. Owen felt the earth beneath them. It was like when he closed his eyes and dug roots into the ground before hide-and-seek, except Clyde's and his roots wrapped around each other, busted up the sidewalk, dug so deep they nearly reached the earth's core.

They pulled apart and the world turned back on again. The sidewalk was crowded with people making their way around the two boys. Gail twirled in Owen's chest. Clyde reached over and placed his hand on Owen's lips, smudged with Clyde's lipstick. His hands were calloused with work and he wiped the smear of lipstick from Owen's mouth with his thumb.

For the first time, Owen felt like he had something to move towards. He wanted to move towards Clyde, to move alongside him. He leaned forward and kissed Clyde again.

They pulled apart and Clyde ran his finger along Owen's elbow, moving down until stopping at his hand. He wrapped his fingers around Owen's, and they walked towards the bus stop. Crowds walked around them, but no one paid them any attention. Clyde leaned his body against Owen's, and Owen traced all the places their bodies touched. The knees. The fingers and palms. Their inner arms up to their shoulders. Once Clyde placed his head on Owen's shoulder, and it was temple against shoulder and top of head against neck.

It was then that Owen felt a hand on his shoulder from behind and it yanked him backwards. He tightened his stance. He remembered that power came from his rear leg, up from the ground. He turned around, ready to fight. The sunlight flared in Owen's eyes.

Clyde's father stood behind him, his hat sitting low on his eyebrows. He spit a wide spray of tobacco on the sidewalk. "What in Christ's name?"

Clyde's eyes filled with water, fear like a waterfall. "Dad, no. What are you doing here? What? No. Don't hurt him."

He slapped Clyde across the face. The lipstick smudged across his lips, still wet. "Goddammit," he screamed. He shook his head no and waved his hands frantically in the air. People shuffled along the sidewalk like a father hitting his gay son was an everyday occurrence for them. He scanned Owen, up and down, spit again. He grabbed Clyde hard by the collar and dragged him past Owen. Owen reached out to grab Clyde's hand. "Don't. Touch. Him." Clyde's dad used his free hand to dip the chewing tobacco deep out from his bottom lip and he flung the slobbery tobacco at Owen's face. "Stay away from us." He dragged Clyde to the truck, *a thief of joy*. The tobacco clung to the side of Owen's cheek. He wiped it with the back of his hand.

He wasn't sure how long he stood in the middle of the sidewalk. The Army of Acronyms was real, and Clyde's father was certainly a member. The day grew colder. Gail sat in his chest. Owen felt the pain of having something perfect taken from him for no other reason than someone else simply didn't like it. It was dark when he rode the bus home.

56

Clyde didn't come to school after that. It was a week before Owen saw him again. During that week, Owen considered calling the cops, certain Clyde's father had killed him. Would the cops care? *Cops are worse than doctors.* He also had to worry about Clyde's father's ties to the Army of Acronyms. Owen was definitely on a list, and there was nothing stopping Clyde's dad from turning him in. A part of him wondered if being caught by the Army of Acronyms wouldn't bring some relief, an end to all his anxieties, like giving in to the pull of the water or the pull of a boy.

Owen wanted badly to call his mother, to tell her about the boy he'd kissed and to ask her how he could weasel his way out of this, find safety. He knew what she'd say. *Run.*

He couldn't call her, and he didn't run. Instead, he went through the motions of school and home and Tennessee's on the weekend, but it was flat and empty. When he'd kissed Clyde, the pull to him had gotten stronger, so strong it outweighed his pull to the water, but he didn't know how to move towards Clyde if he couldn't find him. Clyde had disappeared, and Owen was used to people leaving, but this was the first time he had ever put someone else in danger. He blamed himself.

"Don't do that," Gail said. They sat in the last stall in the bathroom on the third floor at school. A moth fluttered into the window over and over again.

"I didn't know his dad would see us. I forgot about the world and just did it. I wasn't thinking."

Gail tickled his lungs. She spit up the pebble from the beach and then the pellet. "It was a magical moment. I wish we had an object to remember it by." She turned the two objects between her wings.

Owen washed his face under cold water and went to class.

• • •

A week later Clyde and Owen met on the beach at the space where the sand disappeared. Clyde's face was puffy with bruises and scrapes, his hair still buzzed tight to his scalp. Clyde had called and asked Owen to meet him there. "We have twenty minutes," he'd said.

Their time was so limited that Owen was overwhelmed and didn't know how to say everything he needed to. He wanted to unravel his skein of secrets. If he could muster the strength, he'd tell him everything he'd wanted to tell him on the sidewalk in downtown Olympia. He touched the skin beneath Clyde's black eye. Clyde winced. Owen pulled his hand back. Owen kissed Clyde and felt his fat lip beneath his. Clyde pulled away.

"I really don't have long. They pulled me out of school." His words hit with a lisp, his teeth sticking to his bottom lip.

"I noticed."

"You need to stay away from my dad. He's ready to kill you."

Gail straightened in Owen's chest. "I've been thinking about running away. I'm at that age," Owen said.

"You're seventeen."

"I know. That's the age."

"I need another few months of savings before I can leave. I almost have enough. Maybe you can go to San Francisco and I can meet you there."

The water washed up and over the edge of Owen's boot. "I can't go to San Francisco. I'm not strong enough."

"You're stronger than me." Clyde looked out over the water.

"There are things I can't tell you, but you wouldn't like me if you knew them. I'm different than you think I am." Gail stirred in his chest, hung her head low.

"I like you. You. You. YOU. I don't care if you're a space alien." Clyde thudded his hand on Owen's sternum, inches from the hole in his chest.

"I just can't go to San Francisco."

"Okay."

Owen searched Clyde's face for his eyes but couldn't find them. He wanted to take care of Clyde, find a home for him in Montana and lock him inside. He'd teach him the bird migration game and they wouldn't open the door for anyone, but he knew he couldn't keep Clyde from San Francisco. Clyde must have felt a pull to that city like how Owen felt a pull to the water. It was his dream.

Clyde stood up. "I have to go back. Stay here for a few minutes so my dad doesn't see you." He wobbled over the rocks and disappeared around the side of the cliff where the sand spread out wide on the shore.

• • •

School without Clyde was bullshit. Lunch without Clyde was bullshit. Even Tennessee and Megan's house on the weekend with no possibility of Clyde during the week was bullshit. It was the middle of May.

Owen walked the hallways at school with his head down. He barreled through. He looked over his shoulder and remembered that power came up through the ground and through his rear leg.

The Army of Acronyms was real to him again. He couldn't believe he had ever grown so comfortable. Gail tried to let him off the hook, but he wouldn't let her.

"I put him in danger," he said, "and for what?"

"Whatever happened to letting go of scaredy-catted-ness?"

"Out the window," he said.

The bell rang and he went to the next class. He sat in the back of the room and devised a short-term plan. Kissing Clyde had unlocked something inside him that made the idea of wading into the ocean and living with mermaids seem like a worst-case scenario, and Owen didn't know if it was worst-case yet. He wasn't ready to completely disappear forever. Maybe he could be happy alone with the bird in his chest, really alone though. He needed enough money to get to the next town. He would drop out. He just needed to get somewhere where Clyde's father couldn't find him. He would do a better job of hiding this time. This time he wouldn't let anyone in. It would be an afterlife of sorts.

57

I t was three weeks of quiet planning and worrying and anxiousness, and then his mother called. He hadn't heard from her since the last phone call, a year earlier. Her panic fed through the wires, out of her mouth and in through his ear. Her voice shook. The whole receiver shook in her hand, and it thudded against her chin, keeping a quick rhythm. He sat down at the island and slid the phone around to face him. It was midafternoon, the house was empty and quiet. "What's wrong, Mom?"

"I'm going into hiding. I can't call you anymore, ever. He came in again. He walked right up to me and asked if I had a son who had asthma. My god, Owen. It had been a year. I assumed the first time was an accident or maybe I was seeing things, but this was real. I panicked. I told him I didn't have a son. You should have seen the look on his face. Oh god, you should have seen it. I couldn't believe it. He found me. He recognized me. Oh, my heart was pounding so loud. I was scared. I can't believe it though. He said he knows there are others. I cannot believe you're alive."

He knew the look his mother was talking about. It was the same look Owen had seen in the doctor's office, the one that said, *I will find you. There is no escape.* Gail stood upright and tall in his chest, and water filled the backs of his eyes.

He knows there are others.

I don't have a son.

"What should I do?"

"I don't know. Maybe it's best if you don't tell me. That way they can't break me. They have interrogation techniques, Owen. They'll waterboard me. They'll give me truth serum. Whatever it takes to get to you. You should go somewhere else."

"I don't have any money."

"I can't send you any. It'll be too obvious. Ask your uncle."

"What should I do about school?"

"Your safety is more important than school. They'll kill you, Owen. They will kill you." Her voice was strong and solid for a moment, breaths even. She started to cry. "It's too much. All too much. I'm sorry." She hung up.

Silence hung in the air. He slammed the receiver down on the phone.

He knew what he had to do. It was time to run away. He found his inhaler and took a puff.

"But first," Gail said, "one last hurrah."

Book Three

Neither/Both

(How to Unstick When Stuck in the Middle)

58

The Fort show in June was part of the last hurrah, the beginning really. It had been four days since Owen's mother had called. He had done nothing in that time but go to school and try to imagine what living on his own and surviving on nothing would look like. Gail was silent in between jokes, oscillating between feeling responsible for the mood and being a scaredy-cat.

Tennessee and Megan picked him up when the sun was nodding below the horizon, blinking its eyelids orange and purple across the sky.

They pulled out of the driveway and boom, they were off. It was down the hill like a roller coaster. The field was empty, not even Jeez Louise ran next to the fence along the road.

Worst of all: no Clyde.

When they pulled over to the side of the highway, it was the moment before the stars came out, twilight. Lou, Ava, and Comet were all waiting for them on the beach. Comet had a nipper of cheap gin that he passed to Owen as soon as they arrived. Owen brought it to his lips and took a gulp. He passed it to Tennessee, and around and around the bottle went. There was a tangle of moths in Owen's belly at seeing Comet again, but Comet acted like everything was regular, and Owen hoped he'd forgotten the whole incident on the couch. They walked down the beach, the tide climbing higher and higher and the sky darkening. It was a lot of the same, but it was so empty without the possibility of staying here with these people forever. The moon's reflection flickered in the water by the time they reached the boat.

Owen drank more gin on the boat. Moments drifted in and out of focus, like he could blink an eye and be transported further into the evening. Before he knew it, they had reached the island and hiked to the Fort. It seemed his connection to these people was deeper with the prospect of leaving, but his connection to his own body was blurrier and more distant. His feet belonged to someone else.

It was empirically good to be back at the Fort, but the air didn't quite feel right. Everyone was drinking and smoking and making out, but something was off. Gail whispered up to him, "I know you feel it. Be careful."

He rolled his eyes and took the beer Megan offered him. He wanted his fearlessness back for one more night. The six of them stood around the fire. Ava stood next to him and they talked about music and nothing and the fire leapt up at the sky. Ava curled her purple lips into a smile and clasped her hand around Owen's.

"How does she know?" Gail whispered. "Even Tennessee doesn't know."

"She doesn't know," Owen said. Ava let go of his hand and walked towards the Fort. The music rose in volume, the crash of cymbals loud and constant.

Two men stood next to the door. They shoved each other playfully and beer sloshed out of their tallboy cans. They stumbled backwards. Their hair hung over their eyebrows and they each wore a different denim vest, dressed like so many of the other kids here but older, stupider. When they stood upright again, Owen caught sight of a permanent sneer, like the man's bottom lip was stuck on his tooth. No doubt about it, it was Troy and Jon, but no rattail this time, and somehow it seemed they'd each grown denser, a lifetime of destroying brain cells wherever they could. A looping soundbite of Troy calling him *homo* played in Owen's mind. He walked past them, and they didn't look twice at him.

He weaved through the structure until he came to the room where the band was set up. He drank more. He clenched and unclenched his fists. Power came through the ground up through the back leg. He must have looked tense, because Ava grabbed him and twirled him around, dancing. Gail loosened up, too. It was his last hurrah, after all. Owen brought his right hand in and twirled Ava this time. Her long black hair knocked Owen in the face. Ballroom dancing to punk, but it made so much sense. Everything made sense right then. It was stupid how fucking beautiful it was. Owen didn't know if he wanted to kiss Ava or *be* her. Really, Owen just wanted Clyde there, a shame Clyde would never get to see this, a show at the Fort.

Song after song, they spun until the whole world teetered around them. It tipped and curved. Owen stumbled, dizzy and drunk. He liked how Ava laughed at the fun they were having.

Then it was over. The music cut out. The room so silent you could hear a pin drop. Flashlight beams crisscrossed the air. Everyone ran into everyone else with no sense of direction, just scrambling.

Cops.

Cops are worse than doctors.

One of the cops shouted over everyone, "No one's going anywhere. You're all trespassing." His partner pulled out a bag of zip ties. Owen felt Ava's fingertips slide out of his hand.

His ears rang. He scanned the room for Tennessee. Where was she?

It was his luck he'd be captured the week he was running away. He had to get out of here. They would find Gail. Was this the doctor's doing? Were they after Owen?

Oh, Jesus, but Owen could barely stand. His body was nothing but booze. Gail shook in his chest, quiet. He couldn't see a damn thing. The flashlights were too bright, and there was chaos in the air so thick he'd have to swim through it. He remembered the trick his mother had taught him while playing hide-and-seek. He closed his eyes and imagined himself a tree, swaying in the permafrost. He opened his eyes and could see, *bright as day*. The cops lined people against the wall, talking to everyone one by one.

"Gail," he whispered. "I need your help."

"Just wait," she said. "Something will happen. It has to."

The short officer walked over to them. He put his hands out, gesturing a group hug. "Everyone here against that wall. We'll be with

you in a minute. And we have the building surrounded. So don't even
try to run."

Owen walked over with everyone to the wall next to the stage. Troy
and Jon were against the wall across from him. He thought that maybe
they were the reason the cops were here. Trouble followed them. Ava
stood behind Owen. Comet was a few feet in front of him. Comet was
tall and quiet, and Owen could sense him tensing each of his muscles
so that every movement was controlled, nothing out of place.

Troy and Jon started arguing under their breath. "That's it," Gail
whispered, urging them on. "That's our ticket out." Their argument
grew louder. Owen reached behind him and felt for Ava's hand. He
still couldn't see Tennessee or Megan or Lou. Maybe they were with
cops out in the woods.

"Fuck you," Troy yelled at Jon, his permanent sneer tightening.
The taller cop stepped between the two of them and put his hand up.

"Now!" Gail yelled.

Owen felt in his body again. He grabbed Ava's hand. He ran towards Comet. The cop turned around just as Jon reached over him to
punch Troy. The cops swarmed them. Owen grabbed Comet by the
elbow and kept running towards the door. Comet took a step forward,
and they were off. Just like that they were running out of the Fort. The
forest floor beneath their feet. Twigs snapped beneath Owen's boots.
There were no cops outside. *LIARS*, Owen thought. He looked behind
him, and Ava was running at full speed. Her hair and cape flowed out
behind her and any minute she would soar off the ground, lift off. The
three of them were *bats outta hell*. Owen was flying. He bounded over
logs and through blackberry thickets. He twisted his ankle but kept
running, the gin numbing the throbbing pain. Comet ran fast, his
hands pumping up and down with each step. Bats fluttered overhead
in the trees. Ava screamed a holler of pure joy. But where were the
others? Owen thought about turning back, but Gail was yelling in
his chest now. "YES," she said. "YES. YES. YES." And it was constant
rhythm in his body, like his blood pumped YES over and over again.

They reached the water and there they were, waiting in Lou's boat.
Tennessee with her arms wrapped around Megan, crying into her

neck. Lou stood over the motor. The motor sputtered in the water, ready to take off. Owen had never felt such relief wash over him. Gail couldn't contain herself and she whistled loudly in his chest. Tennessee gave him a knowing look and they climbed into the boat. His cousin wiped her face dry. Lou pulled away from the shore and they whooped and hollered. Comet hugged Owen and lightning struck their bodies.

"You fucking saved my ass."

"Mine, too," Ava said. Her nostrils flared up like they did when she smiled big.

Owen laughed. "You both would've done the same for me."

His cousin laid her head on his shoulder. "I was so scared they'd gotten you."

"Fucking pigs." Ava spit hard into the water.

Comet leaned in. "Owen saved the day. Jesus, man." He told the story from his point of view, how Comet thought they were going to jail, but the cops had lied about having the building surrounded. How nutso the whole thing was. How the whole night had gone bonkers. He looked Owen in the eye. "How'd you know those guys were about to fight? You took off a split second before they started throwing punches."

Owen couldn't even remember that far back. He felt pride brimming from Gail in his chest. "I had a feeling," he said, shrugging. The desert sands were thick in his lungs and he needed to get to his inhaler at the house, but still he smiled, and not once did he think about how in a few days, he'd be just a bird and a boy.

Back on the beach and the moon was high and bright in the sky, nearly full. Tennessee and Megan held hands and arched their backs and howled loud and hard. Owen kept quiet, sure the cops could still hear them. Comet, Lou, and Ava joined in, and the air was full of waves pulsing and howls echoing off the shore. The water swallowed the sound. Comet patted Owen on the back. The tide worked its way out from the beach, the task of lowering the sea. Owen wished he were not running away, wished that Clyde's father weren't in the Army of Acronyms, weren't in a long lineage of men taking up space.

"The full moon means the blood is coming," Megan yelled.

Ava laughed and growled, "BLOOD."

That stupid beautiful moon.

Comet gave him the rest of the gin. "Least I can do. In fact, I owe you a whole bottle." They hugged, Owen's blood still pumping.

Slowly Owen's anxiety settled, and he felt safe. They lingered on the beach longer than usual, all the energy surging through them. Owen watched Comet settle back into his body, too. Comet looked out over the water often, across the shore back towards the Fort. He frowned from time to time, and Owen saw it get more permanent, but then Megan told one of her jokes and Comet's mouth relaxed into a smile.

When it was time to leave, everyone stood up and hugged and they slapped Owen on the shoulder. Comet hugged him and called him "brother." "We'll always be bonded," he said. "Best birthday present I could have asked for."

"Today's your birthday?"

"Tomorrow. I'll see you at the party."

"Gemini?" Owen said.

Ava hugged him, and he felt Ava hold his entire body in her arms. He settled into her body. She put her hands behind Owen's head and felt his hair. She pulled her head back and leaned in and kissed him on his lips. It was soft. Owen coughed and swallowed hard to keep the desert sands at bay. He kissed her again. "Just thought you could use a kiss after tonight," she said. "Thank you for dancing with me."

It wasn't like his kiss with Clyde. He felt her tenderness and her love, but their roots did not intertwine in the ground beneath them.

He took a deep breath. The salty air stung his nostrils. Ava pulled away and Owen missed Clyde so hard right then, a deep missing rooted in his belly like a secret. Gail rocked back and forth, and he knew then that the bird in his chest, the thing that he wished weren't there for so much of his life was actually the reason he was still alive. As long as Gail was perched in his chest, he'd be able to survive most things, his greatest asset.

59

The next day, Owen packed, and he listened to an album for every heartbreak he'd known. He shoved shirts and pants and clean underwear into his duffel bag to Morrissey's *Viva Hate*, for Comet. Sleater-Kinney's *Dig Me Out* played while he thought about the first ride he took in Tennessee's car and cleaned up the old bedroom. It was Dirty Projectors' *Bitte Orca* for his mom while he went through his items in the bathroom, grabbing his toothbrush, toothpaste, and hairbrush. He packed his rocks and the jar of water from the Sound to the Mountain Goats' *Get Lonely*, for Natalie and Bob. Finally, he put on the Pixies' *Surfer Rosa* and he remembered the first time he'd played it for Clyde, how it must have cracked him open the same way music cracked Owen open. He thrashed in the backseat, wrapping his arms around the velvet dress and dancing with it so hard he pulled it down. He hugged the dress tight. Rubbed his face in the crushed velvet until the album was over. The music disappeared, and Owen shook off his sweat.

"Missing anything?" he whispered down to Gail, out of breath. "Anything you think we need?"

"I got everything we need right here." She spit up the BB pellet and the rock from the beach and then swallowed them again.

His uncle sat on the back porch, alone. Owen put the duffel bag in the passenger seat of the wagon and joined his uncle. Bob leaned forward and blew smoke through his clenched teeth. He sat up. Both

of them waited for someone to say something. It was always like that
with him. He wanted Owen to speak first, but Owen didn't know what
to say, how to start.

Bob got fed up with waiting. "What's your plan this weekend?"

"I need some money," Owen blurted.

"For the weekend?"

"Kind of."

Bob flicked his cigarette into the lawn. "Oh, I see. It's like that.
How much? I don't have a lot."

Owen didn't know how much anything really cost. How much was
enough to survive on until he could get to the next place? What even
was the next place? "Fifty dollars?"

"Fifty won't buy you a bus ticket. When do you need it by?"

"Tonight," Owen said.

"I wish it was different."

"Me too."

Bob's eyes were dewy, and he placed a hand on Owen's knee.
"You're such a good kid," he said. "Your dad really would have loved
the shit out of you."

"Why?"

"What do you mean why?"

"You're always saying my dad would have loved me, would have
stayed around if he knew I was here. Why do you think that?"

"Your dad was the sort of guy who brought the party with him. He
made people smile. He told the best jokes. Just like you."

Owen wondered if his dad would have taught him about taking up
space. How would his dad feel about him kissing a boy? How would
he have felt about the bird in his chest?

Bob continued. "Your dad and mom only dated for a couple of
months. They were about your age when your mom got pregnant.
Your mom didn't tell anyone. Maybe she was scared. It wasn't like
her, dating a guy like your dad. Your dad left for college and he never
looked back. Couldn't ever stand Montana. Last I heard he was off to
New York."

New York, impossibly far from the Puget Sound, just as far as San

Francisco. "I just don't know if my dad really would have liked me. I don't get along with a lot of guys."

"Your dad was like us, gentle."

Gail whispered up to Owen. "I wish we could hear one of your dad's jokes." Owen smiled wide.

"I'll take some money out and leave it in the wagon for you."

"The wagon?" Owen tried to seem surprised.

"I know you've been sleeping out there. I get it. Sometimes rooms mean different things when people move out of them. Sometimes I think about moving. This house has had so many people live inside it, people who are gone now." Bob pulled out his pouch and pinched a bit of tobacco into a paper. "I'll get you what I can."

60

That night, Owen left the duffel bag in the wagon and took a bus to Tennessee's. When he got to the apartment, Tennessee and Ava were stringing streamers along the walls of the living room. A cardboard pineapple hung from the light fixture in the dining room.

"Festive," Owen said.

"The theme is Glitter in Paradise," Ava said, and she sprinkled her fingertips at her sides for a flourish.

Tennessee dragged Owen into her bedroom and demanded he undress so she could figure out what he could wear. She locked the door behind them. He stood in the middle of the room in his underwear, his arms hanging at his sides.

Posters now hung on the bedroom walls (Kate Bush, an anime-styled image of a woman on a scooter, Sasquatch peeking out of the woods), the bed was made, and the nightstand looked lived-in (empty pipe, cell phone charger, stack of books).

She rifled through her closet and found a romper covered in flowers. "Perfect." She held it up in front of her. She bent down at his chest. "What is it, Gail? What's gotten into him?" They talked about him like he wasn't in the room. She had him step one foot at a time into the outfit.

"My lips are sealed," Gail said, and she zipped her lips up with an imaginary zipper.

"Just thinking." Owen pulled the romper over his shoulders. The fabric was tight between his crotch and his chest and he worried the seams would bust. "It's nothing."

She buttoned him up and tapped his chest. "You look good."

Soon, the apartment was brimming. Comet was there and Lou and some strangers, mostly people Owen recognized from the Fort. Comet wore a long silver cape.

Megan had Owen sit up on the kitchen counter. The back of his head tapped against the cabinet and his heels bounced against the drawers beneath him. His body thought he was in the bathroom ready to jerk off before a bath and so it gave him an erection, which was nearly impossible to hide in the romper. He tugged the material down and looked off at the refrigerator. Megan stood between his legs. Tennessee opened a beer for him and passed it over her girlfriend, and Megan opened her makeup box and went to work on his face. She made him look up and down, close his eyes, purse his lips, relax his cheeks, smile. She spread color around his face. When she pulled the tube of lipstick across his lips, he remembered Clyde's bright orange lips and the taste of the color when they kissed, like crayons. He thought of the wet tobacco flung on his cheek. She held up a mirror when she was done, and Owen was transformed. He was a glittery David Bowie, Star Child. He looked like a Terror, and it was perfect. A blue lightning bolt cut across his left eye. Piles of glitter covered his cheeks like mounds of broken glass. He hopped off the counter and hugged Megan.

He drank beer and weaved through the crowd of people. Ava grabbed him when he walked by and slung her hand around his waist. "Goddamn, you look hot." Her eyes shone with drunkenness.

"You too, honey," and he meant it.

He knew he should be figuring out a way out of town, a way to flee, but the party was such a pure distraction.

"One night," he told Gail. "I want one night with no thieves of joy or the Army of Acronyms, where my only wish is that Clyde could be here with me."

"Our last hurrah," Gail said.

Owen passed her the feeling of wearing a tight romper in a room full of friends and not knowing how to say goodbye, so not really saying anything at all. He stood on the back patio. Comet smoked a cigarette and gabbed at Owen about Against Me! and how they were the greatest band of the 2000s, not waiting for Owen to respond, talking over even himself.

Later Megan gripped Owen's hand and pulled him into the bedroom where Tennessee sat on the bed. Owen's head swirled with beer. He thought it must have been midnight, but when he checked the clock it was barely ten.

Megan led him to Tennessee by the hand and he felt like they were ready to share a secret with him. Tennessee's teeth shone bright white. She blinked twice and pulled the Blossoms Blossom out from behind her back.

"It's time," she said. The flower was completely dried and wilted now, petals clinging to withered stem. Globs of orange light dripped from the pistil.

Owen wasn't sure.

Tennessee reached her hand into the jar. Her fingernails chipped with black paint, she pulled out the dried bits of flower and handed a chunk to Megan and a smaller chunk to Owen. Owen didn't know where he had gotten the idea, but he always assumed they would each eat their respective flower. Tennessee would eat only the orange one and he would eat his purple flower, and then they would experience *everything* together. They were splitting hers, though, and Megan was here.

Maybe this was better.

One last hurrah.

Tennessee and Megan looked into each other's eyes. "The first time we met in person," Megan said.

"Cheers to that," Tennessee said. The three of them held their small bits of dried flowers up and clinked them in a cheers. They stuffed the plant into their mouths. It was dry and tasted like forest floor, dead leaves and bark. The more Owen chewed on the flower, the mushier and fouler it got.

"You just have to chew it enough that you can swallow it. Your stomach will do the rest." Megan's mouth was full.

"To a good time." Tennessee raised her beer and they said "Cheers." Owen drank the cold beer down and it washed the bits of flower, sent them down his gullet to land in his belly next to all his other secrets.

A secret he shared with his cousin and her girlfriend.

Gail was tense in his chest, and she asked a lot of questions that Owen didn't have the answers to. "How does the flower interact with people with asthma? How long does it last? What's it like?"

He answered each question with the same answer: "I'll let you know when I find out."

Bursts of color exploded around him. A person with long pink hair stood near the door, their hair radiating pink like a halo. The Christmas lights around the room were a green aura. Even the refrigerator light spilled yellow across the kitchen. Owen walked around and his back twisted itself in knots. He turned and stretched his spine long. He put a hand to his lower back and applied pressure. Megan twirled around the apartment, now in a nearly see-through slip. She placed a crown on Comet's head. It was made from herbs Tennessee had gathered: rosemary and lavender and sage twisted together.

"For the birthday king," Megan said. Comet beamed and Owen looked up to him then, saw him as someone he could strive to be, and it felt possible, and then the possibility slithered away. Tennessee turned the stereo up loud and the room was full of people laughing and singing, and Owen saw the person with pink hair smile like they were keeping a secret.

"*Is this what you wanted?*" Leonard Cohen sang.

Comet placed a hand on Owen's shoulder and dragged him onto the patio again. Owen worried it would be more of Comet arguing with himself, but he was focused now. "You're a good friend," he said. He pulled out a cigarette and lit it, exhaled fast and hard immediately. "Not a lot of people are good friends like you. I will never forget last night." Why did it sound like Comet was saying goodbye? Did he know?

"You're being paranoid," Gail said. "Just listen to what he is saying."

Owen felt confident then, true, honest. "Comet, how do you do it?"

"Do what?" He took another drag on his cigarette and brought his hand to rest on his elbow. Smoke spiraled up into the light.

"How do you be the life of the party, the person everyone wants to talk to?"

Comet smiled, a small gap between his top teeth. "You are the person everyone wants to talk to. You just don't know it."

Red came to Owen's cheeks. "You will always be my first crush, and now you're like an older brother. You mean a lot to us."

"Us?"

He had meant he and Gail. "Me and Tennessee. Mostly me though."

"I love you," and he leaned in and pulled Owen into a hug. There was no electricity, only warmth.

Owen looked over Comet's shoulder. The person in pink hair was now completely radiating pink, and they moved through the crowd. A pink fog followed them, swirled around the party like smoke. "I need to go inside," he said, and he walked past Comet.

When he slid the door open, the sound of the party burst outside. Everyone sang along loudly with the chorus. *To live in a house that is haunted by the ghosts of you and me.* The horns blared over the speakers. The person in pink strolled through, smiling and singing along, and it seemed to Owen that they were observing the party but were not at the party, attending it from afar or looking back on it like a memory. A large hoop earring hung from their right ear. They pulled their hair behind their left ear, a nervous tick.

He found Tennessee and Megan and Ava in a three-way slow dance huddle near the kitchen. Tennessee's head was dipped back, and her eyes shone with tears from happiness. "How you feeling, Cousin?" she called to him.

He opened the fridge and bathed in the yellow light. "Like a hundred bucks," he shouted to her. Cool air wafted out of the fridge, and he closed it without getting anything. He tugged on his romper and pulled it down off his thighs, relieving the tight cuffs. Gail swayed in his chest.

Comet came to him in the kitchen and wrapped his arms around Owen. Owen wished Clyde were there. Comet placed a firm hand on his back and Owen felt their breaths sync up, in and out together. The whole room buzzed and vibrated and breathed together.

He went into the bathroom and struggled to get out of the body-suit so he could take a piss. "This is family," Gail said. "This is something, isn't it?" she said.

"You're high."

"Who isn't?"

"I wish it could be this forever." He washed his hands and went back into the party. He knew that this was truly his last night, that everything ended here in this room and that whatever happened would be the afterlife. He found the person in pink sitting on the couch now. They pulled their hair behind their left ear again. The gold hoop on the right ear and all the pink light seeping out of their body and Owen saw just a small movement, a little scurry behind their left ear, and he understood.

They were a Terror.

It must have been a beetle behind their left ear, an earring in the right as a distraction. "Terror," he whispered down to Gail.

She froze in his chest.

He walked through the sea of strangers. People laughed and sang along with Fleetwood Mac now. He stood over the person in pink. They had dark brown roots on top of their head. Their eyebrows were dark brown and bushy, and their nose hung to the right. Every Terror must get pummeled and end up with a broken nose at least once in their life. He waved a hand in front of their eyes and so they looked up at him. They looked worried.

"It's okay," he said. He tapped his chest twice, but then realized the person in pink was hiding a beetle behind their ear, so he tugged on his left ear instead. He tried to send them the telepathic message that he had them, that he understood them, and what he was about to do was for each of them, for every Terror. There must have been millions of Terrors, but they were all afraid to say something. That ended now.

He put one foot on the crusty couch and steadied himself, and then put the other foot next to it. He wobbled. He cleared his throat. He could see the tops of everyone's heads. People looked so strange from up there, not like people, and it didn't feel like real life but like a movie. He cleared his throat again. "Excuse me," he said. Megan turned down the stereo, and slowly people realized the kid in the floral romper had something to say.

"I'm Owen," he said. "Happy birthday, Comet."

Everyone shouted, "Happy birthday." They cheered.

"That's not all." People hushed again. The person in pink looked up at him. The top of their head reached his knee. He steadied himself again. "My name is Owen. I have a java sparrow who lives inside of my chest. Her name is Gail, and she has always been there."

Crickets. Dead silence.

He felt the buzz of the room. "I don't care about the Army of Acronyms anymore. They can come and get me." More silence. He pulled the collar away from his chest. "Come on, Gail," he whispered into his shirt. "Say something."

Tennessee stepped forward. She mouthed *no one, never.* "Someone is too high," she said. "Get down from there." She walked towards him.

He shook his head and he felt his chest well up, and then Gail blasted her chirp *poe-poe-TWEET-TWEET-CHIRP-chirp-chirp-poe-POE-POE-TWEET-toe-toe-TWEET-CHIRP-CHIRP-CHIRP.*

A big part of the bundle of secrets unfurled. It was like someone turned the room on again. People scanned the room for the loose bird. Comet took a step closer to him. The person in pink stood up and went onto the back patio and the pink light followed them.

He knew it would only be a matter of time before the Army of Acronyms found him, which meant he had to go. He climbed down from the couch. People were too confused to say anything, worried the drugs they were on meant they were the only one who had heard Gail's chirp. He hugged Tennessee and Megan. He felt weightless. "Good night," he said. "Don't worry. I know the afterlife is all that's left, but we aren't saying goodbye."

Megan grabbed Owen's shoulder and pulled him back.

He had worried her. "I'm not in danger," he lied, "but I am leaving. And I'm taking my bird with me."

Tennessee came between her girlfriend and Owen and put her arms around his neck. She whispered in his ear. "Don't go disappearing."

And Owen could only smile and put a hand on her shoulder.

The air was cold and dark, and he walked towards the Sound, back to his house. The buses weren't running. It was nearly midnight when he started the walk home. Gail bounced in his chest. "That was dangerous," she said, "and I loved it." The air buzzed around them and the sky was full of stars. How good it felt to unfurl his secrets. He walked along the street chanting, *My name is Owen. I have a bird who lives inside my chest. She's always been there* to himself, over and over again. It felt like he was laying a trail of secrets behind him. He was weightless. He had to see Clyde, and then it was sayonara. He was free.

61

The Blossoms Blossom had nearly worn off when Owen got back to the house. The clock above the stove read two-oh-four. He poured himself a glass of water and went out to the wagon. There was an envelope with $237 sitting on the passenger seat. He put the money in the bottom of the duffel bag.

He rolled his Blossoms Blossom out from under the seat and the car filled with purple light. It was so dense he couldn't see but three feet in front of him. The purple was contained to the car, the garage still dark. It crawled into the backs of his eyelids. It stung. Tennessee's flower had been dull with only globs of light, how his flower had looked yesterday. The purple light was edible, and he reached out and it swirled around his fingers. It was begging him to eat it.

"No," Gail said. "This is the worst time for that. You need your head on straight."

Owen responded with a finger to his lips and a shush. He wanted the courage he'd had at the party and he'd need it for what he was about to do: run away and disappear. He brought the jar to his face and looked at the flower, now dried up and wilted, exploding with light. "It's time," he said. He twisted the lid off, reached in, and pulled out the dry flower and all its petals. He shoved them in his mouth and chewed them up. He said, "Round two," and ate the entire flower.

Gail shook in his body. "Bad idea. Bad idea. Bad idea."

"If you say it like that it'll come true, like Beetlejuice."

He put on Radiohead's *OK Computer*, an album for himself. The guitar filled the car. His back ached, and he put his hand on the small curve to straighten his spine. He waited for his *everything* to come.

62

Purple was gone. The car was empty of any color. He went into the driveway and felt the wind push onto his skin. He walked around the house to the backyard. The glass chimes rang on the porch. He felt a glow inside his eyes, a hum in his belly. He straightened his posture. There were small explosions of color around him again: a burst of yellow in the recycling bin, a glow of green coming from the trees, vibrations of brown coming from the earth, a wisp of white from the moon and the clouds, but no purple. Where had all the purple gone?

. . .

Something was off. He thought his head might float off, like a bird ready for flight. The moonlight split through the woods. It felt like a television set. He felt like a giant. Then the trees were like giants. They were alive and he could feel their breath through the bark.

Everything vibrated.

. . .

He thought he could live in the woods forever. Maybe this was where he could run away. Why was he running away again? What was the big deal? It eluded him. Nothing made sense. Baffled by the thought of someone hating someone else. Why? Because they liked dicks in their ass? Why? Because they were Black? Because they were a witch? Because they were a Terror?

"It's just the way it is," Gail whispered up to him. "Can't apply logic to this one."

His rib creaked and he remembered reality. He remembered Troy's face, how he had made Owen a monster he had to destroy, how July had looked on. He remembered wet tobacco sliding down his cheek. The doctor's eyes that said *I will keep you here forever.* How Owen and Gail had been alone but had survived. He was cold in the floral romper and it cut into his thighs. He pulled at the hems.

"I love you, Gail. You're my everything."

"I love you, Owen. It's going to be okay. We'll always make it." He tiptoed over logs and dipped his head beneath the tree branches that were alive. The trees stopped reaching for him. They helped him, pushed him onward.

63

He reached the beach and it was empty, save for him. It must have been four in the morning. His whole head buzzed with the Blossoms and it felt like it could burst. He felt each individual grain of sand beneath his boots. The water washed onto the shore. The Sound was black, swallowing all the light, and Owen was afraid of the water then, but he still felt drawn to it. Then he understood how the people who drew *The Little Mermaid* could envision a new world, underwater. They imagined it. They took the best parts of the world they lived in and transformed them into something magical.

The stars were up there in outer space. The earth was deep and moving beneath him.

He sat down in the dry sand. He rolled onto his back. The world tumbled. The ocean fell away from him. The woods toppled over him. He was stuck in the middle and everything looked so different from that angle. It was like when he sunbathed with Natalie, but it was night, and he was alone. The stars whooshed overhead. He imagined the astronauts up on the moon, missing their astronaut families. And here were the astronaut families, having dinner and missing the astronauts right back.

Concerned with space, Owen asked Gail what it felt like to take up space inside someone else. What did it mean to inhabit space within another being? Had the thought ever crossed her mind that her residence within his chest was the epitome of selflessness? She was willing to share her space within another being. They shared a space and therefore she took up less space. Owen, on the other hand, took up so much space. His arms, his legs, his head, his whole body took up all this space. He stretched his fingers out wide in front of his face. He could barely see where his body ended. What good was it to take up so much space? This was what it meant to be a waste of space. Humans, everyone, took up space with their bodies, but also housing. Humans must use the space wisely, but they don't. They required food to fill the empty space in their bellies. Humans felt the need to conquer the stars and outer space because there must be something out there, something that filled all the space.

Gail thought it might be Owen who was the selfless one. What did it mean that he was willing to shove aside all his organs so there could be a place where he just let her be? And the ridicule? The loneliness?

To take up any space inside another was a great privilege.

• • •

Owen wanted badly to talk to Clyde, to not only talk to him but also be held by him, to run his hands along his body. "I love Clyde," he said out loud, and the words hung in the air above his nose. He could reach out and grab them. After he said the words, it seemed so obvious, like anyone who heard his story would know by now that he loved Clyde. It had indeed been a slow burn, like jellyfish venom or poison, but here he was: in love with a boy. "I have a bird who lives inside my chest. Her name is Gail, and she's always been there," he said next.

"I've always been here," she repeated.

Together they said, "We are a Terror."

Their word not ours.

More secrets spread out on the beach in front of him.

And here came the sun, sprinkles of gold lazily making their way across the sky, scattering at the stars.

"Fresh," Gail said. "Maybe that's enough. Maybe Clyde will like both of us. Maybe he'll love you." Owen felt the sun inside him.

He tried to hold on to the now. He wanted the nowness present in his mind. He wanted his brain's fingers wrapped around it. He felt the earth beneath him and thought about the planet spinning quickly through outer space. That was what it meant to hold on to the now, thinking about the planet barreling through the galaxy, that was now. It made him queasy. He thought about his mother, running food to tables, existing outside himself. He wondered if he'd see her again. That was the future. He had lost the now. It slipped through his fingertips.

The now, the present, was a squirmy little bugger. He wondered if he would know it when he was in the afterlife. Maybe he was there now. The after.

64

The universe's breath was a deep gold. (Maybe it was once purple.)

65

The pull to the water was in the background, not too present. Owen walked to the sea and put his finger in the cold water. It was like ice. "What did this flower do to me?" he said. It was stronger, deeper.

"It's okay." Gail ran the tip of her wing along his spine, vibrations up and down his back. "People take drugs all the time. Just go with the flow."

"Just go with the flow," he repeated. The trees shook under the early rays of morning. His eyes were tired. All the strangeness made sense to him, like of course he was thinking of the way the mind flowed between experiencing the present and recalling the past. It was exactly the same way alligators slipped between swimming in water and running on land. Running on land was nowness, and alligators could run up to thirty miles per hour on land. What else could run that fast?

He stumbled through the woods back to his house. "Things will be back to normal tomorrow," Gail whispered to him. "Tomorrow we will leave."

"There's something I have to do before then." The sky was slate gray, rays of green pulsing through the air, but the woods were dark and so he grasped a tree, wrapped his arms all the way around it and felt its bark on his nose. He closed his eyes. So much darkness it hurt. He pulled away from the tree and his eyes did that trick where it felt like noon out. He ducked under the fallen fir and came up on the other side of the tree. He felt no fear. That was how he wanted to live his life: no fear.

"Goodbye, scaredy-catted-ness," he said out loud to no one, and then, "I'm going to unravel the skein." He tromped through the woods back to the house. The woods were black then, the color of molasses. He shook his head, refocused. Felt some color come back. He spread his fingers out wide and swept his arms back and forth from his front to his sides to his back and then to the front again.

He was sweating by the time he was out of the woods and at the house. The house was all lit up now. Bob and Natalie sat next to each other on the couch. Bob's arm was around her shoulders. Her legs were draped over his. Bob rubbed the sleep out of his eye. They drank coffee. Owen knew they would be just fine without him. Maybe Bob had found someone who would not run away. Owen avoided the house and walked on the gravel. He swept his hand across the rear window of the station wagon. Dust collected on his fingertips. He wondered if the car still ran. He didn't know where the keys were. Maybe he could hotwire it. "Plates are expired," Gail said. "Cops would pull you over in a minute."

"Oh yeah. Cops are worse than doctors." He slipped into the backseat. The air smelled like him and old cigarettes, a little like his mother. "Goodbye, car," he said. He grabbed his duffel bag. The door creaked behind him. It was morning and the birds chirped their tunes. He was comfortable in his skin, despite the sweat that dripped down his back and the tight fit of the romper. He reached the road and walked along the side of it. His duffel bag swung at his knees. His heart paced. He put his hand into the romper and felt his heart. Gail nibbled his finger. Then she chirped and Owen felt easy. He took a deep breath, the wind blew, and he felt it inside him, the whole world breathing. *Got to unravel that skein*, he thought. That was his only plan. He didn't know what he'd do after that.

His gait was long now, and he reached the base of the hill where there was the field and often Clyde. No Clyde, so he placed a foot on the fencepost and avoided the electric wire, and he flipped himself over the fence and onto the ground, flat on his back. The dry grass tickled the backs of his bare legs. The whole world used to be like the woods, and then humans came and knocked them down to build a town, a store, a church, a road.

"Be careful," Gail said.

He stood up, spread his arms wide. He tilted his head back and howled loudly at nothing. A car drove past on the road and continued up the hill. "What if we just lived in the woods?"

"Easier to disappear in a small city," Gail said.

"Yes. Anywhere but San Francisco." He slipped his hand into the romper and felt around until he found Gail's head.

The trees rustled. Jeez Louise came barking out of the woods. Owen thought she might attack him, but her tail wagged, and her tongue hung out the side of her mouth. He picked up a stick and threw it for her and she took off after it. He stood perfectly still, listening to the earth's hum.

Like magic, Clyde walked out from under the trees. No horse, just himself.

Owen felt tears in his eyes. His body released all its tension. "Clyde," he yelled. "Come over here. Oh my lanta, I have so much to share, to unravel." He whipped his hand around in the air, motioning for Clyde to come over.

Clyde walked through the tall grass. "Quiet. My dad will kill you if he hears us," but his grin was so wide. His face had healed, no more swelling, just a crooked nose that now hung to the left. The grass swooshed against his jeans. The sunlight glowed through his buzzed hair like a halo, and when he reached Owen, he put a hand on Owen's shoulder and Owen felt the nowness of the moment, the ground beneath him. He was there.

"An angel," Owen said.

"What is with you?"

Owen was worried he was too fucked up to tell him. Was he speaking gibberish? Gail nuzzled her head beneath his finger. He took a deep breath. "I need to leave because the Army of Acronyms is going to find me."

"What? Let's get you home." He started to walk Owen back towards the road. He looked over his shoulder. "You need to go now."

Owen put his hand up. "No, listen. I love you. I need to say that. It's this thing inside me and it's wrapped up tight and I need to say it. I love you." The earth pulled into focus, stopped its rotation right there in the middle of outer space for a moment. Another car drove down the road.

"Owen," Clyde's voice was hushed. "I love you too." The whole ocean in his eyes. "But you need to leave."

It was too late. The car stopped in the middle of the road and Owen heard his name being shouted. It was the doctor. He was out of time.

"I'm out of time, but I have to tell you that I love you and I am a Terror."

"I love you too." Twice he had said it. Clyde put a hand on his shoulder, and it was jellyfish venom.

"I'm a Terror," Owen said again. "I have a bird who lives inside me."

Clyde looked at him, his eyes worried. He was in his stupid straight-boy uniform, dirty Carhartts and a plain T-shirt that was one size too big, but he looked so beautiful. Why couldn't Owen make the words come out how they formed in his head? His brain felt disconnected from his mouth. The figure from the car walked towards him calling his name. They were getting closer and louder. He leaned forward and kissed Clyde. His heart beat inside both of their heads. Gail beat her wings in his chest. It would be his last kiss, and it was worth it. Nowness. Two boys taking up space, spinning in space. Clyde kissed him back and he was full then. He didn't want to, but he pried himself off Clyde. He was being taken away. He could feel the doctor behind him now. He wouldn't go until he unraveled all the skein, though.

"This is Gail," he said, and he felt in his body and ripped open the buttons from his romper.

Clyde's eyes grew wide and he smiled. Then his smile evaporated. Owen knew it was the doctor. He turned around. The world spun around, and it took a second to catch up. Tennessee stood behind him.

"We have to get you out of here," she said. She pointed behind him.

"I know. I'm running away tomorrow. I had to say goodbye to

Clyde. You're going to say he's not our people, but he is. Oh, he is, Tennessee. I love him. He kissed me. I was now."

"No, we have to get you out of here." Tennessee pointed a finger behind him, past him towards the woods.

He turned around. Clyde's father sat on top of his horse, the rifle from the back of the saddle in his hands. He climbed off the horse and walked towards Owen. "What the hell are you doing here?" He pointed the rifle at Clyde and then Owen.

"I thought I told you to stay away from him," he said to Clyde. "Stay away from our family."

"Dad, it's okay. Owen was leaving."

Owen shook his head. None of this could be happening. He was electricity. He was in love with Clyde. This was not how it was supposed to go.

Clyde's dad looked at him, ran his eyes up and down. "What the fuck are you wearing?"

Owen looked down. The romper was unbuttoned and opened. He pulled it over Gail. The bottom hem cut into the tops of his thighs and then it was pale legs down to his boots. Clyde's father had certainly not seen her. She quivered in his chest. "Careful. I die when you die."

"What are you doing here?"

Tennessee stepped forward. "He's sick. We're leaving. I was just coming here to grab him." She turned to Owen. "Owen, come on. We need to go." She sounded like she was crying.

Owen put his hands up. "It's okay," he said. "I'm going to leave. I needed to say goodbye to Clyde. I promised him I would say goodbye. I love him."

Clyde's father aimed the rifle at Owen and walked towards him, slowly. "What did you say? I can shoot you, you know. You're on my property."

Owen slid his hand under the romper and felt the place where there was no skin just bones and a bird. God, he was sick of the Army of Acronyms. "I love Clyde." He shrugged. "I need to unravel the skein."

Clyde took a step backwards. He waved both of his hands in front of him. "Get out of here, Owen. You don't know what you're doing."

Owen took a step towards Clyde. How could he not? "It's okay," he said. "I love you."

Owen felt the nowness, and Clyde's father took a step forward. He pumped the rifle twice. Tennessee screamed. The rifle popped quickly three times.

66

Owen remembered the boys in the field all those years ago. He felt the wind of one bullet on his right ear. He could hear the wind moving through the barrel. He felt the second bullet hit his thigh. It stung, but it didn't hurt like he thought it should. It lodged itself in his skin. The third bullet passed between his fingers on his chest, right through the hole where there was just a bird. The duffel bag fell to the ground and he followed. "What a shot," he said.

Tennessee and Clyde both ran to him.

"Goddammit," Clyde's father yelled. "It's just a fucking BB gun."

Tennessee and Clyde sat over him. Owen could hear Clyde's dad walking over. He looked at Tennessee. "I die when she dies." Tennessee scooped him up and walked him around the fence and threw him in the backseat of her car.

67

The sun splintered in the early morning and they raced through the mountains. Owen could feel every bit of the earth beneath him. Tennessee was silent in the front seat, all her attention on the road. Clyde was on top of his horse just outside the window, blazing along the highway and keeping pace with the car. Clyde looked straight ahead, never looking anywhere but the horizon, like he was going to beat Owen to Morning. Owen knew that's where he was going. He settled into the seat. The seat belt dug into his hip. He slipped out of it. He was safe. Tennessee was there. Clyde loved him, and that was enough.

It was quiet in his chest.

68

Everything dark and then bright all at once. Like: a dark living room, pitch-black, so much darkness it hurts. Close eyes. Count to thirty. A tree's roots dig deep into the earth, always like that, deeper and deeper. Open eyes, bright as day.

Or: the dark night of sleep and then the bright lights of the bathroom and the roar of the faucet. The cream bathtub full of the way-too-hot water. Lungs won't breathe.

His mother, long hair, short bangs. Lilacs over and over. She rubs circles on his back.

And now, her hair in a short bob. Same eyes, the kind that carry too much worry, not enough light.

His mother whispering: *Shhh. It's gonna be okay. Just focus on breathing.*

Mama's here.

Eyelids flicker. His mother gone again, a ghost.

69

When Owen woke up the first day in the hospital, he had no idea where he was. He was in a bed with a blue polyester blanket stretched down his legs to his feet. He wore a thin blue hospital gown. It was a wide, empty room, his bed the only one. The walls were a taupe gray. A small sofa sat beneath a wall of windows to his right that overlooked mountains stretching far in the distance, cradling the town and the hospital, and he understood he was back in Morning. Slowly pockets of events came into focus. Comet's birthday. The person in pink. His trip on Blossoms. His love for Clyde.

Clyde's father.

His hand snapped to his chest and he reached in to find Gail, asleep. Her body heaved and fell with quick breaths. He was alive so she must also be alive. He sat perfectly still and felt the starched pillow give under his back. With Gail asleep in his chest, he couldn't feel the air. He knew only what was in front of him, the reality that he was in a hospital, and certainly the Army of Acronyms were waiting outside. Wires and tubes hung off his body. One of the tubes ran to an IV on the back of the bed, another to a computer monitor.

He remembered the car ride. Hadn't Clyde and his horse followed behind? Where was Clyde now? Where does someone park a horse at the hospital, even in Montana? Had he actually seen his mother this morning? He could not separate hallucination from life from memory from dream.

And what about Clyde? Had Clyde ever said he loved Owen back? Owen had made a fool of himself. Certainly, it was the last time he'd see Clyde. He was here, in the afterlife, alone. Everyone disappears eventually.

The door opened and a doctor in a white coat came in with a clipboard. He was tall and clean-shaven. His cheekbones were high, jawline deep. Owen slid back on the bed. He pulled his hand out from under the gown.

No one, never.

The doctor stopped dead in his tracks, looked up from his clipboard. "You're up," he said. "Good." He turned around and left.

Owen threw off the blanket. He couldn't figure out how to disconnect the IV from his hand. He had to get the fuck out of here. Where were his things? He stood up. A plastic bag hung on a hanger on a rack in the corner. The floral romper was balled up tight in the bottom of the bag, beneath it was his duffel bag. The floor was cold against the balls of his feet. The air swirled around him and he grew woozy. He summoned his strength. The door opened again.

His mother looked exactly as she had in his dream. Her hair was in a bob and it made her look happier than he remembered her. She rushed over to the bed. "No, no, no, no. Sit back down." She placed a hand on his back and the other on his chest. She smiled at him, though her cheeks were raw from crying.

"Mom, what am I doing here? I need to leave." He grabbed at the IV.

"No, honey. Mama is taking care of it. Just lie back down." She patted the pillow behind him.

He sat down. She put her hand on his bicep while he leaned back. The ache he'd felt for his mother for the past three years subsided, but there was no wash of relief. There was only the absence of missing. He felt Gail stir in his chest in her sleep. "Is Gail okay?"

"She's fine. Wing in a sling. She'll be okay. So will you."

He wanted to apologize but he didn't know how or why. "They're going to run experiments on me."

"No, they won't." A smile spread on her lips. "Everyone knows about you and Gail. The whole world knows. They won't hide you away as long as the media's calling." She pulled out her phone and scrolled through ten different articles declaring: **BOY WITH BIRD IN CHEST IS FASCINATING NEW DISCOVERY**. "Can't experiment when the world is watching," she said.

Owen thought he might be sick. He drew his fingers to his chest. "No one, never."

"I didn't have a choice."

"Is Tennessee here?"

"Yeah, even though I told her she should go back." His mom stood up and put a hand on his forehead. He tried to reconcile this version of his mother, the one who was tender, calm, and collected with the one who left him in the Puget Sound, the one who only called to talk crazy. Now he felt like the crazy one, his daymares of the Army of Acronyms playing in his head. She walked to the door and placed her hand on the doorknob. "I'll go get her."

Tennessee came in a moment later, and the first thing Owen noticed was her hair. Two immaculate braids framed her face and ran down her body, swinging freely at her belly button. She must have been braiding her hair in the waiting room for hours.

She stood over him and placed the back of her hand to her own forehead and then to Owen's, checking his temperature. "You okay?"

"I'm fine."

"Fuck, I was worried."

"I know. I'm sorry."

"Don't apologize. How is she?"

"Asleep but okay. She may never fly again."

Tennessee laughed. "I tried to get them to give me the pellet they removed from her wing, but they wouldn't give it to me."

"It's okay. I have my own keepsake." He was thinking of the pellet Tennessee had left when she had moved out, the one that sat like a pit in Gail's belly.

"So, you and Clyde, huh?" Tennessee sat in the chair next to him.

"Yeah, but I don't know if I'll ever see him again."

"You will. His dad's a dick, but if you like Clyde, then he's sweet, and if he's sweet, he'll show up." She tapped her chest with her two fingers.

"Too late. The whole world knows."

"Owen, the whole world should know about you."

He wasn't so sure. "Thank you," he said, and then, "Work. Aren't you missing work?"

"Yeah, but this is more important. My shifts are covered."

"You should go back. I'm fine, really."

"I know. I'll go back tonight. I needed to talk to you first."

His cousin placed her hand on top of his. She cleared her throat. Her eyes followed the mountains outside the window.

"Out with it," he said.

"It's just—" She gripped his hand tighter. "I'm just so sorry that I left you alone at that house when you needed me. I was so focused on me and Megan that I ignored you."

Owen sat up, crossed his legs under the blanket. "You didn't ignore me. The opposite, really. I'm sorry I broke our promise when I didn't tell you about Natalie." He held his pinky finger out, imagined a drop of blood and the rose quartz.

Tennessee blew air out her lips and waved her hand. "*Pssshh.* That's nothing, like really nothing. It's between me and my dad really, and we're figuring it out." The room grew quiet, just people moving in the hallway, beeps from machines in distant rooms.

"Thank you." He felt himself get a little misty at the thought of not seeing his cousin for a while really.

"No," she said. "Thank you. You're such a badass, Cousin. Can't wait to see what you and Clyde do."

"Yeah, assuming I see Clyde again, assuming his dad didn't kill him, assuming I ever get out of this damn hospital."

"You will. He'll show up. They always do." Then it was just him and his cousin, Gail asleep in his chest. He scanned the room and looked for something to remember this moment by, a small piece of magic, but there was nothing.

70

Tennessee was gone. Owen lay in bed. It seemed there was nothing to do but stare out the window and think about how fucked up everything was. His mind went to the moment with Clyde on the sidewalk, after Clyde had stolen the lipstick, right before Owen kissed him. He tried to conjure the love and desire he'd felt then, the feeling of having something to move towards. Where was Clyde? He thought he'd be here by now. He reached down into himself and searched for the pulling. It was gone, the pull to the water and the pull to Clyde. He was empty. Gail snored softly in his chest, still lights-out for the bird. He worried for Clyde. What if his dad hadn't let him leave? Then Owen worried about Owen. He had done a terrible job disappearing. Barely having run away. No boyfriend. No friends. He was supposed to be in a new town by now, completely off the radar. Not here in a hospital, a boy with a bird and a shitload of doctors who wanted the bird in his chest.

His mother came in. She smiled brightly. Her cheeks were covered in rouge. She petted his head. "Some people have some questions. I promised them one hour with you and then you need to rest. Okay?"

Unsure of what to do, Owen nodded his head yes. Tears filled the backs of his eyes and his stomach twisted in knots.

The door opened and a stream of doctors and nurses and avian veterinarians and ornithologists and zoologists entered the room. It was the beginning of one of Gail's bad jokes. The doctor, the one who'd been chasing him, was not there. Owen sighed some relief. He would not have been able to see those eyes again, feel his hand locked around his wrist. The specialists pushed his mother to the side and gathered around the bed. They shouted questions over each other.

How long has she been there?

Does she eat?

Does she defecate?

Where does she go to the bathroom? How did she get in there? Surgery?

What do you mean she's always been there? That's impossible. No, no, you're wrong.

Very wrong.

A man shouted from the back. *Excuse me. Can you tell me about your experience with Luminous-Essence-Petunia-Blossom? Did you lose sight of colors?*

Keep it down. No one cares about colorblindness.

Get out of here, Gary.

It's just, I wonder if he can see purple or if it's gone.

Owen remembered that the Army of Acronyms was relentless. His mother ushered them all out and shut the door. The room was quiet, empty of the hubbub of the last hour.

His mother walked back to the side of his bed.

"What was that about purple?" he asked.

"Oh, that's nothing."

"Has anyone visited me?"

"Some folks from the diner. People from the town, but they're just interested in looking at Gail. I shoo them away. Tell them to move along." She filled a paper cup with water from the bathroom faucet and brought it to him. "There's one more person you need to talk to. A reporter."

He took a drink and set the water on the table. A few minutes later there was a knock on the door. A woman in a brown tweed skirt and jacket walked in. Her teeth were white, her nose bulbous, and she wore big, clear-framed glasses. She straightened the length of her skirt and then stretched out her hand. A cheap leather watch hung on her wrist.

"Penelope," she said, "with the *Morning Herald*. How are you?" She pulled a chair up next to the bed and sat down. His mother sat in a chair next to the window.

"I'm okay," he said.

"Great to hear. I'm just here to listen to your story. Tell me everything. Leave nothing out." She propped a yellow legal pad on her knee and poised her pen to start writing.

Owen wasn't sure how to start, where to start. He wasn't sure he wanted to tell this woman anything. Everything stacked up to confusion.

"It's okay, honey." His mother nodded. "She's a friend."

"Mom, can you leave us alone for a bit?" Whatever he had to say, he wanted to be able to say it without considering his mother's feelings. His mom stood up and ruffled his hair. The door clicked behind her.

Owen couldn't bring himself to tell the story. It felt so pointless, like what good would it bring, telling this stranger about his life. He thought about what Tennessee meant when she said that the whole world should know about him. Should they? He thought maybe he could start with the information everyone already knew, play it safe.

"I have a bird who lives in my chest," he said. "Her name is Gail. She's always been there." Saying the words out loud never got old, and Owen felt the same relief he always felt when he told someone about Gail. Release. Unknotting the bundle of secrets.

Penelope scribbled on her notepad. "And?" she said.

"And what? That's it. Aren't you surprised? Shocked? Isn't that enough for an article?"

She set her pad down on the floor and took a deep breath. "I'm more interested in you. What does it feel like to have a bird in your chest? What's it been like to live this way?"

"Hard," Owen said, "very hard."

"Hard how?" She pushed her glasses up the bridge of her nose and leaned back and placed her hands in her lap. She waited patiently. Owen thought maybe she did care about why it had been hard for him.

He turned away from her and looked towards the window. Gargantuan clouds rolled like gentle beasts through the mountains. He pretended like she wasn't in the room, thinking maybe it'd be easier if he thought he was alone, sharing his story with no one. He started by listing the ways it was hard having a bird in his chest. The being locked away for ten years. He tried to explain what it felt like to carry a secret like that, forever afraid of what would happen if someone found out, and always wondering if there were others like him, others who were also afraid.

Then he talked about Tennessee. "She saved my life," he said, and he paused because he'd never thought about it like that before, but it was true. Not that he would be dead without her, but he certainly wouldn't be *living*. He talked about the Fort and about feeling like he was invincible. When he talked about music, he got excited and talked quicker.

Then he was really quiet because he thought about Clyde and all the music they shared and how maybe he'd never see him again. He wished Gail would wake up. His chest felt heavy, but he pushed past the feeling and told the reporter about Clyde and what it meant to have someone who he could really just be quiet next to. He told her about Clyde's thick farm boy muscles.

It was strange, this telling from a distance, and it made the next part easier, the part with Clyde's dad, *a thief of joy*. The part with the BB gun, which felt strange since it butted right up against him telling Clyde he loved him.

Afterwards Owen felt empty, like there was nothing left to tell. He turned towards the reporter. The notepad still sat on the floor. Her face was scrunched up with the work of holding back tears.

"I'm sorry," she said. "I'm really trying to remain objective and not cry." She fanned her face with her open palms. "Can I hug you?" Owen nodded, and she came over and wrapped her arms around him. "I think this is against the rules," she said, and then she pulled away. She snapped out of it and became all business again. "Let's get your photo."

He brushed his hair, which he hadn't done since he'd eaten the flower. He asked if he should brush his teeth, too, and Penelope joked that no one could smell his breath through the photograph. He squirmed out from under the blanket and pulled the gown to the left, revealing the hole in his chest. In the photo, his ribs seemed to gleam, and one could barely make out the bird who snored soundly in his chest. He blinked softly in the camera's flash.

71

His mother slept next to him in the bed, her left leg hanging off the side. Her hand lay on his left shoulder. The moon hung high in the air, waning, moving to low tide. The town was lit up beneath the room. It was only the second floor of the hospital, but Owen felt like he was on the top floor of a skyscraper. He wondered for a moment if he'd ever been in a building that high before, maybe school.

A memory came to him from his first last hurrah, when his mother had planted him in a tree and lifted up his T-shirt so Gail could see everything. She'd whistled so loudly. The first time Owen had felt a little bit of freedom. Gail was still asleep in his chest, tuckered from her minor surgery. He ate a spoonful of cold mashed potatoes and turned on the television. The room lit up in the pale blue of the TV screen. It was a rerun of *The Brady Bunch*, a boring show, but he let the voices fill the room. He mostly thought of Clyde.

• • •

Gail woke up the next morning. The room was still. Over the course of the night, his mother had moved to the sofa beneath the window. She was asleep, her arm draped over the side. A half-drunk cup of coffee sat next to her on the floor.

"Good morning, Gail. How are you?" Owen whispered.

"I feel like I got hit by a truck, but I'll survive. Where are we? Where is Clyde? Tennessee?"

"We're in the hospital. You had surgery. Gail?"

"Yes?"

"Everyone knows about you. We're all over the internet. Mom is here. It's been weird."

She paced back and forth in his chest. "This damn sling. I can't even make a fist. We have to get out of here."

"I know. I'm working on it, I think."

"Owen?"

"Yes."

"Where's Clyde? Where's Tennessee? I'm worried."

"Tennessee left. She's okay. Clyde isn't here."

"He's coming. He has to."

"I don't know."

"I do. Listen."

The room was golden in the early morning sun and his mother was bathed in the rays. He listened. He heard hooves over hard dirt and grass. Thunderous hooves, mowing down anything in their path. Clyde's ass bounced on the hard leather saddle. They raced through the mountains in the same golden light. "I'm just not sure," Owen whispered.

• • •

The room burst with movement at eight a.m. on the dot. His mom was up getting coffee and fielding phone calls. More and more people wanted to hear about the boy with a bird in his chest.

He grew restless in the bed, tired and bored. His legs hurt. His heart hurt.

The day passed.

No Clyde.

• • •

Much later, his mother reached over and turned the lamp on. He hadn't noticed how dim the room had grown while the day had waned. She picked up the paper cup full of ice chips that sat on his bedside table, looked at them, and then put them back.

"I'm sorry, Owen." His mother placed a hand on top of his.

"For what?"

"I don't know." She looked at him hard in the eyes. "It wasn't supposed to go like this."

He wondered which way his mom thought this would all go. "No one could have seen this coming," he said. He wanted her to say something about how she wouldn't have left him all alone if she'd known it'd go this way. "How am I going to get out of here?" The room only had one door, and the windows didn't open. He imagined pressing through a throng of specialists, doctors, and zoologists.

The crease in her forehead deepened. "Maybe this was a mistake. I don't know. I thought it would be better when others knew about you, but I just worry all day long. It's all I do. Worry, worry, worry. It's like how it used to be. I want to protect you, but I don't know how. I've never known how." She sounded like the mother who called him in the middle of the night to warn him about the Army of Acronyms, the one who talked crazy, the mother he knew.

And for the first time, he didn't try to console her. "MOM, how do I get out of here? There has to be a way. I need to get out of here." Gail ran her wing down his spine. He tugged at his IV.

His mother closed her eyes and breathed deeply, calming herself down, probably imagining tree roots. She placed her hand on the IV needle in his hand. "You know, when I had you, they wanted to keep you in the hospital." She nodded at Gail in his chest. "She wasn't even here yet and they wanted to run a battery of tests on you and take you away. I answered some questions. I pretended to listen to their advice, and when the time came, I stood up and walked out. You can do it, too. You can escape."

"Then what? I hide more? Longer? Forever?"

"I don't know," she said, her eyes cast down to the arm of her chair. "I have zero answers."

"Everything is so fucked up."

"Would you go back to Bob's?"

"And live next door to the man who shot me? Never. I would go somewhere I've never been. Where I know no one."

She sighed deeply. She shifted in her chair. "There's something you should see." She pulled her phone out of her pocket. "I wasn't sure whether I should show you this or not, but here it is. Maybe they can help you." She unlocked her phone and began scrolling. She pulled up a blog. The screen was basic, only black text on a gray background. The headline read: **WHY IS NO ONE TALKING ABOUT TERRORS?** Beneath the headline was another sub-headline: *Owen Tanner may be sweeping the nation with the bird in his chest, but he is only one of us. There are hundreds.*

He remembered the person in pink, and earlier, July, with his dull, yellow-striped socks. He read the article, and it was like Owen was reading about himself, but some of the details were off: a cricket in a bicep instead of a bird in a chest. A smart bug and funny human, instead of a funny bird and a sensitive boy.

He talks to me. He's always been there.

Owen finished reading the post and stared at the screen.

"Life is not easy for those of us who are different," his mother said. "It is not easy for people who are similar to others. Life will never be easy for you, but I thought you should know that you're not alone. There are plenty like you. You just have to find each other. It will be easier if you can find each other. Then, no more hiding."

He handed the phone back to his mother. His body grew cold and his breaths short. He had never heard another person relate exactly to him like this stranger on the internet. He'd never seen someone like himself declare so clearly and succinctly who they were. *No more hiding.* The possibility sent blood pumping through his body. What would it mean to not hide? He'd spent his whole life afraid of his secret being revealed. What would it feel like to not carry a ball of secrets in his gut? He missed Clyde right then.

His mother smiled at him. "I'll have them take out your IV so you can leave when you're ready." She put a hand on top of his. "No one is ever really that different from anyone else. Life will never be easy, but it can get easier."

She left the room.

"Maybe we can find the others," Gail said excitedly in his chest.

"And then what?" Owen said. "I'm glad there are others, but all I have known is hiding. I have been disappeared for my entire seventeen years on this planet. My childhood was taken from me. I couldn't be a whole person in the world, because I had to cover you up. I can't imagine another way. It sounds amazing, but I can't picture it. It feels like I should be in a world full of Owens and Gails, or in no world at all. I wish Clyde was here."

"Owen," Gail said. "Let's run away. We'll find others like us. We can build our world to look like that." She scratched at her sling, stretched the fabric, and pulled her shoulders back.

Owen didn't know if he had the strength to find others. If only Clyde would show up.

72

After the nurse removed his IV, Owen convinced his mother to stay at her own home. "Promise me you'll say goodbye," she said. "No matter where you're heading."

He promised. She ruffled his hair and wrote down the address of the apartment she shared with Elayne. The room was dark.

. . .

He slept fitfully that night. It felt like the flower still had its hold on him. It swirled purple across his dreams, but he couldn't see it, and so it was washed-out, gray. His whole world seemed gray. He woke up a few times, and Gail thrashed around in his chest, murmuring in her sleep. He woke up around two and he didn't know where he was. The room was dark. He felt a shadow in the room, a stranger, but he couldn't muster the energy to confront them. He fell back asleep. He dreamed of Clyde and him riding horses into battle. Gail sat on a horse, too. They called out, *"BUMP-BADA-DUH! CHARGE!"* He was drenched in sweat when he woke up again at five.

He felt the presence of someone in the room. The room seemed empty. Light came in from the hallway through the small window on the door. The faucet turned on in the bathroom, and Owen shot up in bed. A paper towel was torn off the dispenser. He pulled the blanket off to the side, ready to run out of the room. The light clicked off under the bathroom door and the handle turned. His feet touched the floor.

The door opened and out walked Clyde, that beaming smile. His blue eyes, swirling ocean waters. He looked up and saw Owen terrified on the edge of the bed.

"You're up," he said. "I don't think you're supposed to be up. I was going to let you sleep." That smile so beautiful, it was fucking stupid.

Owen stammered, the breath knocked out of him, and not because Gail had rammed into his lungs. He'd simply forgotten how to breathe. He floated off the edge of the bed. He pinched his arm and felt the sting.

"You are not dreaming." Clyde walked over to him, his arms spread wide.

Owen shook in place, absolutely frozen. He was afraid if he said something, if he reached out and touched him, Clyde would vanish, an apparition.

Clyde stood over him. He smelled like dirt and oil and work and sweat. "But how?" Owen said. "You came here. To see me."

Clyde clutched Owen's chin between his thumb and his index finger. It sent waves of warmth down his shoulders. "I caught a bus the next day. Left home and came right here. Bus was ten hours late, though." He bent down so the tip of his nose was just an inch away from Owen's. "Can't believe you kept that bird hidden from me. You're a trickster."

Owen tried his best to suck in air, but he still couldn't. Clyde kissed him. His lips were chapped, and his breath tasted like gas station baloney sandwiches, and it was perfect. Owen put a hand on Clyde's waist and felt the warmth of his body. Their lips lingered for a moment before Clyde pulled away. "Sorry my dad shot your bird. You freaked him out so bad he couldn't even hit me, though I knew he wanted to."

"It's okay. She's fine."

"Owen, I left. I have two thousand dollars. Let's move away together."

Gail spread her left wing wide in his chest. He passed her the feeling of being kissed by a person who sees you and loves you. The whole room was purple then. A whole world felt possible, anything but this drab hospital room in Montana.

"Let's get the fuck out of here," Owen said.

He went to his clothes in the plastic bag on the hanger, but the romper was sliced in half. Thing was so tight they had to cut him out of it. His duffel bag had been moved under the chair and he pulled out denim shorts and a T-shirt. His heart was beating so fast it felt like a show at the Fort in his skull. He got dressed, and Clyde watched him. Owen felt no embarrassment, just happy nerves and his half erection.

The hallways were quiet. A nurse sat with her back to the door. She watched a video on her phone, propped up on the counter. They walked around the corner and slipped into the stairwell. The stairwell was a cold wind tunnel, and the air felt good. The metal door shut behind them and Owen pulled Clyde close. They kissed again. Owen felt Clyde's body under his clothes, ran his hands along Clyde's skin, bones, and farm boy muscles. Gail spun herself dizzy in his chest. Clyde pushed Owen up against the wall and Owen felt the building beneath, felt all its cement and rebar and glass and wood. He breathed in through his nostrils and smelled the sweat on Clyde's upper lip. He remembered where they were. "We need to get out of here."

Their footsteps echoed down the stairs, and when they opened the door, they were in the ER waiting room. Owen's heart leapt in his chest. He scanned the room for the doctor, reporters, anyone. The room was empty save for an older man in a wheelchair and his toddler granddaughter watching an infomercial together. A phone rang. A security guard's walkie-talkie buzzed with static. They walked through the lobby like they were supposed to be there.

"Confidence is key," Gail assured them. "You're just two guys leaving a hospital."

73

The automatic doors whooshed open and Owen and Clyde were out on the pavement in the parking lot. The sun stretched its red arms across the morning sky, yawned yellow. They were free then, absolutely free.

They sat in the backseat of the cab and their hands lingered in the middle of the seat between them, not touching but floating over the vinyl. Owen wasn't sure where he was supposed to take his boyfriend after sneaking out of a hospital. He wanted to go home, to the old house on the hill, but his mother's warnings of the doctor knowing about the old address crept into his mind.

"Let it go," Gail whispered up to him. "We have time. I can feel it."

The cab driver kept calling them brothers, and they didn't correct him. The town woke up around them. Cars filled the roads, people going to work and to school. *I am in love, but these people are walking around like it's just another day*, Owen thought. The Cedar Creek Mall parking lot was nearly empty. Many of the things in the town were the same. Wyden's was still there. Two doors down was the small cheese shop. But between the mainstays of Morning were condos and sleek new offices. They were jagged and sharp, and they cut into the skyline like the jaws of monsters. The lights on the sign at the Thelma were off, the bulbs dim. He thought about *The Little Mermaid* and his last hurrah. They drove over the bridge and Owen felt the water rushing beneath him, and there was the familiar pull. The desire felt good.

He was exhausted but awake, and there was a heavy pressure on his temple. When they neared the parking lot that sold fireworks in the summer and Christmas trees in the winter, he leaned forward and pointed. "Turn here. The house is up this way."

The front lawn was overgrown with weeds, and the grass stood nearly waist high. It swept across the path. Owen and Clyde ran their hands over the grass. The blades tickled Owen's palms and sent shivers to his elbows. Everything he touched seemed to be softer but also carrying jolts of electricity. The bottle tree was still intact, the glass bottles now gray and dull from sitting out in the elements.

The front porch was a faded blue. He had to press hard to loosen the door from the jamb. The house had grown and expanded and shrunk in on itself over the years, and the parts didn't fit together like they used to.

The air inside was stiff. Clyde waved his hand around in front of his face, trying to stir it up. Owen thought that there would be a flood of memories when he opened the door. He'd thought about which one might be the first one that came to mind when he entered the house, but now there was nothing. It all looked too different. There was years' worth of junk mail piled on the floor, and Owen kicked it to the side.

He reached back and grabbed Clyde's hand, a soft sting. Clyde gripped the hand tightly and let Owen pull him into the front room. Owen pulled his shirt off so Gail could see the house.

"It's so dark," she said. "So different from up here." She nudged him in the rib, and he giggled. A molded cup of half-drunk coffee sat on the floor by the couch. There was a pile of cigarette butts in his mother's ashtray near her window in the dining room. One of her sweaters hung on the back of the rocking chair, a marigold cardigan. Owen took Clyde's hand and pulled him to the back door. He opened the door and let the summer air into the house. The sun was awake and bright now. Clyde stood behind him, a finger loosely in Owen's palm, his other hand around Owen's bare waist.

Gail blasted an extra loud *POE-TWEET-TOE-TWEET-TWEET-TWEET-CHIRP-CHIRP-CHIRP*. Clyde laughed and placed his chin on Owen's shoulder, and it was such a tender gesture that Owen thought he might cry. He thought of Clyde's gentle hand on his horse when they saw the doe in the woods, a soft touching. A tree in the distance swayed in the summer breeze and Owen recalled the time the bird had flown into the house. It had crossed over the yard and swooped over his head and inside with no permission.

"Remember the time that bird got trapped inside?" Gail asked.

"I was just thinking about that." He laughed.

"God, it was a pain to get that guy out."

Clyde buried his face in Owen's back. His nostrils blew out wet, cold air into Owen's neck. Owen turned around and placed his forehead against Clyde's.

"*BUMP-BADA-DUH! CHARGE!*" Gail sang.

The two boys laughed. Owen led Clyde back through the house to his mother's room, where he pulled Clyde onto the bed. They kissed and ran their fingers along each other's arms and backs and shoulders. They intertwined their legs and feet around each other. The room smelled like stale air, and Owen wanted to bring life into it, to fill it with every color (save for purple). He climbed on top of Clyde. He unbuckled Clyde's belt and slipped his jeans off. Clyde's dick was hard and stretched his underwear to the right. Owen placed his fingers around the waistband. He bent upwards and kissed Clyde and looked into his eyes, the wide expanse of the Puget Sound in there. Clyde nodded, and Owen pulled his underwear down. He made his way down Clyde's body, kissing spots along his ribs, the space where there was no bird, just skin, and Owen felt bad for him, no secret animal living inside him, just skin and bones. His hands ran along Clyde's square shoulders and back, and it was familiar, like they'd always known his body. He reached Clyde's cock and he wrapped his mouth around it, felt his heartbeat against his tongue. Clyde arched his head back and pushed the pillows off the bed. Owen tasted the salty skin and swirled it around his mouth. He worked up and down. He wanted to give everything to Clyde, to show him what it meant for him to come here, to leave everything for him. Clyde placed his hands under Owen's armpits and pulled him up to meet his face. Owen hovered in the air above him, a hand on the wall. Clyde kissed Owen's neck and pulled at his belt. He bent down and made eye contact with Gail. "What a lovely bird," he said.

Owen shifted.

"She's beautiful and she makes you beautiful." He ran his tongue along Owen's ribs, and it slid between the gaps in the bones where it was natural, like the space between fingers or toes. A bird chirped near the window and Owen remembered there was a world outside of that room. Clyde drew him back in. Clyde pulled Owen's pants down and grabbed an ass cheek in each hand. He ran his tongue along Owen's dick and then wrapped his mouth around it. Owen felt loved. He felt seen. He disappeared inside himself. No, the world disappeared, and it was only the two boys and the bird in the room, nothing else. Clyde's hair was Velcro against his stomach, and Owen laughed, tickled. Clyde came up and they kissed again, and it was salt. Clyde lay on his back and brought Owen's dick to his ass. He pulled Owen inside of him and winced. Owen moved slowly. It was a dream. He took up space inside Clyde. Clyde made space for him. They were a mess of bodies on the bed. The earth shook. Tremors vibrated in the air around them.

They took turns fucking each other. Owen felt split in two, and the sun sliced a gash through the window and the ray of light cut through the dust in the air. He'd never identified with anything so strongly as a ray of light cast through a dusty room. Afterwards, they lay side by side on the mattress, the sheets tangled around Owen's calves. He watched their reflection in his mother's vanity that sat against the wall facing the bed. From this angle, the strangest thing about them was not the bird in his chest, but the two boys lying next to each other. Gail nuzzled his ribs. Owen wanted it to stay like this, freeze time, live under the sea of this dusty house forever, but he knew he could not.

Clyde got up and went into the kitchen to put on a pot of coffee. "It's old," Owen called after him. "Too old."

"Oh, coffee doesn't go bad. It just gets stale," Clyde yelled from the other room. The faucet ran. The coffee maker sputtered like it used to, spat out coffee. He sprawled out on the bed. Bits and pieces of him were scattered across the room. Clyde was scattered around, too, even parts of Gail. Maybe that was life, creatures breaking up parts of each other and leaving those pieces in rooms and on the sidewalk, making their marks across the globe, small pieces of magic. Gail shook earthquakes in his chest. Clyde returned a moment later with two cups of coffee. "Sorry, cream's expired." Owen lay back and drank the hot coffee in bed. Clyde climbed in next to him and placed his head on Owen's chest.

A few moments later, Owen stood up. Still naked, he went to the window. There was a small glass ashtray. Next to it, an old pack of Marlboro Reds, his mother's from three years ago. He pulled one out and lit it with the lighter on the windowsill. He slid the window open. Cigarettes weren't for him, but it was nice. Clyde walked over and stood next to him. He stretched out his hand, the international symbol for asking for a drag. Owen slipped it between his fingertips. He kissed him again and sucked in the tobacco scent from Clyde's lips. He put an arm around Clyde.

His left rib creaked.

. . .

Clyde said he was made of money, so he ordered a cab and went to get a pizza later that evening. Owen was afraid to leave the house, and he sure as hell didn't want some strange delivery boy seeing him at home, but they had worked up an appetite and he was starving, so Clyde agreed to go alone. Owen sat on the couch and turned on the television. He was in his jeans, no shirt. Gail watched TV with him, some stupid sitcom about a straight family in the suburbs. Owen recognized nothing in the characters.

Dusk settled.

During the second commercial break, there was a knock on the door. Owen pulled on an old T-shirt, from back when he was thirteen, so it came to his midriff. He walked to the front entryway. Clyde would get a kick out of the way the shirt fit, but he opened the door not to Clyde, but to a man Owen did not recognize.

The man was tall and bald with wiry eyebrows. He wore a tan plaid shirt tucked into his jeans. His hands were in his pockets. When he saw Owen, his muscles tensed up under his shirt, and his eyes flashed with anger, pupils shrinking and then dilating.

"Shut the fucking door," Gail yelled, squawking and screeching. Owen slammed the door, but the man placed his brown oxford in the jamb and put his hand up.

"Not so fast," he said. "Is it you?" he asked. "Owen Tanner?"

"I'm Owen." How had they found him so fast? His hand was tight on the door and he pressed the door against the man's foot, hoping it would slowly be squeezed out and he could shut the door and lock the dead bolt. Pieces of his memory clicked into place. He wanted to lie down and let it all end, to surrender to this man. He felt a familiar feeling with him, and that was when he realized it was the doctor. His cheeks flashed red. He tried his best to not look into his eyes, those eyes that told Owen he would do whatever it took to make sure Owen couldn't get away this time.

"I need to see her. Please. Please don't do this to me. Please." There was a soft pleading in his voice, so different from that day in the exam room.

Owen saw him with the stethoscope around his neck, the white lab coat. He remembered the look of horror when he had seen Gail, how Owen had felt like a monster. "Get the fuck out of here. You can read about me on the internet."

"The internet? That's not good enough," he said. "I need to see her again." He gestured his palm at Owen's chest. "Just need to know I'm not crazy." He reached for Owen's shirt. "Please. Please, let me see her." His voice turned guttural. "Now. Let me see her now." And there it was: the man he remembered. The man who would not take no for an answer. It was those boys in the forest. It was Clyde's dad. A long lineage of men taking whatever they wanted regardless of the consequences.

Owen was sick of it, so sick of it.

He leaned back on his right foot but kept his left foot planted firmly in the doorway. He felt the ground beneath him, the whole earth. He tightened his thigh, drew strength from the ground.

The doctor knelt down, begged on his knees. "Please, show me. Do it or I swear I'll turn you in and they'll run all sorts of experiments on you. You'll never be free to see your boyfriend ever again."

"You piece of shit. Don't you ever mention him. Get the fuck off this porch. You're a disgusting little man. This is why no one trusts doctors. The only people worse than doctors are cops. Fuck you."

"Fuck you," Gail yelled.

"Fuck you," Owen said. "Get out." He drew strength through his right leg, felt it pass up his thigh. He rotated his wrist at his right side, his thumb outside the fist like Bob taught him, and he punched the doctor in the nose. He followed through. He took a step around the door so that he stood on the porch with the doctor. The man's head knocked back and he sprung up to his feet. Owen's left fist was waiting for him, and he hit the doctor again.

After that, the punches followed each other, lapped over one another like waves on the shore. Owen shoved him off the porch. The doctor lay on his back, his head on the sidewalk and his right leg draped over the steps leading to the faded blue porch. Owen stood over him. Blood poured from the doctor's nose, his eyes already starting to swell shut. Owen's fists were achingly numb and his knuckles were covered in blood, and he wasn't sure if it was his blood or the doctor's. He drew his fist back again, ready to really pummel the doctor to death, but Gail placed her wing on his spine, a gentle gesture like a hand on a shoulder. Water levied in the backs of Owen's eyes. *The wrong kind of attention.*

The doctor rolled over and spat blood onto the sidewalk.

"Please," Owen said. "Just leave me alone. You've haunted me for years. It ends now. Just leave me be."

The doctor put up his hands. He pinched the bridge of his nose with his thumb and pointer finger and waved the other hand. He turned and crawled out from under Owen before getting up and walking back to his car.

The doctor sat in the car for a moment, defeated. He drove off and Owen stood there, unsure of how to move. The wind passed through the bottle tree and rustled the grass in the lawn.

He went into the bathroom and ran cold water over his face. The soapy water stung his knuckles. His cheeks were puffy, and when he caught his image in the mirror he was horrified. There was something about the lingering rays of twilight that made humans turn into complete monsters. His blood pumped fierce and hard. Owen knew what he had to do. He had to leave. Time to disappear, and this was the worst-case scenario.

When Clyde came home with pizza, he ran to Owen's aid. Owen sat on the couch, the television on. He shrugged off Clyde's concerns. "It's nothing, really," he repeated over and over again, and he grew cold towards Clyde so that he would drop it.

Clyde couldn't drop it though. "Why? Why are you like this all of a sudden? Is it something I did?" Tears streamed down his cheeks. "What happened while I was gone? No more secrets. Don't do this to me. You're all I have."

Owen remembered the night he and Tennessee had drawn blood around the rose quartz. *No more secrets.* This was different, though. He had to keep Clyde safe, had to keep him at a distance. "It's really nothing. Please don't." He placed his thumb on Clyde's cheek and wiped the tear away. "Really, it's nothing. A dumb mistake. It won't happen again."

Clyde leaned his head against Owen's chest.

The night moved over them swiftly. Owen walked around the house, shutting windows and checking the stovetop even though they hadn't cooked anything. He closed all the blinds. "What's wrong with you?" Clyde called from the dining room. "Sit down. Eat."

"I can't." Owen stood over the sink, his palms on the counter.

Clyde came over and wrapped his arm around Owen's shoulders. He kissed the cold sweat on Owen's forehead. "I don't know what happened while I was gone, and you don't want to tell me. Whatever. Save it for later, but let's leave tomorrow. I'll keep you safe. I have money. We can go to San Francisco."

Any place with Clyde seemed impossible to Owen. He'd put Clyde through too much already. Owen would go to California, but not to live there, to leap off the Golden Gate Bridge. He would give in fully to the pull of the water, a sacrifice. *Under the sea.* Otherwise, the doctor would never leave him alone. No amount of salt barrier. No amount of community. No amount of love and fucking. No amount of punk music could disassemble the Army of Acronyms. Not even pummeling someone close to death. Everyone disappeared eventually.

"I don't know about San Francisco," he said.

"Then somewhere else, just as long as it's with you." He led Owen into the dining room and fed him a slice of pizza.

Gail ran her wing along Owen's lungs. The desert sands dusted each inhale, brought on by his anxiety. "Let's have one night of this," she said. "Leave in the morning. Disappear then. Our secret."

"Our secret," Owen whispered back down to her.

Clyde leaned against the dining room table, other hand on his hip. "Where'd you go?" he said. "You don't have to hide her anymore, not around me."

"I didn't go nowhere. Let's get drunk."

They found a bottle of wine on top of the fridge and they had to hack at the cork with a steak knife to open it. Bits of cork floated in the wine, and they went into the living room. They turned on the radio and danced to ABBA and Led Zeppelin and Sublime and Aerosmith and anything else they could find on the radio. They got drunk as skunks. They swirled around. The music thudded the walls and Owen shoved everything out for a moment, told his anxiety it could come back in the morning. Boyz II Men came on, and Clyde tilted his glass back and emptied it. He put both of his hands on the small of Owen's back. Owen put his hand around Clyde's neck, and they rocked back and forth, their foreheads pressed together. Gail rocked in his chest, dancing in her own way. Owen felt his roots dig deep into the earth beneath them and he felt their tendrils wrap around Clyde's roots. They twisted and turned around each other. Owen tried to stop them. He would have to untangle them in the morning.

74

Owen woke up before Clyde the next morning. He slipped on some cutoff shorts and a loose white tank top, making sure Gail couldn't be seen through the shirt. He brushed his teeth with old toothpaste. Gail whispered up to him in his chest. "Don't do this, Owen. Don't disappear on Clyde. Think about how you felt when everyone left you. Don't do it to him."

He spit into the sink. "What choice do I have? If the doctor isn't after me, then someone else is. Clyde doesn't deserve that. He's too good."

"He is good, but he's not *too* good. He's perfect for you."

"I can't. I made up my mind. I can't stay. I can't, I can't, can't, can't."

Gail plopped down in his chest, defeated.

He set the bag by the front door and tiptoed back into the bedroom. He kissed Clyde's eyebrows and hoped he would wake up then. Maybe Owen would stay if he woke up. Clyde smiled gently and then rolled over for more sleep. Owen grabbed his duffel bag and latched the door quietly behind him.

He walked down the hill to the left so that he reached the path that weaved through the woods. He tried to find the old oak tree he'd spent a summer climbing, but he couldn't tell them apart anymore. He placed his hand on the bark of one of the trees and felt the sun's warmth on the trunk. Gail tweeted a nice little song, trying to be supportive of his decision since there was no convincing him otherwise.

He half expected the boys to be shooting in the field, for the pops to erupt in the woods. It was quiet, though. When he reached the field on the other side of the creek, it wasn't a field anymore but a small shopping complex with a natural grocery store, a dentist's office, and a café. Maybe the boys with the BB gun owned all these buildings, taking up space in a new way.

He made it to his mother's place by nine thirty a.m. She lived in a two-story drab, gray apartment complex. Each of the units had a nearly identical patch of grass, and soon he was lost in the maze of buildings. He had to recheck the apartment number several times, afraid he would knock on the wrong door.

His mother answered nearly before he could knock. She wore a T-shirt and jeans. Her hair was wet, fresh out of the shower, and so her cheeks were red. Owen thought she looked well rested, especially given that her son had been in the hospital the day before, that this was really one of the first times she'd seen him since she'd left him in the woods three years ago. She hugged him tight, the kind of hug only a mother can give. "Come in," she said.

She sat him down at the kitchen table and brought him a cup of coffee with a little cream. The apartment was small, a one-bedroom. A broom and a horseshoe hung over the front door, acorns on each of the windowsills. There was a framed photograph in the dining room of the Brooklyn Bridge. A short red sofa and a cream recliner sat around a television in the living room. Two used wineglasses were on the kitchen counter near the sink. *So this is how my mother's been living?* Owen thought. It seemed like she'd completely moved on without him, and he felt like a fool for having missed her so much. She sat down across from him.

"How are you? What do you need?"

He set his hands on the table. "I don't know. I have to get out of here. Maybe I'll go to California."

"I've never been."

For a moment, Owen thought about what Bob had told him, how she had gone clamming with her dad and screamed when it came time to leave the ocean. She pushed the chair out from under her and walked to the patio behind him. She slid the door open and lit a cigarette.

"What's in California?"

"I don't know. Lots of water. It's not here. I don't know how much more of this hiding I can take. The word is out, but I still feel like I need to keep this whole situation under wraps." He swirled his hand in a spiral around his chest. He didn't mention the doctor, tried his best to hide his swollen knuckles.

His mother propped her elbow on her waist and stared out over the patio at the other apartments. She moved to say something and then didn't. She took another drag. "I get it, but I still don't think you need to hide anymore."

"Now? Now you think I can quit hiding?" An anger flared quickly in him. "I've been hiding for seventeen years. All I've ever known is how to stay disappeared. It's too late. It's not like I can flip a switch."

"Owen, I know what it's like to hide your whole life, and I'm sorry that's what I made you do." She took a pull on her cigarette. "I was young when I had you, too young, and I just didn't know."

"It's just—it's a lot right now. Everything feels messed up." He shook his head, trying to shake the anger off.

"I know what's on the other side of hiding. I know what it's like to reveal yourself and be seen and loved. It's worth it. I didn't think so before, but I sure as hell do now."

His mother was being sweet, and it was hard to remember that this was the mother who'd called him once a year to scare him. The mother who abandoned him at her brother's house. But of course, if he had not been abandoned, he would not have met Clyde. He thought about their night together, daydreamed about an apartment like this one, sharing space. An impossible dream. He wondered if the doctor had followed him. The doctor would follow him everywhere.

"Don't go to California," she said. She had to know what he was going to do.

"I have to. There's no other option."

She went into the other room and opened and closed a drawer and returned a moment later, handing him a wad of cash. Stale cigarette smoke wafted off her fingertips. "It's all I got. It'll at least get you to California, and I want you to know Elayne's my girlfriend," she said, smiling wide. "No more hiding."

"Yes, no more hiding. Good." He smiled wide back at her. It seemed everyone got what they needed after they left him.

"I made this mess." His mom leaned forward and placed her hands on the side of the patio door. "I really, truly tried to do the best I could." She clasped her hands in a fist and moved it up and down, punctuating each word.

"You left me there, left me alone in the woods for three years, and you only called to scare me into hiding more." Earthquakes came to his chest, and he tried what he could to suppress them. Gail ran her wing down his spine.

She covered her face with her hands. "I know. I know, I know, I know, I-know-I-know-I-know." She looked up, wiped her face. "I'm so sorry. I wasn't perfect."

He looked down at his shoes. Gail shook her feathers out in his chest, and he had the strongest desire to turn back then, to go back to the house and get Clyde and bring him back here to meet his mom, but he couldn't. He'd taken too many steps on this path. "We're all doing the best we can," he said.

"Why do it, Owen? Why do it at all? Is it because of someone?"

A smile crept to the corner of his mouth.

"Who is she?"

The "she" sat in the air for a moment between them. He shook his head.

"He's a big ol' homo," Gail called out from his chest.

His mother laughed her wide laugh, her teeth stained yellow. "The apple never falls far from the tree." She leaned against the patio door. "Does he know you're leaving?"

Owen shook his head.

"Oh, Owen. You are a beautiful kid who deserves the love you have found. I know I didn't show you that enough. I know it's been hard, but it will get a little easier. It won't ever be easy, though."

"I've made up my mind."

His mother leaned forward in front of him. "And you, Gail? What do you think about this plan to go to California?"

The chatty bird was quiet for a moment. She adjusted her sling. "I think it's his decision. I trust Owen. The boy's in charge."

"Okay, it is what it is." His mother stood behind him and hugged him from above. She rested her chin on the top of his head and ruffled his hair. "I'm sorry. I love you." She patted the hole in his chest with her left hand. "Gail, tell me a joke before you leave."

"A priest, a nun, and a rabbi walk into a bar, and the bartender says, 'What is this, a joke?'"

The room filled with their short chuckles. Owen stood up. His mother opened the door and placed a hand on his back, not like a hug, but like she was passing something to him through his back. He turned around and tears still clung to her cheeks. "Goodbye," she said.

"Goodbye, Mom." He hugged her. Then he went outside and made his way west, so he could jump off the Golden Gate Bridge.

Under the sea.

Book Four

All Grown Up

(How to Survive in the Afterlife)

74.5

I t takes Clyde three whole days to find Owen. When he wakes up and finds Owen gone, he jumps out of bed and goes to Owen's mother's apartment after finding the address on the refrigerator, along with a three-year-old paystub and a shopping list, browning on the edges. Owen's mother hugs him when he shows up on her doorstep. Without a second thought, she gives him the keys to the old pickup truck she'd taken from Bob's. For a moment, Clyde relishes in this, a parent who doesn't give a shit that her son's boyfriend is here. She just wants Owen safe. She tells him Owen went to California, but he knows better. He trusts his gut. For three days Clyde drives around, all over I-90. He never really sleeps, save for an hour here or there in the truck cab on the side of the road.

He finally finds Owen in the coffee shop in Olympia, the one where their knees touched under the table and they shared a cappuccino some months ago, right before the kiss and right before his dad went berserk. Owen sits upstairs by himself one table over from *their* table, even though there is no one else up there and he could pick any table in the room. He takes a sip of his coffee and places a hand to his chest, the left side, where there is no skin, just ribs and that beautiful bird. At first, he barely looks up at Clyde, barely recognizes him, like he's a distant friend he's trying to place, but then he sees him, and Owen stands up and wraps his arms around him. Clyde feels the red-hot touch of Owen. It's the same energy Clyde has always felt between them, even before they kissed, when it was the two of them throwing jellyfish back into the sea. Owen shakes quietly in Clyde's arms and Clyde holds him for a moment. Clyde can feel Gail shaking in Owen's chest, small bird flutters, an equivalent of sobbing. Owen's hair smells like dirt and hot air. His loose Mohawk is wild and strands of hair brush against Clyde's eyelids. Clyde rubs Owen's back in slow circles, and Owen's entire head rests on Clyde's shoulder, dead weight.

When they sit down, Clyde realizes the true gravity of the situation. All this time, he'd assumed Owen was just acting like a little punk, scared of what they were doing or scared of being on his own. Now Clyde sees the relief in Owen's eyes at his arrival, like maybe Owen's life depended on Clyde showing up at this coffee shop today, now, one last chance. His face is dirty, hair tangled. Clyde picks up Owen's hand and turns his fingers over in his palm, hangnails and blisters. Owen's hands are always so torn up, especially for a punk kid who doesn't do much for work, but now there is that red Montana dust stuck under his nails. He even seems skinnier, but he's always been a skinny motherfucker.

Relief washes over Clyde, like wind across a field, and he starts to cry.

Owen tries to smile, but then he starts to cry, too, and they turn into a puddle of tears in the upstairs of the coffee shop. A woman walks upstairs just then, but she sees the two boys blubbering over a cup of coffee and she turns and walks back downstairs. It's Gail who lightens them up, makes room for them to move past the tears. She whistles a quick tune like *chirp-chirp-poe-poe-poe-poe* and it's enough to make both the boys laugh. That bird has gotten so brazen.

"I'm sorry." Owen leans back in his chair and piles his dirty hands on his crossed knees.

Those words, just the two, are two words that Clyde hasn't heard many times in his life. It's almost enough to break his heart, this feeling he has right now for Owen. Red-hot mixed with something like mashed potatoes in the pit of his stomach. Inexplicably, he feels anger rise up in his chest. "What the hell, Owen? I thought we were in this together." He lifts his hand to slap the table but stops short. He is trying to undo generations of men slamming their hands on tables.

Tears form in Owen's eyes again, and Clyde can't stand to see him cry any longer. They are both so tired. Owen swallows hard. "I know," he says. "I really am sorry." He leans forward on the table and wraps his hand around the coffee mug.

"Where were you going?"

"San Francisco."

"Without me?" Clyde leans back and looks at the bookshelf to his left. Louisa May Alcott. Kant. Faulkner.

"Maybe I wasn't going to go all the way. I don't know. I didn't know what I was doing. Don't know what I'm doing. I had to go, though, like had to get the fuck out of Montana." Owen closes his eyes tight when he says *fuck*.

Clyde shakes his head. "So you came here, back to the one town where neither of us are safe?"

Owen drums his hands on the table and then stops. He does that thing where he disappears for a moment, and Clyde knows it's Gail, urging him to chill out, to talk to Clyde. "Look," Owen says, "I left because I love you and I don't want you to have to live a certain life. It's not going to be good. I will always be on the run. We will never be able to settle. I was saving you from that. You should be able to settle."

Clyde lets a little bit of the anger through, just enough that he feels it, but not so much he becomes it. "We—" Clyde motions his hand between Owen's chest and his own. "This thing we are doing is something we're doing together. You don't get to decide things for me."

Owen leans back in his chair and pulls the hem of his tank top down past his rump. "I'm sorry," he whispers to his right shoulder.

"The night after my dad found us downtown, I thought he might kill me, and I thought he would surely kill you in the field that morning. Both times I was mostly worried about never seeing you again. There you were, standing in that romper." Clyde can't help it, he starts laughing, but the laughter turns to tears quickly, always so sensitive. "Standing in that romper covered in flowers and high as shit. Jesus. I thought you were dead for sure. My only relief was the BB gun."

"I die when she dies."

"Yeah, well, I didn't know about Gail yet. Didn't know you had a bird in your chest. Anyways, I thought we had made it, like we were at your old house and we just *were*. We existed in that space, fucking and eating pizza and dancing. It was a dream, Owen. *My dream.* Then you were gone, and it was that fear all over again. I can't do that. I can't keep getting these moments and then having them taken away from me. I need safety, but I don't need to settle. I need to be with you, something like a family."

"It's just—I'm too much." Owen's hand goes to his chest, so obvious, too on the nose.

Clyde grips Owen's hand over his chest. "Yeah, no. You're not. She's not." He nods to the bird. "You're both perfect. There's some place out there for all of us. Anywhere but Montana and here."

"I don't think I can go to San Francisco."

There is something in Owen's breath, short but exhausted, that tells Clyde that Owen can't go to San Francisco because he'll want to die there. He was going to die there. "Then we definitely don't need to go to San Francisco. I don't have to go all the way to San Francisco to get away from my dad. I'd stay on the run with you."

Owen smiles deep and wide. He raps his knuckles on the tabletop and their knees knock together under the table. The smile fades. "I can't ask you to give up your dream." He looks Clyde hard in the eyes.

Clyde can't help but smile. He loves Owen's eyes so much, deep hazel with flashes of green. They are like moss on the trunk of an oak.

Owen crosses his arms at his elbows and clasps both of his biceps. He bites his lower lip and knocks his boots against the hardwood floor a couple of times, kicking down with his heel. All those years keeping Gail a secret tucked tight in his chest. He sips his coffee.

Clyde takes the cup from him and takes a drink. He puts his hands up in the air. "I've been thinking about this, and the whole reason I wanted to move to San Francisco was to get out from under my dad, to build a new family far away, and that was the first place that came to mind, but we could do that anywhere." He leans over and kisses Owen. Red-hot. The way his heart flutters makes him feel like he must have a bird in his chest, too. "You are my family."

Owen leans forward, both elbows on the table.

Clyde continues. "There are people all over the internet who are coming out as Terrors. We can set up camp somewhere and keep them safe, or we can move somewhere and not tell a single other person about the bird in your chest. I don't care. I just don't want to be anywhere without you. It's cliché and not punk rock, but I'm not punk rock. I'm a fucking hick. Hicks get sentimental."

"I've never thought about living past seventeen. I never thought about making it past this summer. It's always been one foot in front of the other." Owen drums his fingers on the rim of his coffee cup.

"But here we are." Clyde spreads his arms wide, gesturing to the room around them. "I mean, really, let's do it. Let's at least go see the ocean, like the real Pacific Ocean that stretches to Asia and back."

There is a soft whistle from Owen's chest, and Clyde knows that Gail must be in there telling him she loves him, that Clyde loves him. She must be telling him that San Francisco is the worst place to kill yourself and that he can carve out an Owen-sized hole somewhere between the Sound and San Francisco. "I want to go to the ocean."

"Fuck San Francisco." Clyde's hand slams on the table, but it's for joy not anger, still busting up that lineage. "Let's go somewhere where we can thrive." Clyde reaches across and puts his arms around Owen's neck. "Let's go look at the ocean."

74.8

Owen's mother is nowhere near the old GMC truck, but he feels her all over it, like the station wagon but fresher. Smashed pack of Marlboros on the dash. Pine tree air freshener on the rearview mirror. That old stale cigarette smoke. Two dirty coffee mugs roll around on the floor beneath his feet. There's a note on the speedometer: *Slow down*, and a small heart beneath it, a note from Elayne.

His mother always had a lead foot.

The bench is wide, and the stick shift takes up much of the floor between the two boys. Owen buckles himself in and then scoots as close as he can to Clyde. His knees jut to the right so Clyde can put the truck in reverse and back out of the parking spot in front of the café. When they reach the highway, the rain thunders on the roof of the cab. Clyde is quiet and Owen thinks he's worried that if he says something, Owen will change his mind. He is like Gail in that way, the way he tries to make ideas seem like Owen's when really, they are his. Trick is, though, that Owen really does want to see the Pacific. He wants to see it during the day, try to map the expanse, see if he can see China. His mother's Pisces fish. He wants to know what it's like to stand next to his boyfriend while he watches the big ocean pulse on the shore.

The truck rattles on the windy road along the Sound, and without prompting, Gail starts blabbering loudly, projecting her voice so it fills the cabin. "Maybe," she says, "there is a space between hiding all the time and becoming the leader of a movement. Like what would it look like to catch up on life a little bit, not live in fear but just kind of live for a minute, you know?"

Clyde reaches across and pulls out a cigarette from the smashed pack on the dash. He cranks his window down with his left hand and lights the cigarette with his right. Eyes on the road the whole time. It is just like how Owen's mom used to open the window, and he loves him so much then, not because he reminds him of his mother, but because he reminds him of family. Wind and rain whip around the cab, and Clyde rolls the window up so it's a bit cracked. He blows a puff of smoke at the cracked window.

"I don't even know what it's like to just live," Owen says, waving the cigarette smoke out of his eyes. "It is always hiding and how can I stay disappeared and when will I have to move. Where can I go next?" The tension and tiredness of the last few days has settled into his shoulders. There was a rush of relief when he first saw Clyde, his body grateful that his life was saved, but now he just wants sleep.

Clyde smiles and it wakes Owen up. "What if you were just a Terror living next to the ocean for a minute?" The cigarette rotates left and right with the steering wheel. He slows down around the curves. They hug the one-oh-one and it is nothing but dense forest, a world full of water and green. And then suddenly, no warning at all and they are on the side of the ocean, the water right there.

It seems corny, but Owen cannot help but feel hope in what he sees: the wet forest, bright green; the wide ocean, swirling gray waters; and that light beam, orange glow in deep water. Owen is a kid again, playing at bird migration patterns in the living room. Gail chirps and it echoes around the cab. Clyde flicks his cigarette out the window and cranks the window all the way down, the rain having softened. Owen rolls his window down, too. It is cold but he doesn't care. He needs the salty air and the smell of fresh rain in his nostrils. He runs his finger along the car door. His nailbed is still dirty with that Montana red dust. "I want nothing more than to live next to the ocean."

"The ocean it is," Clyde says. "The end of the world."

"Or the beginning." Owen leans far across the bench and grips Clyde's hand and kisses him on the cheek. Patches of stubble bristle against his lips. He smells like dry hay and horsehair. His hair is nearly an inch long. He's kept it shaved for the entire time Owen has known him.

Like he can read minds, Clyde's hand jumps to the side of his hair, briefly letting go of the steering wheel. "Maybe I'll even grow my hair out."

Gail whistles, a response.

75.1

It is early evening when they reach the Astoria–Megler Bridge. A line of cars crosses the long bridge from Washington into Oregon. A Ferris wheel and a boardwalk dot the coast. Pine trees cover the hills. Gail runs her wing along Owen's side. She whistles. He passes her the sensation of being in a truck with the boy you love and not a goddamn care in the world. Thoughts of the doctor and the Army of Acronyms far from his mind. Out the window they go. A sign reads: *Astoria: Where River Meets Sea.* "Maybe this is it," Owen says. He definitely wants to live here with Clyde, to wake up next to this every day.

Clyde pulls off the bridge on the other side, the Oregon side, and he drives towards the water. He drives until he finds a sandy beach, just south on the coast. They park on the side of the road. The homes are small beach cottages, mostly weatherworn, and the sunlight is fading to strips of orange across the sky. The pop and creak of car-door hinges. Clyde's hand wraps around Owen's hips and he settles into the feeling. The gravel crunches beneath their feet. They walk down the waterlogged and chipped stairs to the ocean. Owen wraps his arm around Clyde's neck. The wind blows fast and hard on the beach. The ocean roar is loud. They wobble in the loose sand.

The two boys unravel their limbs and Owen has the desire to wade into the ocean like always. *Under the sea.* He throws his jacket in the sand. He peels his tank top off. He's a boy in dirty cutoffs in the middle of the beach. Couples walk by and no one seems to notice the hole in his chest where there is no skin, just ribs and a gabby bird. Gail is light as a feather, and she is freaking out at an ocean so beautiful it's fucking stupid. It is her first time seeing the wide expanse of the sea. She coughs up the small pebble and the pellet and rolls them in her wings. Owen takes off running for the water. Clyde follows. His boots pound the soft sand. He gets to the water's edge, arches his back, and howls viciously at the sky and the moon that is beginning to rise. Gail does the same in his chest. Clyde is laughing and howling, too. Clyde's eyes shine so bright at Owen, and Owen knows what it feels like to know the slow poison of love. He sucks in the salty air, and it seems like the most natural thing in the world to be *him* right now, a boy with a bird in his chest, standing at the beginning of the world.

Clyde stands behind him and puts his arm around his waist, his chin on his shoulder. The ocean laps waves around them, but they are sturdy.

"Time to get rid of these guys." Gail holds up the pebble and pellet. "Need to lighten the load."

"No more magic?" Owen asks.

"Got all the magic we need right here," Gail says, tapping the top of his heart, her words light and breezy.

Owen knows she is right. Anyway, there are millions of pebbles all around them and he can always pick up another. He's got all the time in the world.

"Bye-bye, pellet. Bye-bye, pebble," he sings, and his voice comes out like bird chirps. He can feel Clyde's face tighten in a smile behind him.

"Bye-bye," Clyde says.

"Bye-bye," Gail says, and she throws the small pebble and then the BB pellet out of his chest and into the water, one after the other. *Plop, plop.* She sings her song.

Acknowledgments

Endless thanks to my editor, Melanie Iglesias Pérez, and the rest of the team at Atria Books who saw the possibilities of this novel and helped make it a reality.

So much thanks to my world-class agent, Cassie Mannes Murray. Your belief in this book and in my writing career has been invaluable. Thank you for finding it a home and for always having the right GIF for every occasion. How do you do it?

Thank you to Zoe Tuck and Davey Davis, who each read a full version of this book at its messiest. Zoe, thank you for the phone conversations about art and life that end up lasting hours. Davey, I am so glad we're littermates.

Thank you to my Mills College cohort who put up with early scenes from this book when it was my thesis. Thank you to Cornelia Nixon for the title and for direction. Thank you to Micheline Aharonian Marcom for teaching me that sometimes we have to make hard decisions.

Andy Greer, thank you for always supporting my career and for teaching me early on that a writer can be queer and out and still find success. You made the possibility visible. Thank you to every queer and trans artist who came before me and who will come after me. Every time we share a piece of our art with the world, the world knows us a little better.

Thank you to all the queer and trans siblings in my life. I cannot believe I get to live on this planet at the same time as you all. It's a big piece of magic.

Thank you to the teachers who encouraged my writing early on, especially Mrs. McCann at South Salem High School and Susan Reese at Portland State.

Thank you to Noah Emmet. Your support means the world to me. Long live Pope Elections.

Thank you to my parents, who raised me to be me and have always loved and accepted me, and thank you to my sisters, Hannah and Kelsey. Sisterhood feels so good.

Thank you to Literary Arts and the Oregon Arts Commission for your generous support.

Thank you to Iris, who sat in the room with me while I wrote this book and listened to me read sentences over and over again. Thank you for the snuggles. You will be provided with a lifetime's worth of kibble as a reward.

And how do I say thank you to someone who has supported me more than any other human on this planet? Thank you, Stelleaux, for the pots of black tea when I needed them, for the late nights full of belly laughs, for loving me wholly, and for being my most avid reader. Watching you make art pushes me to be a better artist. This book is for you.